GRANDMA'S ATTIC

SHANE DIETRICH

NOTEBOOK
PUBLISHING

First published in 2019 by Notebook Publishing,
20-22 Wenlock Road, London, N1 7GU.

www.notebookpublishing.co

ISBN: 9781913206253

A CIP catalogue record for this book is available from the British Library.

Typeset by Notebook Publishing.

To David and Stella;
two of the most influential people to me growing up.

CHAPTER ONE

April 22, 1945

I checked my watch. Just after 2300 hours. I heard a muffled explosion to the east and glanced in that direction. The rhythmic staccato of machine gun fire erupted, followed by a pair of flashes against the night sky. The larger explosions shook the ground, and I felt the shock waves in my gut. The Russians were close, and I needed to get out of there, quick. "What is taking them so long?" I wondered, glancing back toward the pier.

I had just put my wife and two small children on a boat. I knew I had to get them out of Germany before the whole country collapsed, and I breathed a shaky sigh of relief that this part of my dreadful task had been successful. I'd managed to get Stella and the boys to the docks without anyone detecting I was a man of service age. I left them in the hands of an old fisherman—a friend of my father, now deceased—who was leaving port in Rostock to head south along the coast. He had agreed to take this risk out of respect for my father's memory. I'd asked him to get them to Spain, or at least close to it. Stella had a sister in Spain, and barring my capture or death, I would meet her and the family there later. Under cover of darkness and amid the shadows, I crouched in an alley between the shipping warehouses and watched as they left port. I didn't move until they were completely out of view. I didn't know if this would be the last sight I would have of Stella and my sons. Now, if I could only get myself out of this without being shot, I would have truly succeeded.

This was a tricky situation for me, abandoning my unit, the 2nd SS Panzer Division, Das Reich, but I had to get my family out. My plan was to head west and surrender to the Allies, preferably the Americans, knowing I'd get better treatment from them. No matter what, I could not stay in the east. And certainly not in Berlin. Doing so would mean certain death. Russian soldiers were shooting every SS soldier they came upon, no questions asked. The Nazis had their own death squads out as well. Any citizen caught without papers was considered a deserter and shot on the spot. No trial. No explanation.

Moving at night and hiding out in the daylight, I made it to Hanover in a little over six days. I found it in ruins, no different from every other town or village. I'd heard rumors the Americans were not far away, so I would hold tight there and make it appear as if I was going to make my last stand. There wasn't a single building still intact. Most had either collapsed completely or were missing entire sections, like a cutaway, exposing interior floors as if it were a model. From the street, I looked up to where I'd call home for now. The doorway was now a hole about the size of a dump truck. I saw stairs going up to a second level where half the exterior wall was missing. A couple of pictures hung crooked on the interior wall over a small couch covered in dust and plaster. In the doorway to an adjoining room, a wooden door hung at an angle, only the bottom hinge holding it in place.

I could see through the broken windows to the ground floor. On the right side was a small kitchen; a few old appliances sat crooked along the wall, which was also partially missing. I glanced around quickly. Not seeing anything of significance, I walked through the hole that looked like someone had literally driven through it. I walked toward the kitchen, the sound of crunching glass under my boots. There was a loud squeak as I opened the icebox door. Empty. I rummaged through the cupboards next. Nothing to be found there either. Giving up hope I would find food that night, I took my MP 40 from my shoulder and carefully went up the damaged steps. Although my stomach was growling, groping around in the dark was dangerous, so further searching for food would have to wait until morning.

At the top of the stairs was a bedroom. The bed frame was in pieces, and a stained mattress lay on the floor. There was a dresser with all the drawers pulled out, empty and scattered on the floor. A broken mirror sat in the corner. I found an old blanket in a closet under remnants of the plaster wall and pulled it out, shaking the dust out of it. Removing the two grenades from my belt, I unbuckled it and set everything down next to the mattress. When I sank down on the mattress, I became engulfed in a puff of stale dust. Against my better judgment, I removed my boots and socks. The air felt so good between my toes; a lengthy time in the confines of a boot had left them damp with sweat. *Damn*—I had a new hole in one heel. *No wonder my heel hurts,* I thought. I grabbed a broken section of the mirror and looked myself over. *Pathetic! Some dignified officer you turned out to be. This will never pass inspection. Your uniform is filthy and ripped, and your boots have absolutely no shine!* I berated myself. There was nothing to be proud of in the man who looked back at me in the mirror. I looked like a beaten man from a defeated country.

Not really expecting to sleep, I lay on the mattress and covered myself with the blanket. Looking at the stars through large holes in the ceiling, I wondered how this would end. Would I die in a hail of bullets? Or would I make it back to my love someday? Total chaos had enveloped the land we now occupied. The Bohemian Corporal was bringing all of us down in flames with him. God, how I would love to get my hands on him now! I heard people scavenging through the rubble on the street and an occasional gunshot somewhere in the distance. As the night dragged on, it became eerily quiet, and I fell into an uneasy sleep.

I woke the next morning to my foot being kicked. I looked up and saw a young lieutenant staring at me.

"Sir," he said, "I need to see your orders."

Rubbing my eyes and yawning, I sat up, trying to look calm despite my apprehension at being caught off guard. "What did you say, lieutenant?"

"I need to see your orders, Sir."

Groaning, I stood up. I towered over him. Not that I was that big, only around 5'9" or so, but this kid looked all of about fourteen and was maybe five feet tall.

My only recourse was to bluff. "Lieutenant, I was lying in a hospital in Hamburg when it was bombed. I'm trying to get to my unit now," I lied, "so I don't have any orders."

"Sir," he said. "You're lying. You're a deserter, aren't you?" He drew his Luger pistol from the leather holster on his hip.

I said, "No. Now put that damn thing away before one of us gets hurt."

Pointing the pistol at me, he ordered, "Put your boots on, and we'll go see the commander. You can explain it to him."

"What did you say to me?" I bellowed. "You realize I am a superior officer, don't you?"

Fear flooded his body, and his hand began to shake. In one quick motion, I grabbed his wrist with my right hand and bent it up and back. He grabbed the gun with his other hand and tried desperately to get free of my grip, but I was much stronger. I pushed him back until he was trapped against the wall. I heard his wrist snap, and he screamed in pain as I yanked the pistol from his fingers. Throwing the gun on the bed, I placed both hands around his throat. He fought hard to no avail. As he struggled to breathe, he used his broken arm like a club, attempting to break my grip. I lifted him slightly by his neck so his feet were just off the ground. His breathing became more labored, his eyes bulged from his head, and blood vessels showed in his forehead. His face turned bright red, and in a moment, his body went limp. I let go, and he slumped to the floor. I knelt over him, checked for a pulse, and ran my hand over his vacant eyes, closing them. He was dead.

My eyes filled with tears. I didn't want to kill him. But I knew if I let him go, he would come back with help. It was him or me. "Damn kid didn't belong here," I muttered. Another life ended way too soon. I removed his belt and took the holster off, putting it on my own belt as I wrapped it around my waist. I looked at his feet. *A bit small,* I thought, but I removed his boots anyway. I took the socks off his feet and slipped them on my own. "Not bad... at least they're new." I slipped my boots on, grabbed my weapon, stuck the grenades in my belt, and put on my hat. Gathering the rest of my things, I started for the stairway.

Suddenly, I heard rapid gunfire. I tensed for a moment, thinking it was a firing squad that had probably just executed some poor fool. I knew I needed to leave before they came here and discovered the kid. I went back down the failing staircase and checked both directions before stepping into the street. Seeing no one, I started walking, dodging and weaving around the piles of rubble. A wood stove, looking conspicuously out of place, sat in the middle of the street, most likely blown out of someone's home in a bomb hit. I trudged about a hundred yards when I came to a building that had been an old cafe. I squeezed between the falling door and crumbling wall and stepped inside. Two kids with arms full of scavenged wares saw me and startled. Terrified, they tried to run past me. One got by, but I grabbed the second one by the collar of his jacket. He dropped the load he carried, and I let him go. I knelt, thinking, *Jackpot!* There were two unmarked cans of something, and a couple of potatoes, which I placed in my coat pockets, and a half loaf of stale bread. I broke a piece from the loaf, and it dissolved into crumbs. I scooped them into my mouth, knowing it would taste like sawdust, but also knowing I was a desperate man and would need every calorie I could consume to keep going. I removed my canteen and shook it gently. It sounded empty, but even a few drops would moisten my mouth to help the breadcrumbs go down. I shook the droplets in, but they disappeared on my tongue, not even enough to provoke a swallow. "Time to find some water."

Looking around the cafe, I saw some tables and chairs strewn about and tipped over. There was a piano in the corner by a picture window devoid of glass. The piano had bullet holes in it. I walked over to it and lifted its top, hoping for something hidden inside but noted only several keys missing. I squeezed back out the door to the street and had only taken a few steps when I heard the faint sound of vehicles approaching. Gunshots and explosions began to fill the air, and I searched for a place to defend myself. This had to be it. The Americans were finally here, and today, I would either live or die. On the corner, I saw a single level building that was once a bakery or other small shop. I ran to it and climbed through the empty front window. The entire back of the building was gone. *Damn*, I thought, *this is no good.*

Heading back out the window, I noticed a puddle on the floor and stopped in my tracks. Dying of thirst, I got on my hands and knees. I sniffed it first. *Smells okay*, I thought. I dipped my finger in it, rubbed my fingers together, and determined it was water. It was filthy, but I wasn't about to be picky. I bent over and slurped at it like a dog drinking from its bowl. It didn't taste good, but at least it was wet. I thought about how I must look, lapping at the floor like an animal. I thanked God that Stella wasn't here to witness my disgrace. I stood up and went out the back of the building into a courtyard. There was a small trash heap covered with weeds. Rummaging through it, I looked for anything usable and found an old paint can filled with water. I scraped the scum off the top and poured the rest into my canteen. Until I found clean water, this would have to do.

The sounds of battle were getting closer. I ran to the next house down, which was a three-story apartment building. There were no windows on this side, so I maneuvered my way to the rear of the building and discovered several windows on each floor from where I'd have a good vantage point. A door just ahead of me was entirely blocked by rubble, so I navigated around it to a ground level window and was surprised to find it still had glass. I rammed the barrel of my rifle through the glass and around the frame, clearing it of sharp pieces, and crawled through the window.

No sooner had I brushed off when there was an explosion in the courtyard where I had just been. The concussion threw me to my belly. I lay there, ears ringing, blinking the dust out of my eyes, thinking if I had still been outside, I would've been dead. I stood up, my legs rubbery, and looked out the window. The shell hole, most likely an errant mortar round, was a mere ten feet from the wall. Smoke seeped through the dirt from several places in the hole. I figured I'd head upstairs where I'd have a height advantage and see them coming from a block away. I turned to go up the stairs when I heard a loud whistling noise. I instinctively ducked, and there was another explosion. It shook the building under my feet, knocking me down again as dust and plaster from the ceiling fell all around me. I heard a groaning sound, followed by crashing noises. I half-crawled, half-ran for the window as the ceiling came thundering down behind me.

With no time to think, I threw myself back out the window. I looked up and watched the entire top of the building come down, each floor pancaking onto the next one. This was too many close calls for my liking. As I moved through the courtyard, my nerves frayed, and I felt terrified. Suddenly, two GIs appeared around the corner of the building in front of me. They saw me and fired wildly in my direction. Instinctively, I raised my submachine gun and opened fire. It was kill or be killed, and my training took over. They collapsed as my bullets ripped through their bodies. A third soldier stopped short of the corner and raised his M1 Garand, firing when it got to his shoulder. His bullets zipped past my head. I adjusted my aim and fired a third burst in his direction, emptying my magazine, but he was solidly behind the building for cover. I dropped to the ground and took out one of the potato mashers I had. I removed the end cap to expose the string and white ceramic ball. Pulling it sharply, I got to my knees and hurled it in his direction. He fired at me again, the bullets biting into the dirt beside me. I heard the *ping* of his clip being empty, and then my grenade exploded.

I slapped a new magazine into my sub gun, grabbed my Luger, pulled out its magazine, and counted the rounds. Eight, including the one in the pipe. I had one grenade left and two magazines for the MP, including the new one I'd just put in. I turned and ran back to the building I'd just come from, running along the outside, staying close to the wall. At the front, I stopped. I heard it before I saw it. About a block in front of me and heading my way was an M-4 Sherman with at least two squads of infantry, one on each side of the street. They were going house to house. This was not good.

I turned around and ran back to the courtyard. I stopped short when I saw an American. His back was to me, and he was on his knees giving first aid to one of the soldiers I'd just shot. I knelt so he wouldn't see me if he turned around and said a prayer. I asked God to forgive my sins and to guide me through the days ahead, to watch over me and protect me from evil. I pulled out my Bible from my lower coat pocket, turned to Psalm 23, and read.

The Lord is my shepherd; I shall not want.

He maketh me to lie down in green pastures.

He leads me beside the still waters.

He restoreth my soul.

He leadeth me in paths of righteousness for His name's sake.

I put the Bible back in my pocket, stood up, and removed the Luger from its holster. I quietly walked up to the man on his knees. He had a red cross painted on his helmet. The most coveted targets in the world were officers, radio operators, and medics. This would have been a great notch in my belt if I was still fighting for

Germany and not just my own survival. I put the barrel of the gun in his back between his shoulder blades. He raised his hands, never once looking at me. I raised the gun and tapped it on his helmet, signaling him to get up. He turned his head, looked at me, then turned back, and continued to attend to the injured man.

A calmness suddenly washed over me. It felt like I was being showered in peace. I was tired. Tired of fighting. Tired of killing. Tired of trying to survive. Before I realized what was going on, the medic rose to his feet and turned to face me. I could see the fear in his eyes, expecting he was about to die. A tear rolled down his cheek. As I peered into the man's eyes, I wondered if he was married. Did he have children as I did? Here was a man willing to die for the sake of a suffering fellow soldier. This wasn't chivalrous at all. Killing an unarmed man was murder. If I did this, I would be no better than the lunatics in command that I had just left when I'd deserted my unit. This was what I wanted to get away from. I had done more than my share of unthinkable acts, and I would need to atone for my sins. As I inhaled the newfound serenity that had enveloped me, I made a vow. From that moment on, I would not kill another human being as long as I had breath in me.

I motioned to the wounded man with my pistol. The medic looked at me quizzically. I motioned again. "Up," I said. The American nodded understanding. Not knowing what my next move would be, he looked at me warily as he bent over, wrapped the injured man's arm around his neck, and attempted to pick him up. I placed the Luger back in its holster and grabbed the wounded man's other arm, wrapping it around my shoulder. This time, I saw astonishment in the medic's eyes. The man who seconds ago was about to kill him was now helping him. The two of us carried him back toward their unit, the American and I looking at each other from time to time. I wondered what I was seeing in his eyes now. Relief? Questions no doubt swirled in his mind, as they did mine, but I felt God was with us. I hoped this would help me to surrender without being killed.

In short order, we were met by other American troops, all chattering wildly as they surrounded us. I was pushed away and replaced by one of their own to carry the wounded soldier. Without warning, I received a rifle butt to my back. I dropped to my knees and was kicked in the head. My vision blurred. I knew I was being kicked, pummeled, and pounded, and there was nothing I could do but curl up in a ball. Thankfully, it wasn't long before I lost consciousness.

CHAPTER TWO

May 1978

I hopped into the backseat of my father's 1975 LTD, next to my baby brother, Aaron, who was buckled into a car seat in the middle, wearing his tiny blue coat and hat. Dad was already in the driver's seat, and as my mother slid into the front seat beside him, he fumbled with his keys, dropping them on the floor. He cursed under his breath, getting a disapproving look from my mom. With only a slightly apologetic expression, he started the car, and we were on our way. It was a Saturday morning, and we were headed to my grandma's house— my dad's mother. She lived about twenty miles away, so I passed the time playing my electronic football game.

When we arrived, more than half of all my cousins and relatives were already there for the birthday party for me and the two cousins I shared a birthday with in May. Since there were three of us, the family celebrated them all on one day. My family was quite large. My dad had seven brothers and two sisters. Everyone was married and all but two had at least one child.

As we walked into the house, there were hugs from Grandma and a couple of the aunts and even a, "There's the birthday boy!" from one of my uncles. I was a whopping twelve now—old enough to understand adult conversations but young enough to still enjoy the fuss my family made over my special day. There were balloons and streamers in every doorway. In the living room, presents covered in bright wrapping paper were stacked neatly in the corner by the large console TV. I sauntered over to the pile, casually trying to see which ones had my name on them. In the dining room, three cakes were lined up on the dinner table, each with the appropriate number of unlit candles. As I walked past the table, I resisted the urge to swipe my finger in the frosting, which was so tempting for a boy with a sweet tooth. I heard laughter coming from upstairs and went to investigate, thinking I needed to distract myself from the cake.

Following the noise, I found some of my younger cousins involved in a serious game of Monopoly on the floor of one of the bedrooms. I sat and watched for a while, then wandered back downstairs and outside to see what my older cousins were doing. They had a touch football game going, and I joined the team that had fewer players. I loved doing anything physical, anything outdoors.

In an hour or so, we were called in to eat. A huge spread was laid out on several card tables in the screened porch. There were hamburgers, hot dogs, and chicken, all from the grill, veggies, chips, and side dishes, as well as several desserts. Each family had contributed, and it made for quite a feast. Piling my plate high, I went inside to the living room where the kids' table was set up on a thin, clear plastic sheet covering the carpet. I sat eating with my cousins, talking about school, sports, and what we hoped to get for our birthdays.

The parents spread out around various tables in the house and porch. Uncles gathered around coolers drinking beer; any get together was reason enough for beer. The aunts convened in circles, catching up on the local gossip. I don't think my uncle Erik sat down at all. He was in charge of the grill and was constantly bringing platters of raw food out to cook on the porch and hot food in to serve. Second helpings were encouraged, or even thirds.

After eating, everyone sang "happy birthday" to us as the candles were lit on each of our cakes. I made a wish, blowing out my candles. One uncle asked, "What did you wish for, Michael?" and I reminded him that wishes didn't come true if you shared them. My younger cousin, Theresa, was the only one of us who couldn't get all her candles out in one breath, which led to ribbing from the rest of us about having a boyfriend for each candle still lit. Next on the agenda were the birthday spankings from the uncles. Not having much choice, I bent over one's knee and he counted, "One... two... three..." all the way to twelve and said, "A pinch to grow an inch and a sock to grow a block," pinching and punching me as the words left his mouth. This was repeated with each uncle until they had sufficiently tortured us. I was thankful I wasn't fifteen years old like my cousin, Justin. Following that abuse, we each got the biggest piece from our respective cake and double scoops of ice cream, so I decided maybe the sore butt was worth it.

After our cake was finished, the presents were handed out, and as I ripped the paper off, I had to feign excitement. "Oh, yay, a new pair of jeans! Just what I wanted! Thank you, Uncle Ernie and Aunt Jill." I did get some neat things, though, like a new baseball glove for the upcoming little league season, but nothing from my ever-expanding list of desires.

Once the presents were opened and the discarded wrapping paper was cleaned up, the parents gathered around several tables playing bridge or 500. All of us kids went back to playing, generally making a racket, constantly being told by an adult to "tame things down." Several hours passed until the darkening sky signaled it was time to go home.

The next day, Sunday, my mom's father came over and took us out to lunch to celebrate my birthday. We never combined family events; it was always just Dad's side or just Mom's side. This grandpa was my idol. He was not a big man, maybe 5'8" or so, and well into his fifties. He was a WWII vet, an Army combat medic. He'd been wounded at one point and carried around several pieces of German shrapnel in his face. The doctors had removed what they could, but the pieces left behind they wouldn't touch. They were too close to his eyes, and as long as he didn't have serious problems with them, the risk to remove them was too great. He worked at a local hospital as a pharmacist and had gained the respect of doctors and patients alike. I wasn't the only one who looked up to him.

Once we entered the restaurant, the hostess was at the ready, asking, "How many? Smoking or non-smoking?" I knew what the answer to that question would be. The only one who smoked was my dad, and Grandpa wasn't about to sit at a table where his son-in-law would smoke after dinner. Weaving in and out of other tables, the waitress led us to an empty one in the center of the room. As we sat down, the waitress handed out menus. Mom and Dad shared one since Mom held baby Aaron. Grandpa didn't even look at his and said, "I know the fish is really good here." That was all I needed to hear. All you can eat fish and fries was a meal made for the gods, and even though I was a mere mortal, I would try to demolish the restaurant's fish supply.

In a few minutes, the waitress came back to take our orders. She smiled at me and said, "You first, honey." I wondered if she could sense this was a special day for me. As we waited for our food, I looked around the room. Every table had a candle on it in a yellow glass container covered in a net-like fabric. This was a steak house, adorned with the typical Western decorations. A wagon wheel in one corner, horseshoes, spurs, cowboy hats, and ropes hung on the walls. A few saddles were placed on shelves high behind the bar, and lots of artwork depicted cowboys and the Western way of life. I had never eaten at the Chuck Wagon before, but the food looked good, and I was happy to be anywhere with Grandpa.

I looked at my grandfather sitting across from me and wondered, as I often did, how it felt to have pieces of metal buried in his face. He had never told me the story of how he was wounded. He didn't want it to seem like he glorified war. He knew, however, that World War II was a piece of history that had captured my interest, so while we waited, he handed me a small box, slightly bigger than a watch box. I slowly opened it, and I was blown away! Inside this box were all the medals he had received while in the Army. There was a purple heart, a bronze star and a silver star, a European victory medal, and the Japan victory medal, since my grandfather had been sent to Japan once Germany surrendered. This was the best birthday present ever! I was so excited, I couldn't contain myself, which I'm sure was obvious because I wiggled and squirmed in my chair, thanking Grandpa over and over. And the best part was that it was from him, the most important man in my life!

I was forced to settle down once the food arrived, and as we ate, Grandpa asked if he could take me to Canada on a fishing trip. After very little discussion, my parents consented. Grandpa turned to me with a teasing smile and asked, "Do you want to go?"

I'm sure he knew the answer even before I squealed, "Yes!" Of course, I jumped at the chance! I would spend every day with him if I could.

As we waited for the waitress to clear our dishes, Grandpa told me he had one more gift for me in his car. We walked out to the parking lot and he opened his trunk. To my surprise, it was a P-51 Mustang, remote-controlled airplane. I looked at him with my eyes wide and mouth open, speechless.

"I'll come over in a few days and we'll put it together and go fly it," he said.

This was amazing! This was like a big kid toy! I had never been given anything this fancy!

We went back inside to where my parents sat at a now cleared table. I excitedly told them about the airplane. Mom smiled, but shushed me, pointing at Aaron, sleeping on her shoulder. Grandpa made me promise I wouldn't touch the plane until he came over. I crossed my heart, promised, and had to listen to my father preach about responsibility. The waitress returned, and dessert was ordered. I took out the small box again and held the medals in my hand. Again, I asked Grandpa how he got the Purple Heart. He said that was a story for another time. I was disappointed, but not surprised. Sometimes I wondered if I would ever hear the real story.

Soon, the waitress brought our dessert, a few other waiters following her. They sang "happy birthday" to me and left us alone to finish eating. As we stood up to leave,

Grandpa threw some cash on the table to cover the tip and went to pay the bill.

In the parking lot, we said our goodbyes, and I climbed in the back with my knees on the seat and my elbows resting on the rear dash so I could watch as Grandpa drove away. I had so much to look forward to and couldn't wait for Thursday, which was usually the day he'd come over if he was available. I daydreamed the whole way home—my RC airplane cruising through the sky, shooting down imaginary German Bf 109s.

Getting up early Monday morning, again fumbling with the medals that had once been my grandfather's, I decided to take them to school. I stuffed the box in my backpack, had my breakfast, and left for the bus stop. This was an obsession now. I'd had an interest in the subject before, but now! Now, I had something authentic that I could hold in my hands! Something with meaning! I was also more determined than ever to hear my grandfather's heroic stories. I wanted to know about the things he did and the people he saved.

Once at school, I caught up with a couple of friends who, like me, were interested in WWII. I motioned for them to follow me to a table against the wall, just inside the school doors.

"You're not going to believe what I got!" I told them as I slowly removed the box from my pack. I opened it and set the contents on the table.

They stood in awe of what lay before them. Mouths agape, they looked at me simultaneously.

"Real?" Jerry asked.

"Yes!" I told him. "My grandpa just gave them to me for my birthday."

They wanted to know the stories behind each one.

I told them I wasn't sure yet. "He wants to wait for the right time to tell me about it, I guess."

They picked them up one by one. "Man, they're heavy!" they marveled. The bell rang, cutting short the show, so I quickly gathered the medals, put them gently back in the box, placed it in my pack, and went to class with a promise to the guys that I would show them again when we had more time.

The week flew by, and before long, I was headed home on Thursday. It felt like the bus driver was going as slow as possible. I ran all the way home from the bus stop. As I rounded the corner, our driveway came into sight. There was no car! He wasn't there. I couldn't believe it! I had been dying for this day to arrive, and now I felt crushed! As I walked up the driveway, my mother came out to greet me.

"Where's Grandpa?" I puffed, trying to catch my breath.

"He had to run to the hobby store for some different glue or something," she answered. "He'll be back in a few minutes."

Hope was restored in my little world, and I sighed in relief.

"Awesome." I ran in the house to change and tackle some of my daily chores before he got back. I had most of the dishes in the dishwasher when I heard him pull up. I dried my hands as I ran to the door. I rushed over and gave him a huge hug just as he got out of the car.

"So glad to see you," he said.

I replied, "I've been so excited all week for you to come over!"

We walked into the kitchen of our small house and sat down at the table. It was covered in newspaper and a few small tools set off to one side; a couple of screwdrivers, an exact-o knife, some sandpaper, and now Grandpa added a bottle of glue.

"Finish the dishes before you start on that thing," Mom said.

I was about to protest when Grandpa said, "It's okay. I have a few things to organize before we can begin anyway."

Within five minutes, I was done and pulled up a chair next to him as we began taking the pieces from the box and setting them aside.

Mom came into the room with baby Aaron on her hip and said, "I'm headed to the grocery store. I won't be too long."

We heard her start the car and back down the driveway.

Immediately, Grandpa cleared his throat and turned to me. "Do you still want to hear my story?"

"Yeah!" I exclaimed.

He took a deep breath. "It all began in 1943 when I walked into the Army recruiting station."

My grandfather, being a devout Christian, didn't believe in the taking of another man's life, no matter what the reason. So, instead, he'd decided he would try to save lives by becoming a medical corpsman. He told me about his basic training at Fort Benning, Georgia. The men responsible for instructing the new recruits, the drill sergeants, had been harsh on him. They all thought that if you didn't want to kill Germans or Japs there was something wrong with you.

"It wasn't like it is today," he said. "Back then, they would beat you with a baton if they wanted. They would kick you and slap you—even hitting with a closed fist was acceptable."

"What if you hit back?" I asked, realizing that I was not paying attention to the airplane anymore.

He said, "Then they would court-martial you." He explained that was a military court, and they could punish you by taking your money, your rank, or even your freedom by putting you in a military prison.

"Why would anyone volunteer for that?" I wondered aloud.

"Well, it was a different time," he said, briefly looking away from me and out the window. "They believed it would teach you to be tough and get you ready for combat," and under his breath, "It wasn't even close." He turned his attention back to me. "So, after six weeks of that, and four weeks of medical training, I graduated."

"What did you have to learn to become a medic?" I asked.

"Lots of things," he started. "We were taught how to apply a compression bandage, which applies pressure to a wound to stop the bleeding. We learned how to splint broken bones, start IVs—"

I interrupted, "What's an IV?"

"It stands for intravenous. It's where a needle is put directly into a vein and it's attached to a tube connected to a bottle of medicine. It makes the medicine work faster. Kind of like two months ago when you were really sick and dehydrated. They gave you an IV, remember?"

"That's what that was called?"

"Yes," he said, and continued. "We learned how to perform CPR, sanitize and dress wounds, and apply a tourniquet. Do you know what a tourniquet is?"

Tipping my head to one side, I said, "Mmm... not sure."

Grandpa gave it to me straight. "If you had a serious cut on your arm and we couldn't stop the bleeding, I would wrap your arm in a cloth..." He paused. "Wait a minute. Go get that dishcloth and I'll show you." He wrapped my arm with the towel and tied the ends around a screwdriver he picked up from the table. "You can use

anything long enough that won't break, even just a stick."
He began twisting the stick. "See how it's tightening? It
would cut off the blood flow to the cut and stop the
bleeding. But this is only to be used in emergencies.
There's a lot of risks involved."

"Like what?" I asked.

"Well, do you feel your hand getting numb?"

I nodded.

"That means there isn't much blood getting to your
hand. The tissues need blood to live, so if you leave it too
long, your hand will die." As he untied the tourniquet
from my arm, he chuckled. "Now don't you go trying this
on any of your friends!"

"Okay, Grandpa," I grinned.

Grandpa's story went on. "We also learned about
chemical weapons. They are a gas you can't see. It attacks
a person's nervous system making people vomit and can
even kill them. We had to carry atropine injections in
case we encountered that. You had to jab the syringe into
your heart within just a few seconds to counteract the gas
and survive."

I began to see why Grandpa waited until my mom
had left before telling me this story. She would think it
was too gory for a twelve-year-old, but I was fascinated.

The story continued. "We also learned how and
when to give antibiotics and painkillers, like morphine.
Our job wasn't to heal a person, just stabilize them and
keep them alive long enough to make it to a field hospital

where doctors could fix their wounds properly." Grandpa leaned back in his chair, stretched his legs, crossed his ankles, and kept going. "After graduating, I was shipped to my unit, the 1st Infantry Division. We were called 'The Big Red One' because of the red number one on our unit patch." He smiled at the simplicity of it.

"Shortly after arriving at my unit, we boarded troop ships headed to England. Some of our soldiers had to stay with English families because the Army didn't have enough space in the barracks for everyone, but I wasn't one of them. Eventually, there were so many soldiers in England that between us and the British soldiers, we outnumbered the civilians. The equipment kept arriving, and the troops kept coming. Skill training and physical training, PT, made up everyday life. We knew that we'd be invading the beaches of France at some point. When and where was anyone's guess."

I jumped in. "You mean D-Day, Grandpa?"

"Yes," he said, "but at the time, we didn't know where it would be or the timing of it. In fact, the original invasion was supposed to take place several days before June 6th." Looking at his watch, he shook his head as if to clear it. "Let's concentrate on our project now for a while," he said. "I'll need to go soon, and it would be nice to get the wings attached so we can let the glue dry before I come over next week."

I could have listened to Grandpa's story all night, but I said, "Okay, Grandpa."

We did what we could on the airplane and set it aside where it wouldn't be disturbed. As we cleaned up our work area, he asked what I was doing over the weekend. I told him I'd be staying at my other grandma's because my mom and dad were going somewhere out of town.

He said, "Alright, I'll still see you next Thursday, I hope."

We heard Mom's car pull in, so I gave him a quick hug and went out to help her bring in groceries as Grandpa got in his car. I lingered on the steps to the house with an armful of bags so I could watch him drive away.

CHAPTER THREE

When I got home from school on Friday, Mom and Dad were already gone, and Uncle Lyle, my godfather, was waiting to drive me to Grandma's. I dropped my school bag in the house and grabbed the duffel bag I had packed last night. I slammed the door behind me as I went through it and bounded off the stoop, making the three steps in one.

"Whoa, Buddy!" he laughed. "Are you sure you have everything?"

I nodded as I crawled into his F-150. On our way, we talked about music and baseball. I think I looked forward to the ride with him just as much as the weekend with Grandma. He was my favorite uncle, and I liked knowing he was my godfather and would raise me if anything happened to my parents. When we got to Grandma's, I jumped out of Uncle Lyle's truck just as fast as I had hopped into it, grabbed my bag, and after a quick hug for Grandma, took my stuff upstairs.

"Dinner will be soon, Michael," Grandma hollered to me as I rounded the corner at the top of the steps.

I heard, "Goodbye, Michael," and yelled back, "Bye, Uncle Lyle. Thanks for the ride."

Grandma made a tasty meal, as always, and after dinner, we sat watching television. She let me watch *Hogan's Heroes* even though she wasn't a fan. Around nine o'clock, I knew it would be time for bed, so I asked Grandma for some ice cream.

"My goodness, Michael! After all you ate for dinner, you still have room for a snack?" she asked, pretending to be shocked.

This was our little routine every bedtime.

I said, "Of course, Grandma! The ice cream just melts in my belly and fills in all the spaces around the other food!"

"You eat just like your father," she chuckled.

We each had a small bowl of ice cream, chocolate chip with chocolate sauce, and she added a couple cherries on top of mine. When we finished, Grandma asked if I wanted her to tuck me into bed.

"No, thanks, Grandma," I replied. "I think I'm getting too old for that. But I promise to brush my teeth."

As I dashed up the stairs, I played a musical game in my head with the creaky stairs. I knew where every squeaky step was and what sound it made by how much pressure was applied. Sometimes, I would even add words and have a little ditty in my mind by the time I hit the second floor. Once upstairs, I went into my room, the room that had been Uncle Lyle's when he still lived here. Grandma had redecorated since he'd left, of course, but some of his things were still scattered around the room. His high school picture, some trophies, and his baseball memorabilia made me feel like I was never alone in this room. I hollered "goodnight" to Grandma. She didn't answer, so I listened closely and heard a faint snoring sound and knew she had fallen asleep in front of the television again. I closed the door, turned on the small fan that sat atop the dresser, and opened a window. My favorite thing about this room was the little balcony attached to it that looked over the backyard. I opened the door to the deck, the door sticking momentarily, and stepped out to look at the stars. The sky seemed especially bright tonight—it would be like a night-light in my room. I looked to the ground below and saw a bunny in Grandma's garden. *Oh, if grandma could see this,* I thought, *she'd be out there with her broom!* I made a mental note to talk to Grandma about it tomorrow. Maybe she'd let me trap it.

I took a couple deep breaths and headed inside, leaving the door open. I turned off the light, letting the stars illuminate the room and crawled into bed. With the fresh breeze coming in, it wasn't long before I was fast asleep.

Saturday morning, I woke up to a bright, sunny day and knew it was going to be a warm one. I sleepily walked downstairs and saw Grandma, already busy baking her German coffee cake. She had baked four pans of it every Saturday for as long as I could remember. When she asked me how I slept, I said, "Like a rock!"

"Good," she said. "Now go watch some TV for a while, and as soon as I get these cakes in the oven, I'll make you some breakfast."

I went into the living room and turned on the big console TV, plopped into the closest easy chair, and watched cartoons. This was my favorite way to wake up. An hour later, I finished eating, changed into clothes, and sat in the sun on the front porch in a large wicker chair, wondering what kind of adventure I could drum up. *I know!* I thought. *I'll sneak up to the attic!* It had been a long time since I had been to that mysterious place, exploring the odds and ends Grandma had stored up there, although I never really did have permission. Uncle Lyle had always told me, "It's easier to ask for forgiveness than to ask permission." I told Grandma I was going to my room to do some homework.

She replied, "Okay, Michael, that's my good boy."

I noisily ran upstairs, only instead of going to my room, I went to the bedroom across the hall from mine, walked to the closet, and opened the door. Right inside the door was a dark stairway that led to the attic. I flipped on the light switch and a small lightbulb in the ceiling slowly came to life, dimly lighting the way. I quietly took one step after another to the top, slowly raised the doors over my head, and peered into the expansive storage space. I saw nothing alarming, no spiders or rats, so I opened the doors wider and went through.

There were several lightbulbs hanging from the ceiling by old electrical wires. Cobwebs hung thick in every corner, and there was an inch of dust on everything. Most of this sizable room was empty, but there were boxes stacked together in several places, almost as if certain items were being kept together. The boxes weren't labeled so it was anyone's guess what was really inside without looking. They weren't taped shut, but rather, the corners were folded over each other to keep the tops closed. It was already getting warm up here, so I went to the lone window and slid it open. The cool breeze that entered felt so good. I closed my eyes and inhaled deeply, smelling the flowers from Grandma's garden.

I turned back into the room and saw that the breeze had stirred up the dust. I could see the particles being lifted into the air and drifting through the shaft of sunlight coming through the window. As I scanned around the room, my eyes lit upon several boxes and two old trunks on the opposite side. The streak of sunlight hit one trunk squarely in the middle as if calling me to it. The few times I'd been up here, I didn't recall seeing it. "I'm sure it has been here," I reasoned with myself, "I probably just missed it in the dim light." But now, with the sun shining directly on it, it stood out like a turd in a punch bowl.

I walked over to it and looked closely. It was undoubtedly old and appeared like it hadn't been opened in many years. I looked at the items around the two trunks and realized there weren't even any old fingerprints in the settling dust. I assumed they most likely hadn't been opened since being stored here. I didn't wonder long what was inside as my curiosity was getting the better of me. I gently blew on the cover and dust flew everywhere, including about a pound up my nose. "Not so smart," I coughed. When it had subsided a bit, I flipped the latch and slowly lifted the lid, my eyes growing big as saucers!

Spread before me were German WWII artifacts. I had been told that my grandparents fled Germany just prior to WWII, settling here and moving into this house when it was new. I'd never met my grandfather. He'd passed away when I was a baby, so I only had a few stories of him instead of memories, and those were only the things that had happened here in America. Now before me was finally some evidence of a life in Germany. There were uniforms with patches neatly sewn on, crisply folded and stacked. There were medals thrown loosely in a small wooden tray on top. There were letters galore, wrapped in a broken and decaying rubber band and a pile of black and white photos. A small book was stuffed in the middle that I guessed was a diary or journal.

I looked at the other trunk, and my imagination ran wild. I slowly opened it and found the contents just as amazing! There was a helmet, a bayonet, an old Luger pistol, and other Nazi memorabilia including a couple of swastika armbands, a swastika, and an SS flag among other items like belts, leather boots, a canteen, and smaller objects a soldier might carry. I wondered how this got here if my grandparents had left prior to the war. I knew my grandpa had a brother who'd stayed in Germany and was eventually killed in Stalingrad, or so I'd been told. Maybe this wasn't what I thought it was. My eyes darted back and forth between the two open trunks, my brain racing wildly with all the possibilities. I had to know more. I had watched WWII documentaries with my father, like *World at War*, so I already had a grasp of what lay before me. But who did it belong to? That was the true question.

I heard Grandma call "Breakfast!" so I quickly closed the trunks and hurried down the stairs, closing doors and turning off lights as I went, wanting to make it look like I had never been there.

"I'll be right down," I hollered. "I just have to wash my hands."

I couldn't stop thinking about what I had just found. I raced downstairs, thinking the sooner I ate, the sooner I could get back to the attic.

As I rounded the corner into the kitchen, Grandma asked, "Where have you been? You're all dirty, for Heaven's sake."

I looked down to see I was covered in dust, I thought quickly and fibbed. "I lost my super ball and had to crawl under the bed to get it." I had forgotten that Grandma was a meticulous housekeeper so there never would have been dust under the bed.

She looked at me suspiciously and said, "Uh huh." Then she said that maybe my ball was more of an outside toy, hinting I should go outside with it.

I agreed, and as soon as I finished eating, I ran out the back door to play. At least, that's what I tried to make it look like. Instead, I snuck around the house and quietly came in the front door. I scurried up the flight of stairs, avoiding all the creaky spots, and headed straight to the trunks. I opened the one with the uniforms first. As I held up one of the jackets, it seemed very heavy. The first thing I noticed was a band that ran around the bottom of the left sleeve that said, "Das Reich." I grabbed a nearby piece of paper and jotted some notes. I sorted through the wooden tray, finding a ring and a few colorful ribbons I knew had to be awards of some kind. I assigned imaginary names to unfamiliar things I came across so I could write them down and do some research later at home.

Next, I grabbed the letters and the journal, setting them aside. I figured I could take them home to read them. I could easily sneak them out in my bag, return them the next time I came back, and they'd never be missed. I pulled out the photographs and set those with the letters. I began to rummage through the equipment. I felt like I was playing with stuff I shouldn't even be looking at, but I couldn't help myself. Suddenly, I realized it was getting darker and knew it was close to supper time, so I packed things back in the trunk as best I could and quietly lowered the lids. I closed the window, grabbed the letters and pictures, and scurried back down the stairs. I could hear Grandma's pots clanging in the kitchen, so I knew I was safe walking across the hall to my bedroom without being seen with my treasures. The smell of dinner wafting up the stairway made me hungry. I washed my hands—this time remembering to brush the dust off my clothes—and followed my nose to the kitchen.

Grandma always made German food for dinner. The *spaetzle* she was making tonight with a pork roast and gravy was the best. There was so much food, I thought we might be feeding the whole German army!

"Are we having company?" I asked.

She nodded. "Your uncle Lyle is coming. He should be here soon."

As if on cue, the door opened, and my Number One uncle walked in. Smiling, he greeted us in German. Grandma used German as much as possible. The Fatherland and our heritage were very important to her. She had insisted that all her grandchildren learn the German language at an early age. I had started speaking and writing German from the time I could read and write. So, in dinner conversations, I was expected to keep up. I sometimes had to search for the right words, but eventually, I'd get it. Often, I would learn new words at the table and get quizzed the next time I visited.

After dinner, I was excused and immediately went to my room. I began looking at all the black and white pictures. There were men in uniform, some with vehicles and equipment such as tanks, trucks, and artillery pieces. I tried looking for the common denominator. And after a few minutes, I noticed one man in most of the pictures. I had to find out who this was. Having no recollection of my grandfather, I couldn't tell if it was him. On the bottom of the stack were several pictures of him in what appeared to be a dress uniform. I saw the tabs on his collar and realized that this man, whoever he turned out to be, was an SS officer.

I reached for the journal and opened it carefully, noticing the dates at the top of the delicate pages. The first entry was 1942 and the last was from 1945. I opened to a random page and read the words:

"We fought what I believe was the largest tank battle in history today. Thousands from each side clashing on the Russian steppe. Trying a classic pincer movement, we attempted to encircle two Russian armies and over a hundred thousand men. After the first day, we are woefully behind schedule. I got 4 1/2 kills today and one truck. Hunting was good. However, I lost sergeant Dietel and 4th squad. First squad's Panther was damaged, but it was repaired. Now we're down to three Panthers. I have a bad feeling about the future of this operation. Seems they were waiting for us. One round, HEAT, T-34 in the open, 11 o'clock, 500 yards!"

I flipped a few pages and read some more as the hour hand on the clock flew by. I was enthralled and lost in my own little world, or rather, someone else's world from years ago. Like a person gasping for air, I couldn't stop. I was excited and nervous about what I might find. When I heard Grandma coming up the creaky stairs, I quickly put everything in a pile and shoved it under the blankets. She knocked on the door.

"Michael, it's time for bed."

"Yes, ma'am," I said, and went to the restroom. I went tinkle, or piddle, as Grandma called it, washed my hands, dried them on the towel in the squeaky brass towel holder, and began brushing my teeth. I stood looking in the cracked, stained mirror that opened to the little medicine cabinet. I pictured my grandfather looking in this same mirror and imagined the things he must have seen and done. I took longer than I realized to brush my teeth, daydreaming the whole time. I said goodnight to Grandma and gave her a hug and kiss. Sliding my feet along the smooth wooden floor, I got to my door, grabbing the brass door handle so I could make the corner into my room. I flipped back the blankets on my bed, scooped up the pictures and journal, brought them to my lips and whispered, "See you tomorrow." Laughing at my silliness, I tucked them into my backpack. I turned on the fan on the table by the bed and flipped off the light. In total darkness, I felt my way to the bed, crawled in, and pulled the sheet and thin blanket over me. Closing my eyes, I tried to sleep, but my brain had other ideas. My mind took me to the Eastern front, imagining what it was like wearing that heavy wool uniform and being surrounded by death every day. Thinking of those words in the journal, I pictured myself in a tank, rumbling across the Russian steppe. Eventually, I drifted off, dreaming so vividly, it felt like I was really there.

CHAPTER FOUR

July 4, 1943

As I stood looking over my men in the predawn morning, I wondered how many of us would survive the upcoming battle. At 0400, our artillery opened up. Round after round whizzed overhead like a freight train. We heard loud explosions on the near horizon. It was slow at first and then picked up the tempo until every gun was firing on the Russian positions. Soon, the Nebelwerfer 42 (multiple launch rocket system) joined in. The screaming rockets flying over us made me thankful I was not on the receiving end. Within minutes, Russian artillery attempted to answer back. The confusion caused by shells passing each other in mid-air only added to the apprehension of what was about to take place.

Momentarily, I fell into a trance-like state, thinking back to just last night when my men had gathered around after another crappy but warm meal provided by the field kitchen, talking innocently, and were relatively safe. Now, I was putting them in harm's way, yet again.

I went over the operation again in my head: the movement order, rally points, and code words. Initially, the Panzerkampfwagen VI (Tiger) would lead the way, along with the few Elephants, sometimes referred to as the Ferdinand. Then, we would follow in our Pzkw V (Panther) with the Pzkw IV keeping on our flanks. Our job was to support the infantry. I was brought back to the present by my platoon sergeant.

"Sir, are we ready?"

I looked at him, thinking, *this could be the last time we ever see each other alive.* I told him to "Start 'em up."

He turned toward the tanks, raised his right arm over his head, and made a circular motion with his hand. The Panthers fired up, rumbling in the cool darkness. The Maybach V12 was a good engine, but this was a heavy tank. Actually, it was classified as a medium tank because of its gun size of 75mm and being smaller than the heavier Tiger with its 88mm gun. There were some growing pains for this tank and some bugs to work out, but overall, it was a great tank, and we knew it. The biggest issue was its transmission, often leaving us stranded on the battlefield until it could be recovered and repaired. We prayed that today, all would go well for us. It was imperative we struck like lightning and overpowered Ivan.

As the eastern horizon began to lighten, the dew that had formed on the horizontal surfaces seemed to retreat from the rising sun. The small water droplets danced with the vibrations of the engines, gathering into bigger puddles and running down sloped surfaces. I pictured this being the Red Army under our advance, running for their lives as we crushed them under our tracks. Our first targets would likely be infantry or improved fighting positions such as bunkers or sandbagged machine gun positions, so our course was to have a few high explosive (HE) shells loaded in the breech first.

I went to my tank, crawled on top of the turret, and took one last look around. The sky was light blue with a few wisps of clouds with their edges painted in shades of orange and pink. It was beautiful, even through the gathering smoke and dust that filled the air with increasing fury. I took a deep breath, tucked my head, and crawled into my commander's cupola. I grabbed my headset and placed it around my neck. "Ready?" I hollered down to my crew.

Driver Private Williams, gunner Corporal Helmut, loader Private Rundle, and radio operator Corporal Hoffman, all gave me a "check." Private Williams was out of Mannheim, only eighteen years old and barely beginning his life. He came from a large family and was the oldest of four brothers and two sisters. His family owned a hardware store where he had worked until being called to serve.

Corporal Helmut was twenty years old but with a baby face that could have passed for about fifteen. He came from the small northern town of Tessin where his family raised sugar beets. His father was in failing health, and with only one sister, they needed more hired help in the fields. With most of the young boys and men off fighting the war, farm workers were hard to come by and were usually women. I once overheard him talking about being able to send more money home now that he had been promoted to corporal.

Private Rundle, eighteen, was an only child and hailed from Stuttgart where both his mother and father worked in a bake shop. His father had lost his hearing as a child from a severe case of measles, so was not fit for service himself, but I guessed that he would be quite proud to have his son serving. And if the care packages that came to the boy from home were any indication, my guess was right. A box came at least every two weeks, sometimes more, filled with the fanciest of cakes and cookies. The private was always gracious and shared.

Corporal Hoffman, a confident nineteen-year-old, came to us from a small town east of Berlin named Strasberg, very close to Poland. It was so close, the other members of his unit teased him about having a Polish accent. He took it well and laughed at himself right along with them. I suspected he was glad to be mocked for that and not something else, like the fact that he was engaged to his high school girlfriend who came from a wealthy family. And maybe they had, just not within earshot of me.

I looked back at the convoy, raised my right arm, and swung it forward in the traditional "follow me" motion. The large iron beast under me leaped forward, the suspension catching up to the forty-four tons of iron set in motion. We crawled out to the clearing, the tracks clanking and screeching the entire time. This certainly was not a stealthy vehicle. I pulled my headphones over my ears and heard excited radio chatter from the first elements that had just crossed the berm. Instantly, I could hear the large booms of the Tiger's 88s going off as they fired at the enemy. The 5th SS Panzer division (Wiking) had just taken out several Russian T-34s at long range with high explosive anti-tank (HEAT) rounds. Even from a thousand yards away, it was like shooting fish in a barrel. The strong smell of cordite filled my nostrils. I loved the smell of burnt gun powder, but this became overwhelming. Columns of thick, black smoke rose into the air from several locations, each of them representing burning Russian tanks and dead soldiers. I grabbed the binoculars from around my neck and peered ahead. Suddenly, I saw him.

"Target at one o'clock. T-34 at 800 yards. HEAT round. Fire when ready!"

As Rundle scurried to remove the round from the breech, I saw the Russian fire in our direction. A puff of white smoke emanated from his muzzle. A *whoosh* in front of us, and the round hit the ground, throwing chunks of sod and dirt in the air for sixty feet. Rundle yelled, "up!" and we fired back. *Boom!* The huge gun recoiled from the explosion, and the tank rocked back on its tracks. Within a second, our shell hit between the hull and the turret. A large fireball rose above my target. I blinked instinctively and watched his turret hurling skyward. The awesomeness of such an event always shocked me. An explosion so violent it could throw several tons of twisted metal high into the air. I knew that those inside would be shredded; limbs torn from torsos and bodies flung against the metal bulkheads. There was no chance of anyone living through such a horrendous blast.

Quickly, I scanned the horizon looking for more threats. A Bf 109 fighter plane caught my attention when I heard him shooting. I looked up behind me and saw he was angled toward the ground in front of us. Some of us carried a swastika flag attached to the rear deck lid, just so we wouldn't get strafed by our own Air Force. I didn't have one on my tank and became immediately concerned that I was the target until I turned around and saw mini dust clouds form where his bullets were hitting the ground.

The Russian steppe was an unforgiving place. There were patches of open ground where fires had burned away the tall grass and weeds, and other spots where the grass was three feet tall. It was quite easy for Ivan to conceal a minefield, an anti-tank ditch, or an improved fighting position. And the worst thing was, you'd never know it until you were smack dab in the middle of a shit storm. The fighter passed overhead and pulled up abruptly at the end of his run. The Panther belonging to 3rd Squad fired. The spot where the fighter had just been shooting exploded into a cloud of dirt and dust, the debris hanging in the air momentarily, like being suspended without gravity, then falling to earth. The larger chunks first—the finer stuff took longer to dissipate, like an evaporating cloud.

We continued our advance, the infantry forming up behind us, the artillery shells and rockets still passing overhead. That would all end soon as the possibility of hitting our own troops was too great. It was good we were getting close air support now. The Bf 109s and Fw 190s would clear the skies of Russian fighters and revert to a ground support role. It wasn't long before I noticed a blinking light to our front. I heard bullets zing past me. I lowered myself into the iron hulk and closed the hatch. The bullets started beating against us like hail on a metal roof. *Tink... Tink... Tink*. Every once in a while, a bigger one would hit, like a .30 caliber. *Bang... Bang*.

I peered out the small slits positioned around the turret made of thick, bulletproof glass until I picked out the enemy machine gunner. I told Rundle, "One round, HE, machine gun nest at three hundred yards."

He soon yelled, "up!" but Helmut already had him in his sights and before the word could leave the loader's lips... *Boom*. The 75mm recoiled, kicking back into the turret. I was briefly blinded by the smoke, but we drove through it in a second. I saw our round burst just past their position. I called for another round of HE. "Drop twenty-five," I yelled, meaning the number of yards I wanted the gunner to adjust to hit the target. Rundle opened the breech, and the empty brass shell went clanging to the floor, a thin wisp of smoke appearing from its hollow casing. He slammed another shell into the breech and again yelled, "up!" The gun firing again and immediately afterward... *Boom*! As our tank hesitated in its forward movement, I witnessed the gun position disintegrate before me.

I opened the hatch and slowly raised myself up, looking to the rear. I saw the infantry running and dodging. Some would throw themselves to the ground on their bellies, then pop up and run some more. I turned back to the front and saw it right away. "HALT!" I yelled. The big tank locked up the tracks, skidded on the dirt briefly, and tilted forward as everything came to a stop. Just yards in front of us was a huge ditch, concealed by tall grass. It was approximately fifteen yards wide and around twelve feet deep. This ditch was designed to swallow us whole. These ditches were a common tactic. Some were bigger, some smaller, but this one was just big enough that if we hadn't seen it, we would've gone in and been unable to crawl up the other side, and steep enough we wouldn't be able to back out, rendering us useless until we could get extracted. I looked left, then right. The trench went on several hundred yards in each direction. The machine gunner we just took out was supposed to keep us buttoned up in our tanks so we wouldn't be able to spot the ditch. Maybe half the squad would've ended up in this hole if I hadn't seen it in time. Now the trick was to find a way around it. Often, though, the only way around included crossing a minefield or some other tank trap.

The idea behind this ditch tactic went something like this: one or two tanks would find the ditch, and if speed was a critical element, they might look for an easier crossing. Eventually, the ditch would come to an end, followed by a stretch of land, twenty, thirty, maybe even fifty yards wide. Then another ditch would start. Anyone using this land bridge might be crossing into a minefield that would take out the first tank, or armored personnel carrier (APC) like an Sd.Kfz. 250, or 251, blocking the land bridge and causing a backup. Or they would have artillery and mortars zeroed in on that location. Essentially, it would create a bottleneck and back everything up, grinding the attackers to a standstill, leaving them in the open and vulnerable, causing delays and buying themselves time, maybe even calling in air strikes. It was cheap, and effective, but it didn't last forever. However, troops used the time they gained to fall back to another defensive position.

Rather than looking for an opening, I decided to try something else, so I called for the Pioneer Battalion and told them I needed a temporary bridge to cross a tank ditch. They asked for my location, so I removed the map from my pocket, spread it out, and quickly calculated my position. After relaying that, I was told to hold tight and they'd be there shortly. I ordered the tanks into a defensive posture, kind of half-moon shape, with thirty yards between us. Staying ever vigilant, I told my men to "smoke 'em if you got 'em" and to be watching for Ivan. When I checked in with my commander, telling him of our situation, understandably, he was not happy. "Get moving as soon as the bridge is up," he said. We were beginning to fall behind schedule already. The infantry had already caught up with us, crossed the ditch, and continuing their advance.

It was approaching 1200 hours by the time the Pioneers arrived with prefabricated bridging sections piled onto a five-ton truck. Their men raced to unload and connect the pieces. Soon, a bulldozer approached and began working on filling in a section of the ditch. This way, when they were done and the ditch was passable, the Pioneers could take their bridge sections to another trouble spot. It wasn't long, and their commander announced the bridge was ready to cross. I hollered, "Fire 'em up," and we crossed one by one, leaving the Pioneers behind. I suspected we'd need them again before the battle was over.

As we trekked over a slight rise, I couldn't believe my eyes. Everywhere I looked I saw tanks, either engaged in combat or the hulks of metal, burning red-hot. This had to be the largest tank battle in history. There were thousands of tanks from both sides as far as the eye could see. Clouds of dust and columns of smoke rose from numerous places across the field. I felt overwhelmed. I felt confused about where to even begin looking for targets. As we started down the opposite slope, the tank to my right, 1st Platoon's tank, commanded by Sergeant Hummel, exploded in a shower of sparks and smoke. It came to a screeching halt as the track on its right side broke apart and fell off its road wheels. Undeterred, they began firing the mounted MG-42 at a spot in the distance. I focused on the direction they were shooting and saw an enemy soldier, armed with an anti-tank rocket, the RPG-1, stand up and get hit multiple times. He flailed his arms, dropping the RPG as he fell to the ground. How many more of these weapons were on this field was anyone's guess. Our infantry, which was now directly in front of us, gathered the courage to advance again, now that we had arrived.

Hummel, my 1st Squad leader, gave me the thumbs up that everyone in his tank was okay. I told him not to wait for maintenance if they could help it. "Try to repair that road wheel and track, then catch up with us." Either way, they could only fight and shelter from their current position, effectively being taken out of the battle, albeit temporarily. We could ill afford this right now. We needed every man and fighting vehicle we had.

What we encountered ahead was best described as organized confusion; bullets, shouting, explosions, and planes overhead. Bodies lay everywhere, blanketing the earth; wounded men cried out in pain, while the dead were forever silent. It overwhelmed the senses, and I began to feel numb, thinking every minute I was able to take a breath was a mini victory.

I picked out a target just to our left and hollered below, "One round HEAT, T-34 in the open at 11 o'clock, 500 yards." The turret whined as it rotated left, the gun depressing ever so slightly. I heard the familiar response from my well-trained crew, "up!" then *boom* as the gun fired. "Damn!" I yelled. "Short! Send another! Add thirty!" The T-34 was preoccupied with a Tiger on its left and never even saw us. "Up!" ... *Boom*! The tank jerked back. Our shell entered our opponent from the front right side of its hull, the T-34 exploding into a large red and orange fireball and a shower of sparks, then thick, black smoke billowing from its interior. Within moments, secondary explosions followed. Obviously, the tank's magazine had been compromised, and now its own shells were cooking off.

The radio was alive with chatter as excited voices called for maintenance, air support, medics, fuel and ammo, and even artillery. Unit commanders gave orders—armor and infantry working hand in glove. The going was slow; the advance of maybe a mile had been completed. We should've been at least ten times that far by this point. We kept moving forward, the infantry using the tanks as cover. I crawled into the turret and closed the hatch. An explosion close to us showered our Panther with dirt and rocks.

"Where did that come from?"

Private Williams, my driver, replied, "Right front, two o'clock."

I looked and another T-34 had us dead to rights. Helmut was turning the turret as fast as it would go, but I was willing it to go faster. He fired at us again, the shell just nicking the turret. A loud *ping* echoed through the tank as it bounced off to the rear. "Faster!" I barked. "HEAT round, T-34 at 575 yards. Fire when ready!" Again, our gun went off, the shell streaking toward its target and hitting just behind the turret. The T-34 ground to a stop, its engine compartment set ablaze. The main turret hatch flew open, as did the driver's hatch, the crew scrambling to get free of their stricken vehicle, like ants parading out of their hill.

This was a target rich environment. Armored vehicles were everywhere; disabled ones from both sides littered the expansive steppe and added to the mounting confusion. I scanned in front of me and locked onto another target. A Russian KV-1 appeared to be out of commission, but not destroyed, a Tiger close by burning ferociously. Like two dueling gunfighters, they shot each other at close range, the Tiger getting the worst of it. I knew we'd need to close the distance first before being able to give any assistance. The KV-1 was Russia's heavy tank. This monster had armor so thick that our 75mm couldn't penetrate it from the front, only from the rear, and we'd need to be within three hundred yards. Suddenly, I saw movement on my left. It was one of our

Stug IIIs from our Assault battalions coming alongside. I looked behind us, wondering where my 4th Platoon sergeant, Dietel, had gone. He was engaged with an enemy tank to the left, driving toward each other at slow speed. The Russian fired, and his shell penetrated the gun mantlet of the Panther, exploding in its interior. The Panther jerked several times in its death throes and came to a stop, its main gun hanging angled and resting on the hull. The driver popped his hatch open and tried to crawl out, only making it about halfway before collapsing, half hanging out of his hatch, the Panther now on fire. I felt helpless. There was nothing I could do.

I looked back to the right and said to Williams, "Come left thirty degrees. One HEAT round, T-34 in the open at 560 yards."

Rundle hollered, "Up," and there was a pause.

I looked at Helmut and yelled, "What the hell are you waiting for?"

"I can't find him in my sights!"

Suddenly, the Russian fired at us, the round smashing into the ground directly in front of us, giving us a bath in dirt and sod.

Helmut yelled, "I see him!"

The quick-thinking Williams had stopped in the shell crater that had just been created. Although it wasn't big enough to hide us, it would offer a smaller silhouette to the opponent. The 75mm cracked, *boom*, and we finally answered back. But the Russian had never stopped moving, and in addition to our momentary delay, our round went long.

The waiting was extremely strenuous. Waiting for that next round was like two prize fighters exchanging blows. Waiting for death was like the punch to your head knocking you out. Waiting could drive you crazy with anticipation and stress. You wanted to help and encourage but needed to stay clear.

The Russian fired again, his round just going over the top of us. If we hadn't been in the shallow hole, we'd all be dead right now. Rundle popped the breech open, but the empty shell case was stuck. He closed the breech plug again and reopened it. The case was not extracting, and I could see the Russian was still coming. "Hurry! He's going to fire any second, and he won't miss again!" Finally, the casing came free, Rundle yanking it out and throwing it against the rear bulkhead where it bounced and clanged against the floor, resting at my feet. I looked out again, wondering why the Russian hadn't fired yet when I noticed the Stug had engaged him also. Apparently, he figured the Stug was the bigger threat at that moment, so he was now traversing his turret to his left. "Drop eighty and fire when ready." Rundle crammed a new round in the breech and tapped Helmut on the knee. *Boom!* The Panther's gun belched fire and smoke at the communist threat. The HEAT round sliced through the tank's metal like a hot knife through butter. The right track popped off, coming to a rest on the ground while the tank slowly came to a stop, smoking badly. Williams applied some throttle and the diesel engine revved, pulling us out of the hole. We turned slightly and continued forward.

I said, "One round HE, truck at twelve o'clock, 740 yards." Rundle again had trouble extracting the empty case, but in short order, had the required round in the chamber. Again, we fired. "Direct hit!" I screamed as the truck and cannon it was towing flew into the air, exploding in a million pieces. As we kept advancing, I asked Williams how our fuel situation was. "Less than half a tank, Sir," he replied. I told him to get behind the KV-1 we saw. "Let's take it out and get in to refuel."

The KV-1 crew, amid attempting a field repair, saw us coming and scrambled up into their dead tank. In minutes, we were in position, and I sent one HEAT round into it, but the heavy Russian beast just shuddered. It was almost as if the tank just swallowed it up. So, I called for another, and this time, the shell burst in its engine compartment, setting the whole thing on fire. As it quickly became an inferno, I deliberated on putting another in her. Just as I was about to say "fire" the Russian opened his main hatch. The crew filed out of the tank one by one, on fire and flailing their arms wildly. My radio operator fired our coaxial machine gun at them as they came out, putting them out of their torment.

It was approaching 1500 hours when we pulled up to the fuel site. We were below a quarter tank. While we sat in a long line of tanks, trucks, and APCs, I told the men to grab some food and asked Helmut to bring some back for Williams. I told Williams when he was done fueling and checking the fluid levels to meet me at the Battalion Command Post. "Oh, and have that breech looked at. We can't afford to have shells sticking in the muzzle." After that, we'd need to go to the ammo dump and rearm before going back out.

I hailed a passing motorcyclist and hopped in the sidecar, setting my submachine gun on the floor and my brown leather satchel in my lap. I told the private to take me to the battalion. As we drove, I closed my eyes. I could hear the battle over the motorcycle's engine. Just being able to disconnect briefly was relaxing, and I began to fall asleep. No sooner had I dozed off, when the motorcycle stopped in front of a large gray tent. "Sir, we're here." I opened my eyes and stretched. Crawling from the sidecar, I grabbed my MP 40 and slung the leather satchel over my shoulder. "Thank you," I told the driver. He answered with a salute, which I returned and dismissed him.

The tent was filled with soldiers ranging from sergeants to colonels. Most pored over maps, a few listened to radio communications. I spotted my company commander, Captain Kinsler, and approached him, telling him I had one tank under repair for a broken track, and I had lost one, along with my platoon sergeant, Sergeant Dietel, and four others.

He said, "I'll try to get you replacements, but I doubt it will happen any time soon." He led me over to a large map spread out on a table.

It had small flags on pins stuck in many locations. I saw ours in supply. This was how they tracked the units and their progress.

He pointed to a spot on the map. "You need to get into a defensive position here, before dark. In the morning, we'll renew the offensive with another artillery and rocket barrage." We were woefully behind schedule now and desperately needed to pick up the pace. "Radio, light, and noise discipline after dark," he said, which meant no radio communications, no fires, no running engines, and talking at a minimum. We didn't need Ivan dropping artillery on our positions in the middle of the night. He pointed to another spot on the map. "This is your objective in the morning."

Trapping and capturing a couple hundred thousand Russians would not be an easy assignment, but I told him I understood and saluted before heading outside. I found a quiet spot to sit in a patch of grass, pulled out my map, and plotted tomorrow's course. It wasn't long before my squad's Panthers came rolling up the road. I waved to Sergeant Hummel.

"Glad you finally decided to fix that track and get back into the fight!"

He laughed. "I tried to get here quicker, but my men wanted to take naps first, Sir."

Turning serious, I told him he had just received a promotion. "You are the new platoon sergeant."

I crawled on top of my tank and told Private Williams to go to the ammo point. Each tank topped off their magazines, and we rolled out, back to the battle. Fortunately, by the time we got to our position, the infantry had already secured the location. We spaced the tanks about thirty yards apart and added clumps of grass for camouflage. I posted a guard duty rotation, which included radio watch, and told the men, "Remember, if you're going to smoke, it'd better be inside the tank." Then I said, "Get some rest. Morning will come early." I looked at my watch. 1900 hours. I was starving and realized I hadn't eaten all day. I pulled a piece of bread and a can of meat from my pack. It wasn't much, but on an empty stomach, it would have to suffice. I sat down, resting my back against one of the road wheels, and opened the can. The meat was more like a paste, so I used my bayonet to spread it on the bread. Amazingly, it didn't taste too bad tonight. I drank the warm, tasteless water from my canteen. I refilled it from the water can in the tank's storage bin and put it back in its canvas cover, ready for another day.

Taking a deep breath, I knew it was time for my dreaded task of writing to the families of the men I'd lost in this last round. Sergeant Dietel's was the most difficult.

We had shared some personal moments, so I knew more about him than the others. I wrote with a heavy heart.

Dear Mrs. Dietel,

It is with deep regret that I must inform you that your husband was killed in action. His tank suffered a fatal hit from an enemy tank.

Hans shared with me his joy at the birth of your first child. I hope that when your son is old enough, you will tell of his father's valiant fight against the enemy to the end. That he fought honorably for the Fatherland.

I hope it will console you to know that he spoke of you with pride, and the love he had for you was evident in his face. I know that you will esteem his memory as you live.

I wish peace for you, for all of us.

Sincerely,

Lieutenant Heinz Dirden

I wrote another three similar letters, but none were quite as personal. It was a cool and cloudless night, so I chose to lie by the tank. I spread my blanket out and told Helmut to wake me at 0330 hours. As I removed my boots, I wiggled my toes. "Now that feels good!" I pulled off my damp socks, setting them out to air dry. I yanked a new pair from my pack and put them on thinking, *it's surprising that when your feet feel good, it makes the rest of your body feel better too.* I lay down, looking at the stars. I thought about Sergeant Dietel and his crew. I wondered, *is he watching us now? Does Heaven really exist?* I just prayed when it was my time to go it would be quick and painless. I thought of my wife, Stella. *What is she doing right now? Is she thinking of me?* I thought about writing her a letter, but I was just too exhausted to be careful with my words. I wanted to say enough to inform her, but not enough to worry her. *Maybe I'll have time in the morning before we head out,* I thought.

I pulled another blanket over my head, took out my journal from my satchel, and opened it to the next empty page. Turning on my flashlight, I wrote the date at the top of the page. I could write anything in my journal. I could let my mind spill out onto these pages, knowing it wouldn't be read until after this was all over. I figured, if I survived this war, my great grandkids might be able to see what we endured. And if I was killed, maybe my wife, or whoever found this, would hopefully see how valiantly we'd fought. I wrote until my mind was numb. I tucked my journal back in my bag, clicked off the flashlight, and pulled the blanket off my head. I closed my eyes and was asleep in minutes.

CHAPTER FIVE

1978

I woke up Sunday morning to Grandma nudging me slightly.

"It's time to get up and get ready for church."

I mumbled something and rolled over.

"You have twenty minutes," she said, and left the room, closing the door.

The dream last night was still vivid in my memory. I swore I could smell the smoke and hear the tanks. I rolled over and sat up, rubbing the sleep from my eyes. As my feet hit the floor, I was almost surprised to feel the cold hardwood floor instead of dirt and grass.

I put on my dress shirt, making sure each button lined up properly, picturing it was a stiff, gray uniform. My socks were clean and folded neatly, but as I put them on, I envisioned them dirty and damp from air drying on the field. My pants and belt came next, in my mind, loaded with a canteen, bayonet, and ammo pouches. Finally, lacing up my dress shoes, they became boots with laces up the ankles. Looking at myself in the mirror, I was forced back into the present.

I left my room and navigated the long, creaky staircase. At the bottom, Grandma, wearing her flowered dress, waited by the front door. She smiled at me, saying, "There's my *guter junge*, my handsome boy." After a few minutes, my uncle Don pulled up in his Cadillac Eldorado convertible. Uncle Don always had the coolest cars. I especially loved his 1932 Ford Roadster with its open engine compartment, huge racing tires on the back, what looked like little bicycle tires on the front, and a rumble seat. It was a blast to ride in, but it wasn't Grandma's style, so the Caddy it was.

It was a short drive to the church. Uncle Don pulled up to the front to let Grandma and me out. I always admired the look of this church with its tall, medieval-looking doors stained a dark cherry and rounded at the top with wrought iron hinges and door handles. Once inside, there was a huge stained-glass window behind the altar and smaller ones on each wall. Each window told a story, depicting scenes from the Bible: Noah's Ark, the Last Supper, David and Goliath, the birth of Jesus, Daniel in the lion's den, Moses and the Ten Commandments. And when the sun shone in, the whole church came alive with glimmers of color. There were lanterns hanging from pillars, the classic, slippery wooden pews, the glistening gold goblets that held the communion offerings, and the pastors in their long, flowing, white robes. We were at the early service, and every pew was full. My aunts, uncles, and cousins took up the first two pews, and Grandma and I slid in too. The service lasted about an hour, and I did my best to listen, but in moments of silence, my mind would drift off to my dream; remembering it, reliving it.

When the last song concluded, we were ushered out to begin the long, slow march to the back of the church to shake the pastor's hand. Uncle Don was already waiting for us with the car at the curb so Grandma didn't have far to walk. Once back at Grandma's, the family began to arrive, just like they did every Sunday. Grandma relished this family time, meeting at her house after church for coffee and German coffee cake that she had lovingly and faithfully made every Saturday. Topped with cinnamon sugar and some butter, it was to die for.

My parents arrived at ten o'clock to have their share of coffee cake and told me to gather my things. I ran to my room, grabbed my bag, and threw in my pajamas and dirty clothes. I grabbed the bundle of pictures, the stack of letters, and the journal. I wrapped them neatly together and placed them in a clean sock. Grabbing both handles of my bag, I struggled down the stairs. My parents were just wrapping things up and saying their goodbyes. I gave Grandma a hug and said, "Thank you."

"*Bald kommen*," she said, "come back soon."

Walking out the screen door, the spring creaking as it stretched, it caught my bag handle and just about tore it off my shoulder. I gasped, hoping it wouldn't rip and spill the contents on the steps.

Luckily, it didn't, and Mother said, "Careful! Watch what you're doing."

"Yes, Mother," I said, and she didn't know just how much I meant it.

Once home, I went to my room and dumped my bag on the bed. I took out my dirty clothes for the laundry and removed my bundle of goodies, separating the items. I spent the afternoon looking through the pictures.

At dinner that night, my dad asked me what I did at Grandma's.

I replied vaguely, "Not much." He pressed for more, so I told him, "I read and played outside."

"Well, I hope you were good," he said.

I tipped my head innocently. "Of course, I was." As I was excused from the table, I headed to my room.

He called, "You have one hour before bedtime."

"Okay, Dad," I said over my shoulder and ran to my room, not wanting to waste another minute. I flopped down on my belly across my bed, grabbed the stack of letters, and took one off the top.

February 21, 1942
Dearest Stella,

I finally arrived at my unit today, just west of the Volga river. Our unit is in a brief rest and refit, it seems. I met my platoon this morning, and they seem like good men, one and all. My platoon sergeant, Dietel, appears very knowledgeable, and I know I will look to him for guidance early on. I hear we'll be getting new tanks soon. Exactly when, I am not sure. Currently, we have the long-barreled Panzer IV. They've been up-armored though, to give us a little extra protection.

I miss you already, Stella. I'm wishing I could come home to you.

Please take care, and I'll write when I can.
Heinz

I grabbed some pictures from the stack and knew the man in the uniform was my grandfather, Heinz. I realized if this letter was true, then they did not flee prior to the war like I'd been told. Now I had more questions than ever. I kept looking at the pictures, wanting the man to talk to me. I was brought out of my thoughts by my father yelling from his chair, "Brush your teeth and get ready for bed, Michael." Once again, I wrapped things up and tucked them in my pack for school. I did as I was told, said goodnight to Mom and Dad, and crawled into bed.

I lay there for what seemed like hours. My brain did not want to shut down. A sudden flash of light caught my attention through my closed eyelids. I opened my eyes quickly, blinking. Seconds later, I heard the rolling thunder. There was another flash, followed by more thunder. My bedroom made up the entire top of the house. It was the attic space converted into a pair of bedrooms, but until my brother was old enough, the whole place was mine. Soon, I heard the rain pounding on the roof. This sound, along with my dreams the other night, and now my recent findings, made me feel anxious. I imagined the flashes of lightning were the artillery going off, and the thunder was the explosions on the battlefield. I couldn't understand how anyone could retain any composure in such horrendous conditions. Without even realizing, I fell asleep until my alarm went off at 6:00 am.

I awakened abruptly, my first thoughts going to my discoveries of yesterday. My mind re-capped the entire weekend in my head as I dressed and headed downstairs. I ate my breakfast, sitting next to baby Aaron in his high chair while Mom made my lunch. I thought about how this man, Heinz, whoever he was, left his wife and babies to fight in the war. I gathered my school bag, gave Aaron a kiss on the top of his head, and started out for the bus stop.

Last night's storm had left behind a fresh smell in the air. Walking down the street, I tried to watch where I stepped as worms littered the road. A few small branches lay on the street from the wind. A couple of the neighborhood kids were already waiting for the bus and talking about the storm. I kept to myself. First of all, I was really tired, but also, all I could think about was the letter. I was about to take my pack off when we heard the bus approach. It rounded the corner, the brakes squealing as it came to a stop. Everyone filed on, I grabbed the first seat I came to and stared out the window for the entire ride, formulating a plan in my head about what would be my next move. I needed to learn more of this story to get answers to my growing list of questions.

I went straight to my classroom, but I knew it would be a while before I got a chance to get to the library. The bell rang, and our lessons started, but I was so lost in daydreams, I couldn't remember one word the teacher said. A couple of hours into the day, when we finally got a break, I walked quickly to the library. I didn't stop to talk to any friends who greeted me, breezing past them with, "I'm in a hurry. I'll catch up with you later." I walked in and went straight to Mrs. Turnbull, knowing it would save me time, not that I couldn't have found it myself.

"Could you help me find WWII books? Mainly German ones."

"Of course, Michael."

Within thirty seconds, I was standing in an aisle with row upon row of just what I was looking for. I was amazed at how many books there were. I looked up and down and thought, *Where do I start?* I began reading the titles and ignored anything that didn't say "SS," Schutzstaffel, Hitler's elite fighting force, on it. I selected four books that I thought would help my quest.

I hurried back to class and started looking through the books. All I wanted to do was read. I felt like a sponge soaking up everything I could. But I was told to put my new books away and take out the math book instead. *Yuk,* I thought. *Doesn't she know I have more important things to do?* I did as I was instructed, but it made for a very long day.

I had a one-track mind as I headed out of school, and once on the bus, I took the books from my pack. As soon as I opened the pages, I was totally lost, not paying attention to anything around me. I didn't even know the bus had stopped until the driver, clearing his throat loudly, looked at me in his overhead mirror, and called out, "Are you getting off here or not?"

"Oops, sorry," I said as I closed the book and stuck it in my pack, being careful not to damage the other items I had in there. I realized I had never taken out my priceless pieces all day. *Tomorrow*, I thought, *I'll just leave them at home.*

I walked briskly home, thankful I didn't have much homework. It was a humid day and Mom had turned on the air conditioner, so the house felt cool. I sat in front of the A/C to complete my math homework.

Mom looked it over when I was finished and said, "Very good."

"Thank you," I said, pleased at the praise from my mother, but more pleased that my homework was done and I could get on to more interesting things. I was like a dog with a bone, and there was only one way I was going to get any satisfaction. I took off to my room where I pulled out my new library books and began reading. After dinner, I again buried myself in the books, but I was getting rather disappointed, realizing the ones I had checked out weren't doing me any good. Yes, I learned some things, but not the information I'd been looking for. I put them in my pack so I could return them the next day and get new ones, then, removed the letters again and read.

March 13, 1942
My dearest Stella,

I was wounded today in a slight altercation with Ivan. We were traveling to a sector that needed help, and I was standing in the hatch when our tank was hit by a Russian partisan armed with an RPG. The outer armor that had been added to our sides was penetrated but not the hull. It left me with some minor shrapnel wounds in my arms. I'll be okay, so not to worry, darling. Looks like I'll get a wound badge now. Will write again soon. I miss you and long for your arms around me.

Heinz

I grabbed the next one.

April 8, 1942
Dear Stella.

I finally received your letter yesterday. I'm so happy you are well. I can't wait to be a father again. Do you have a name picked out yet? Tell the neighbors I'm sorry they lost their dad. This is going to be a long war, darling. I only hope our generals can swing the tide of bad luck we've had lately. I have confidence I'll be home for Christmas though. With any luck, maybe I can get back for the birth of our child.

I love you always.
Heinz

I wondered, Who was this baby to be born? I went on to the next letter.

June 22, 1942
Dear Stella,

I know it's been awhile, my love. Know that I am well. We've been extremely busy here lately. Things are not quite going as planned. I lost a tank today. My whole 4th squad was killed. Losing men is hard, writing their families is equally as difficult. Give Karl my love and I will write again when I can.

Heinz

So, obviously, the baby wasn't Karl. I grabbed yet another letter.

August 19, 1942
Dear Stella,

I was wounded again the other day. I am being sent to Hamburg in a few days. I'll write when I get there. I'm hoping you can come to visit. I must warn you, however, my left leg is not very pretty. Our tank ran over a mine, and the shrapnel penetrated the belly, killing my driver and wounding myself and my radio operator. Gotta go, darling. Will be in touch soon. Please don't worry, I'm in good hands and I'll be alright.

Heinz.

I suddenly realized how tired I was. *Investigating is exhausting,* I thought. So many thoughts swirled about in my head. I hurried through my bedtime routine, anxious to get my head on a pillow. I slept soundly that night and rose the next day to another morning routine. "Twelve-year-old boys have a lot of routines," I said to myself, "and I'll bet soldiers have even more."

When I got to school, I took the first opportunity I had to return the books to the library. I asked Mrs. Turnbull if there was something more specific I could look for. "Like what?" she asked. I told her I was interested in the German SS during WWII. She again led me to an aisle, only this time, she helped me to find particular books. I took another four books, and this time, I was more confident than ever I would find what I needed.

I was doing my chores after school when the phone rang. My mom picked it up.

"Hello?" Then, "Sure, Dad, hold on just a second." She handed the receiver to me and whispered, "It's your grandpa."

I took the phone. "Hi, Grandpa."

"Hi, Mike, how are you?"

"I'm good. Looking forward to tomorrow."

"That's kind of why I'm calling," he said. "Something has come up, and I won't be able to make it tomorrow."

Dejected and looking at the floor, I said, "Okay, I understand."

"Mike, are you okay?"

"Yeah, no big deal," I said, knowing he would only feel worse if he knew how disappointed I was.

"I'll be there next Thursday, for sure," he told me. "I can't stay away from my grandson too long, you know."

Smiling, I said, "That will be great," and we said goodbye.

Mom asked, "What did your grandpa want, Mike?"

I told her he wouldn't be able to make it tomorrow.

"Are you okay?" she coaxed, knowing the feelings of an excited twelve-year-old could be fragile.

"Yes," I assured her. "He promised he would come next Thursday." I headed to my room before my mom could interrogate any more.

Taking out my new books, I first looked at the one with the medals in it. It had medals from all countries, so I flipped the pages until I found the German ones. I matched the badges I found in the trunk and determined one was a wound badge in silver, indicating he was wounded at least three times, but not more than four. The silver tank badge, according to the book, meant he had at least fifty tank kills, but not more than seventy-five. To me, that seemed like a lot! I also noticed a small book that each soldier carried called a *Soldbuch*. This document would give the soldier's history of which unit he was attached to and where, decorations received, and so forth. It also allowed the soldier to draw his pay, so this was a very important document. I needed to search those trunks better to see if there was one in there. That would help my cause. I also found an Iron Cross First Class medal and a Totenkopf ring. The ring, I read, was only awarded to SS officers by Heinrich Himmler and was stamped with the name and date awarded on the inside. I was definitely going to look closer at that ring in the trunk the next time I was in Grandma's attic.

Next, I went to one of the SS books. It said that, initially, the 2nd SS Panzer division was made up of police officers. I had heard that my grandfather was a policeman before they left Germany, so this started to make sense. *But why the big lie all these years?* I wondered. I couldn't wrap my head around that part. After dinner and a bath, it was time for bed. Trying to go to sleep wasn't getting any easier for me. I had questions. Lots of questions. Things a book couldn't answer. I needed to devise a way to ask detailed questions without letting on that I knew everything I had been told before now was a lie. I plotted and schemed until, eventually, I fell asleep.

Thursday came, and by the end of the school day, I had way too much homework to enjoy my new obsession. *I guess it's a good thing that Grandpa couldn't come over,* I thought.

Lying in bed that night, I felt restless, like I needed to do something, anything, to move my search forward. This obsession was like a drug. Even if it wasn't a harmful one, the addiction was still a fixation, and it gave me cravings. Craving for knowledge, for answers. Thinking of the dream I'd had at Grandma's house last week, I quietly got out of bed and grabbed one of the library books that told of the SS battles and statistics. I grabbed my flashlight and crawled under my blankets. I opened the book to the date July 4th, 1943. Operation Citadel, or the battle for Kursk, the book said, was the largest tank battle in history. Depending on which sector one was in, it lasted for about two weeks or so. I looked at the pictures. *Just like in my dream!* I thought. *This is creepy.* I wanted to press on, but I felt my eyelids getting heavy. I fell asleep with the book beside me and awakened in the morning with it on the floor beside my bed, my flashlight next to it with a very dim light. *I'll need new batteries if I'm going to do this again,* I thought.

Thankfully, it was Friday, and the school day passed quickly. Riding the bus home, the bus driver remarked how quiet I had been lately and asked if I was okay as we came to my stop.

"Oh yeah," I said. "It's just a huge research project I'm working on," I told him, getting off the bus.

He nodded. "Okay, Mike. Have a good weekend."

His words trailed in my ears as I had already started walking up the street toward home, but I turned and gave him a wave.

At the dinner table that night, I began asking my dad questions. "What was Grandpa Heinz like?"

Dad looked at me quizzically. "What do you mean, Mike?"

"Like... What did he like to do? Did you ever do stuff with him?"

Dad took a deep breath and squinted like he was thinking hard. "Well, I know he loved to fish and hunt, especially pheasant hunting. But he had a terrible limp as he got older and had to give that up."

"What was wrong with him?" I asked.

"He said it had something to do with an incident when he was a police officer back in Germany. The 1930s were a rough time, and supposedly, he got beaten up pretty badly by some Nazis when he was ordered to break up a rally Hitler had organized. His left leg had been burned badly and was scarred. He tried not to let it slow him down, but as he got older, it got harder for him."

"What did he do for work when they came to America?" I asked.

"He worked for the post office, just like me."

"That's cool. Did you work together?"

He shook his head. "No, we worked in different facilities."

I finished eating and asked to be excused.

Dad said, "Go ahead." He paused. "And Mike? If there's more you want to know about your grandpa, you can ask anytime. Okay?"

"Thanks, Dad," I said, knowing he was thrilled that I was taking more interest in his father.

I went to my room with my mind racing. This was further proof I was on the right track. Grandpa's left leg was wounded, plus, Dad's explanation fit, but either my dad didn't know the truth, or it was a well-orchestrated lie, and a lot of people were in on it. But again, why? What were they covering up? I took the journal out of my desk and opened it to the spot I had read before my dream. I flipped through a couple pages, but there was only one other entry regarding the battle.

July 10, 1943
Some units are over a week into this disaster. We've lost hundreds of tanks, assault guns, artillery, and soldiers. This was a misguided venture, no doubt. Russia has lost probably twice as much as us, but they can afford it. I'll bet history will show we had 5:1 odds against us. Maybe if we had launched on time instead of waiting months, then possibly we could've achieved our goals. But Ivan used his time wisely. Row upon row of defensive belts, tank ditch after ditch, and minefields. Coming up on almost a week, and we're nowhere close to making our objective. Word is, we'll be retreating to our original positions within a day or two. I'm afraid we'll never recover from this terrible decision. I wish this would all end.

I flipped back to earlier pages.

August 22, 1942
After being wounded the other day, I've been well taken
care of. The doctors are excellent, and the nurses are
pretty. I told my nurse after I was healthy enough to walk,
she had better watch out, I'll chase her all over the ward. A
few operations are necessary, but they feel I'll make a full
recovery with little side effects. A long road of therapy is in
my future.

The next twenty pages or so talked about recovery
and therapy. Amongst them, I came to a page that
fascinated me. I grinned to myself. Now this is
interesting, I thought.

September `7, 1942
I was able to spend a few hours with Karl and Stella today
during their visit. It was great. My God! I miss them both.
I can't wait for this terrible war to be over. We talked
about names today for the new baby since it'll soon be
here. We settled on Arnold if it's a boy. I think little Karl
will make a great big brother.

Oh my! That baby is my dad! I thought. *This puts a*
new twist on things!
Feeling like I couldn't comprehend any more that
night, I said goodnight to Mom and Dad, brushed my
teeth, and went to bed. I was so mentally spent that I fell
asleep   almost   immediately.

CHAPTER SIX

August 1942

I woke up and heard the rain on the roof of the tent. A breeze caused a loose portion of the canvas to flap rhythmically. I rolled to my side, tired from the last few days of operations. *Good sleeping weather*, I thought, knowing I wouldn't be able to stay here. Ivan loved to make us miserable and, if nothing else, would send us an artillery present, most likely when it was raining hardest. Twenty minutes later, I sat up, looking around to see if anyone else was stirring. I looked at my watch. It was almost 0600. I gently shook Sergeant Dietel.

"Sergeant, get up."

"Yes, Sir, I'm awake."

"Good," I said. "Get the men into formation. We have crap to do today."

"Yes, Sir," he said, sitting up immediately. He rose to his feet, grabbed his uniform, hurriedly put it on, and dashed out of the tent.

It was cool and damp inside the canvas. My clothes felt moist even though they were dry. As I dressed, I could hear the men in the nearby tents moving about, and within minutes, they were lined up in formation. I grabbed my MP 40, donned my cap, and walked out to address them.

Sergeant Dietel yelled, "Ach-TUNG!"

The way he said it always impressed me. The men became rigid at attention. I walked to the front of the formation, clicked my heels together and returned Dietel's salute.

He said, "Sir, all men are present and accounted for."

"Thank you, Sergeant." He made an about-face to stand beside me, and I began my instructions. "Today is a maintenance day. After breakfast, I want you cleaning personal weapons and equipment. After lunch, we'll pick up the tanks from the maintenance crew. Oil changes and tune-ups will be complete by then. When you get them here, I want the toolkits cleaned. Every vehicle needs to be topped off with fuel, magazines filled, and all the water cans filled. I also want each platoon to draw two days rations. This lull we're having isn't going to last long." I turned to Sergeant Dietel. "Sergeant," I said, "dismiss the men to the mess hall and get them on task."

He replied, "Yes, Sir," and saluted again.

I returned the salute and headed to the latrine. I heard Dietel dismiss the men, and they hurried off to the mess tent while I went to make a mess of my own. Every day, I seemed to become increasingly ill, and the latrine was both my friend and foe. I had to find time to see the doc today.

Once I finished, I made my way to the mess tent. I grabbed a tray and stood in front of each station as the cook slopped on some runny eggs and shriveled up stuff that appeared to be bacon. *Only the cook knows what this really is,* I thought to myself. I grabbed some bread, an apple, and a steaming cup of coffee, and found a spot by Dietel.

He looked at me in concern and said, "Sir, are you feeling alright?"

I told him I did not feel well, but I would try to get to the infirmary later. I changed the subject by asking about his family and what he planned to do after the war. He shyly told me of his young wife at home, pregnant with their first child. He told me he didn't care what kind of work he would do after this was over, he just wanted to be a good father. After a little of this sharing, Dietel excused himself to get to work, and I was left alone at the table. I picked at my food, knowing I needed to eat something, but also knowing there was a good chance it would go right through me. By the time I had finished, the tent was almost empty. I grabbed another cup of thick black coffee. *This looks more like tank oil,* I thought. As I walked away, I wondered if it could be these coffee dregs that were wreaking havoc on my innards.

I made a beeline for the tactical operations center (TOC). There were people milling about and lots of chatter over the radios. I saw Captain Kinsler looking at the map table and talking with another lieutenant from 4th Platoon. After their short conversation, the lieutenant left. I strode up to the captain and came to attention, saluted, and said, "Sir."

The captain looked at me, returned my salute, and said, "What can I do for you, Lieutenant?"

"Requesting permission for my men to get leave, Sir. A quarter of the platoon each week for the next month. The men are pretty tired and could use a break, Sir."

He thought for a moment and turning back to the map table, said, "I'll see what I can do." He twisted his head to look at me again and said, "Lieutenant, you're not looking good. Are you okay?"

I felt my stomach turning. "I've been feeling under the weather a bit, sir," I admitted, "but I'll be okay. I'm going to see the doctor later if I can find some time."

The captain said, "Lieutenant, you will make time. I can't afford to have you laid up in a hospital right now. Take care of your men, but don't neglect yourself! They need you, too," he said.

"Yes, Sir."

He added, "Oh, and Dirden? There's going to be an anti-partisan operation later. Will you have your armor back by 1300?"

"I expect to."

"Good. I'll most likely send you out with Captain Hinske to support his company. There's been an uprising in Kurchatov. We need to put it down before things get out of hand. I'll call on you when I need you."

"Yes, Sir. Is there anything else, Sir?"

"No," he said. "Now get to the infirmary."

***

I walked into the medical tent where there were about a dozen soldiers in for various minor ailments or complaints. In short order, the doctor, Major Bassett, came over with a slight smirk on his face.

"Lieutenant, so nice of you to come to visit us."

The doc knew I hated coming in here unless it was to visit one of my men.

I ignored his ribbing and said simply, "Sorry, Doc, but this isn't for enjoyment. I've been under the weather lately, and it's only getting worse."

Major Bassett became serious and said, "Well, tell me what's going on with you?"

"I feel like I've been running a bit of a fever, and I have stomach cramps and diarrhea. Plus, I've been getting headaches."

"It sounds like you have a classic case of dysentery," he declared.

I groaned. I knew this was a common ailment among servicemen, but I never thought about the possibility of it hitting me.

"Just increase your fluid intake so you don't get dehydrated, and you should be over it in about a week." After noticing the annoyed look on my face, he added, "Don't worry. Everyone gets it sooner or later. It's just your turn."

I thanked him as I left the tent and went to check on Sergeant Dietel. The men had just finished cleaning their weapons. I looked at my watch: 1126. I instructed Dietel to have all the drivers ready to go to the motor pool in fifteen minutes. It was time to collect our armored steeds from the maintenance company. I told him I'd be back soon and left the tent.

It seemed like each time I went outside, it was raining harder. With the puddles ever expanding and heavy vehicles navigating the soft, earthen road, it didn't take long for deep ruts to emerge. Wheeled vehicles were already getting stuck in some areas. *This is going to be a miserable day,* I thought. I went to see Captain Kinsler again to ask if my men could get a ride to the motor pool. The captain, busy in the operations tent as usual, told me he'd have a truck in front of our area of operations (AO) in a few minutes.

Then he asked, "Hey, did you see the doctor?"

I told him, "Yes, and Doc said it's nothing. It's gotta run its course. I'll be okay."

He nodded, and I went back out into the pouring rain.

Dodging the bigger puddles, I reached my tent, eyeing my bed—I badly wanted to crawl back in. I grabbed my weapon as I heard an approaching truck and stepped out to see Sergeant Dietel heading toward me with the five drivers. The truck came to a stop in front of us with a squawk of the brakes. Dietel and the other drivers hopped in the back, the gray canvas cover keeping them mostly dry. I jumped in front with the driver and told him to take us to the motor pool.

"Yes, Sir."

Letting out the clutch, the truck jerked a few times before rolling forward steadily. The wipers were moving, but not keeping a consistent speed and squeaking on the upswing. The normally five-minute drive turned into fifteen as the driver made every effort to avoid getting stuck.

Pulling up in front of the motor pool, the men and I filed out and headed to the main tent. The sergeant in charge came to attention as I asked if my tanks were ready.

He saluted and said, "Yes, they are." I was about to turn and walk out when he said, "Sir? In about two weeks, you'll need to turn these in again. You should be getting the new Panthers soon. I hear they're applying the *Zimmerit* now and will be putting them on the train in the next couple days."

"Very well," I said. "Thank you, Sergeant." This was good news!

Outside, I told my men to go get the tanks. They ran off like children going to play. While they were gone, Sergeant Dietel and I chatted, mostly complaining about the crappy weather until the tanks rolled up within minutes. I clambered aboard my command tank while Dietel boarded his. The idiots in the motor pool had left the hatches wide open, allowing the rain to pour in. Everything on the inside was soaked. I stood in the hatch the whole way back, feeling miserable. I told Private Trollheim to pick up the pace, so he revved the engine, and the tank surged ahead, spitting mud out the back. The other tanks followed suit, and within minutes, we were back in our area.

"Have the men clean the equipment and clean the tank guns," I instructed Dietel. "Also, get a few spare road wheels and sections of track from supply just in case we need to perform emergency field repairs." Then, thinking of my gut and my bed, I told him, "I'll be back in an hour," and headed to the latrine. Hoping for a short nap, I went back to my tent, peeled off my wet clothes and crawled into my bunk. I had no sooner warmed up when I heard the messenger at my door.

"Lieutenant Dirden, Sir?"

Annoyed, I replied, "What is it?"

"Sir, Captain Kinsler would like to see you in operations, Sir."

"Tell him I'll be there in five minutes," I snapped.

"Yes, Sir."

I heard him squish off through the muck.

Damn. I just don't feel like doing this today, I thought. I flipped the covers down and grabbed a dry uniform, but I had no spare boots, so the wet, muddy ones went back on my feet. Grabbing my cap and my weapon, I headed to the TOC.

I walked into the tent, came to attention, saluted, and said, "Sir, you wanted to see me?"

"Yes, I heard you have your tanks back."

"Yes, Sir."

"Good. Meet Captain Hinske in twenty minutes outside his TOC. He needs armor support to deal with these pain-in-the-ass partisans."

"Will there be any others?" I asked.

He shook his head. "Dirden, these are just ragtag civilians, not professional soldiers. I think you'll be pretty bored as it is."

"Yes, Sir. Anything else, Sir?"

"No. Now get moving. You're burning daylight."

I went directly to my men and said, "Finish up what you're doing and mount up." The men, upon hearing my command, changed gears and picked up their pace. I directed my next words to my platoon sergeant. "Dietel, we're heading to Captain Hinske's company. Partisan issues, I guess."

"Great," he said, rolling his eyes. "Shall we bring one deck of cards or two?"

"Funny," I said without expression.

I noticed the spare parts I had asked for attached to the outside of each tank's hull. My men had done a good job once again, and at that moment, I thanked God for every one of them. Soon, all five Panzers were rumbling. The V12 was a gas hog, but fuel shouldn't be an issue today. I was more concerned with its twenty-five tons on muddy roads with a narrow track. I ducked inside the turret to make sure everyone was ready. The steel was cold, and it felt like sitting inside a refrigerator. I hoped it would warm up once we started moving. Water dripped from a couple of spots where things had been mounted on the outside but not sealed.

I went back up and stood in the turret and yelled, "Move out!"

The tank jerked, and the tracks clanked and squealed. The rain never stopped as we journeyed. At times, it would downpour, then it would lighten up to a drizzle. I hated this Godforsaken country. It certainly wasn't worth fighting and dying over.

No one got stuck during our trek through the mud, and it wasn't long before we were lined up with Captain Hinske and his company. We rolled out together, the captain in a half-track (Sd.Kfz. 250) led the way, followed by myself and my 2nd Squad. The rest of the captain's company and my other three tanks covered the rear. We arrived at Kucherov within the hour, and from a mile away, the captain and I looked through our binoculars. Not seeing anything unusual, we formulated a straightforward plan. My other three tanks would head out and approach from the north while we rolled in from the east. Anyone trying to escape in any other direction would be easily spotted and captured.

We waited in a semi-concealed position while the other tanks left and got into their own positions. About twenty minutes later, they sent word that they were ready, so we advanced at lightning speed. The trucks carrying the infantry slid to a stop, and the men piled out, rushing to separate spots like a well-orchestrated play. They'd bust into shops and homes, breaking down doors and windows to gain entry. My tanks blocked all exit points.

I could hear soldiers smashing dishes and glass and breaking furniture as they tried to find weapons and explosives. I think it was just an excuse to destroy stuff and release built up frustration, albeit at someone else's expense. We saw people being rounded up in the street and held at gunpoint. Then they were separated, women and children being kept apart from the few men there were. Most of the men were very old or just young boys. Suddenly, we saw two women take off running, holding what looked like two babies in their arms. Moments later, shots echoed through the streets as soldiers opened up on them. Bullets riddled their bodies as they slammed to the ground face first, their children flying from their arms as they fell and bouncing off the ground. A young private went out and smashed the buttstock of his rifle against their heads. It was like smashing an over-ripe watermelon. They left the babies there to die if they weren't already dead.

Twenty-five women were singled out by the captain and lined up shoulder to shoulder with the empty steppe as the backdrop. Sitting in his half-track, with an order from the captain, the machine gunner cut them down in seconds. The remaining women and children became hysterical, crying out for mercy. Another twenty-five women with their children were lined up where the others lay dying. The gunner opened up again, the bullets turning living flesh to hamburger. Blood sprayed against the tall grass, painting it a crimson red. I saw the captain counting out another twenty-five, children and young boys mixed in this time. Mothers clutched their children in their arms, trying to shield them from impending death. Some would be ripped away while other parents got a bullet to the head, making them release their grip.

My stomach turned and I couldn't believe what I was witnessing. The kids were lined up and as they cried, the gunner opened up again, killing only half before his belt of ammo ran out. He was trying to reload when I jumped down from my tank and ran over to the captain.

"Sir!" I said.

He looked at me.

"What are you doing, Sir?"

"Reprisals for the uprising, Lieutenant. You should know the rules by now, don't you?"

"But Sir," I said, "the children are innocent, and you know that!"

Just then, the machine gun opened up again, killing the rest. I looked on in horror as the parents fell to the ground crying and convulsing in the muddy street.

"Lieutenant, get back to your tank before I have you written up!" the captain growled. "I am acting on Reichsführer Himmler's orders and if you don't like it, take it up with him."

I slowly turned and walked dejectedly back to my tank. I heard another twenty-five counted out, but I couldn't watch. The shots rang out, and I wanted to scream. There was no honor in this! This was murdering innocent, unarmed civilians whose only crime was living here. When they were finished, the captain walked among the bodies. Anyone who appeared to have life left in them, received a shot to the head from his Luger. Next, he had his men set fire to half the village, burning homes and businesses. The bodies were left there for the inhabitants to take care of. We mounted up and headed back to our AO.

It was dark before we were halfway back, and we had our blackout lights on, with just enough light to illuminate the road in front of us. The thought of those little kids dying in such a horrific way made me nauseous, and I vomited all over the turret. I thought of my own children and how I would feel if the role was reversed. *We had better win this war,* I thought, *or Germany will be ravaged like no other country ever has!* How could anyone think this was a good policy? I couldn't wait to get back. I needed to speak with Captain Kinsler.

"Private Trollheim," I bellowed. "Drop me off at the TOC and put her to bed for the night." As we pulled up, I didn't wait for the tank to come to a complete stop before I jumped off. I hollered my instructions for the men to Dietel as they clanked down the muddy road. I gathered my thoughts and my composure and walked into the tent. Saluting, I said, "Captain Kinsler, Sir."

He looked my way, returned the salute and said, "Glad you're back, Lieutenant."

"So am I, Sir," I said. "May we talk in private, Sir?"

"Of course," he said.

I walked to the entrance, and pulling the flap back, I stepped outside, and the captain followed. I noticed it had stopped raining. I was grateful for that, at least.

A bit impatiently, the captain asked, "What is it, Dirden?"

I spoke hurriedly, "Sir, Captain Hinske is out of control! He shot a hundred innocent women and children today! Pure execution!"

I had hardly gotten the words out when he pulled me closer by the sleeve of my uniform and in a whispered voice said, "Dirden, shut your mouth and never speak of this again!"

Shocked, I looked at him, my eyes wide.

"Himmler himself gave the order to all units. A company commander just last month was shot for not following orders. So, unless you want the same fate, I'd forget this ever happened! Hitler wants to see all Jews, Slavs, and Bolsheviks exterminated. It's beyond our control, so just do what you're told, Lieutenant. Now, go get something to eat and get some rest. You'll feel better in the morning. And the sooner you forget about this, the better," he said.

"Yes, Sir," I replied weakly, but came to attention and saluted.

The captain returned my salute and sauntered back into the tent. I couldn't believe my ears. Never in my wildest dreams had I thought Captain Kinsler would have spoken those words. I stumbled to the mess tent, grabbed a tray and got in line after my men, making sure they were fed first. I took a piece of black bread and some watered-down stuff that looked like chicken soup. I never did find any chicken, but the flavored water was easy on my stomach. I sat next to Dietel again.

He leaned his head closer to me and spoke low and incredulous. "Sir, can you believe what happened today?"

No, I told him and said not to mention it again. "Captain Kinsler won't do anything about it." Soaking my bread in the soup, I ate about half, got up, and said, "Get the men to bed, Sergeant. I've got an uneasy feeling about tomorrow."

With heavy feet, I strolled to my tent. I lay on my cot, disgusted with what had happened today. The children's faces were etched in my brain. Tears began to form and soon I was sobbing uncontrollably. I wanted to run away. Get my wife and kids and leave this horrible place. Then, something flickered in my memory, and I thought of some words my father said to me once. He said, "Son, if you want to change something, you attack the problem, not run away from it."

I heard Sergeant Dietel shuffle in, and I stifled my cries, thankful the tent was dark. I rolled over and wiped my eyes. Breathing into my pillow, sheer exhaustion, both physical and mental, took over, and soon, sleep enveloped me.

I woke earlier than usual the next day. Hearing Dietel snoring, I wondered what time it was and looked at my watch. 0400. I lay there with memories of yesterday flooding my brain as soon as I could make a conscious thought. *This war would be so much easier if we had the people on our side,* I thought. But instead, we fought the soldiers and the local militias once we took over a territory. When we first invaded this rotten place, the people looked at us like liberators. They would've done anything to help us. And what did we do? We crapped on them. We stole their belongings, shipped them off to concentration camps, killed their wives and children, and burned their homes down. *God help us if we don't win.* I couldn't get rid of that thought. It made me shudder, thinking what the ramifications could be.

I decided to get up. There was no sense laying there with my head spinning. I hastily dressed, grabbed a piece of paper, and began writing to my wife. That always made me feel better. With things as desperate as they were, I saw no reason to sugarcoat things for her any longer.

August 1942
Dear Stella,

I witnessed horrible things yesterday, darling. Women and children being slaughtered for no reason other than being in the wrong place at the wrong time. Promise me that if I don't survive this terrible war, and the Russians invade the Fatherland, that'll you'll escape to the West at the earliest possible moment. Things will get ugly if we don't win this war, darling!

My love for you keeps me pressing on.
Heinz

Sergeant Dietel rolled over and saw me writing feverishly. He asked, "You okay, Sir?"

"Yes, Sergeant." I quickly went on, avoiding any further questioning. "I think it's time to get the boys up and moving."

"Yes, Sir," he said, sitting up in his cot. Stretching and yawning, he spoke the words I was sure all of us were thinking. "Hopefully, today will be a better day."

When he left the tent, I knocked the dried mud off my boots, placed the letter in an envelope, addressed and sealed it, and ran it over to the mail room.

Sergeant Dietel had the men in formation and standing at attention when I came to them. At attention himself, he greeted me with a salute, and said, "Sir, all the men are present and accounted for."

Looking over my men, I could see the apprehension in their faces. "Boys, let's try and forget yesterday. I've spoken to Captain Kinsler and he promised he'd investigate. Now, let's get back to business and do our jobs. Sergeant, release the men to chow. After that, we're going to do some gunnery training." As Dietel dismissed the men, I turned and headed to the latrine again. Right on time, just like a freight train.

After my morning business was taken care of, I, too, headed for the mess tent, settling on just fruit and some hot cereal today, hoping it would be easier on my stomach. I grabbed a hot cup of coffee and sat next to Sergeant Dietel again. This was becoming a habit I rather enjoyed. We talked about what scenarios to put the men through when a messenger ran in and yelled, "Is Lieutenant Dirden in here?"

I raised my hand slightly, so he could see me, and replied, "Yes, Private, what is it?"

He came rushing over, saluted and said, "Sir, Captain Kinsler requests your presence in the TOC."

"Fine, Private. Tell him I'll be there in a minute." I returned his salute and dismissed him. The private dropped his salute and ran back out. I looked at Dietel and said, "What do you think this is about?"

"Don't know, Sir. Maybe the captain needs you to put his boots on for him?"

"Very funny, Sergeant. Better watch how loud you say that."

I took one last bite and told the sergeant to turn my tray in for me. I put the apple in my pocket as I headed out. Even though it was overcast and a bit cool, at least it wasn't raining, thank God, and the puddles were drying up. Once at TOC, I went straight to Captain Kinsler, and we exchanged salutes.

"Dirden, I need your platoon to go with Captain Hinske again. There was another uprising close to where you were yesterday."

I started to protest, but I was stopped short.

"Lieutenant, you're most familiar with the area, and besides, Captain Hinske requested you. How would it look if we turned him down?" He spoke quickly, hardly taking a breath. He didn't want to give me a chance to interrupt. "It'll be fine, Dirden. Just do your job and look the other way if you must. Now, get moving, you have thirty minutes to get to his AO."

"Yes, Sir," I said, keeping professional. I saluted again, and without waiting for the captain to return it, I stormed out of the tent.

The platoon was just filing out of the mess tent. I said, "Hold on, guys." I looked over at Sergeant Dietel and he could tell it wasn't good. "Drivers, get your tanks and top them off. We're heading back to Captain Hinske's company again for another quelling." Instantly, I could see the crestfallen look flood their faces. "Sergeant, draw one day of rations. We'll be out past dinner, I'm sure. okay, guys. Get going. We're leaving in fifteen minutes."

I went to my tent and sat for a second, looking up at the ceiling. "God," I said, folding my hands in prayer, "please don't let this happen again. Watch over us and protect us. And please, Lord, let me drive over Captain Hinske's half-track. In Jesus name, I pray. Amen."

I stood up, grabbed my weapon, and went back outside to where our tanks were camouflaged. The platoon was just finishing up their checks: oil levels, tracks, road wheels, and communications (Comms). Barrel shrouds were removed and ammo loaded into the machine guns.

"Let's move, gentlemen," I bellowed. The engines started up, filling the air with rumbles and exhaust smoke. I climbed aboard and called for checks. On "Okays" from everyone, I yelled, "FORWARD," and we crawled out of our hiding spot behind a pile of brush.

We were a little late getting to Captain Hinske's company, despite the improved road conditions. They were already loaded up and the captain looked at me with a perturbed look on his face. Giving the command for our tank to stop next to him, I climbed down.

"Sir," I said. "Captain Kinsler said you requested our support?"

"Yes, Lieutenant." He pulled out a map and pointed to a spot about ten miles from where we were the day before. "There's been another uprising here." He jabbed his finger again into the map. "My dispatch rider was killed this morning. I want to strike while the iron is hot.

You lead the way, Lieutenant. Now, let's get going, shall we? Speed is everything," he said.

There was nothing I could say but, "Yes, Sir."

I told my driver, Private Trollheim, to go, and the hulking beast leaped from its spot, going through the gears like a racecar. I turned to look behind me, and the captain's company was keeping a good tactical distance. A couple of miles down the road, and I again looked behind me. Seeing they were still there, I turned to the front. I knew we were getting close, and was about to tell Trollheim to slow down, when there was an explosion. It was the loudest I'd ever heard, and it lifted the tank in the air. It slammed back down, the tracks grinding to a halt and the mud, debris, and smoke covering us instantly. I fell inside the tank, my world spinning wildly around me. My ears rang, and my vision blurred as I lost consciousness. I awoke sometime later in the infirmary. Dr. Bassett was checking my vital signs. My head hurt like hell and was pounding like crazy. I looked over and saw Sergeant Dietel sitting across from me.

"Well, good morning, Lieutenant. How do you feel?" Doc asked.

"Like I was run over by a Panzer IV!"

He smiled. "I think you'll make a full recovery, but we'll need to ship you to Hamburg for a while. The therapy you'll need is more extensive than what we can handle here. Besides, you'll need a few more surgeries that I can't perform."

I was suddenly excited at the prospect that I might see my wife again. "Okay, Doc," I said. "Whatever is best."

He smiled at me and went on to the next patient as a nurse changed my bandages.

I looked at Dietel. "Sergeant, what the hell happened?"

"Sir, we were ambushed. They must've known we were coming. Your tank rolled over a mine, we believe, and it threw the left track and killed Private Trollheim. Corporal Schnizzell was severely wounded. He'll probably recover, but I think the war is over for him. He'll most likely serve out the rest of his time as a concentration camp guard or at a radio school or something." It was almost as if he was talking more to himself than to me.

"What about Corporal Helmut and Private Rundle?" I asked.

"They'll be fine. They only have concussions, they'll get back on their feet. You just concentrate on recovering yourself now and get back here quick."

The nurse finished my bandages and left.

Dietel turned his head away, looking off across the room somewhere and spoke without looking at me. "I gotta say, Sir, I think you're the best officer I've ever had the pleasure to serve under."

I cleared my throat and said only, "Thank you, Sergeant." I didn't want the situation to become any more awkward for us. I told Dietel to go take care of the guys and not to let some other guy squander their lives. Not that he'd have any control over that, but I wanted him to know that I supported him if he chose to speak up to authority. With that, he stood and saluted. Clumsily, I returned the courtesy from my bed and he left, saying "I'll see you soon."

Within hours, I was on a train bound for Hamburg with thoughts of my darling, Stella, and my son, Karl, filling my mind. Despite my intense pain, I couldn't be happier at that very moment.

CHAPTER SEVEN

1978

I awoke Saturday morning and still felt exhausted. My dreams were taking a toll on my mind. I felt as if I was reliving my grandpa's experience, sort of like traveling back in time. My sheets were soaked with sweat like I had run a marathon in my sleep. I wasn't sure what to make of it all. Wanting more information, I went directly to the books. Skipping cartoons was uncharacteristic of me, but I could only think of one thing right now.

I took a break from the German side for a while and started reading about the Americans. I read about how the Japanese were interned in the U.S., mostly on the west coast, for fear that they were spies and would invade the mainland. The Nazis had relocated millions of people just because they didn't like their ethnicity, and even though we didn't slaughter the Japanese, we forced thousands of them to give up homes and businesses, and essentially give up most of their belongings. After uprooting them, they were put in primitive camps. *How unfair,* I thought. And yet, most were still patriotic to America. I thought, *If I was one of them, I'd leave this country first chance I could.* The thought of treating innocent people that way made me feel sick. I guessed it must have been different back then, like Grandpa said.

I came upon the chapter that covered D-Day and found myself caught up in it. I finally looked at the clock when Mother called me down for breakfast. It was almost 11:00 already. I ran downstairs and said, "I'm really not hungry, Mom. I'll just skip breakfast." Concerned, she asked if I was sick. "No, why?" I asked.

"Because you didn't even watch TV this morning, and now you're not hungry."

"I'm fine, Mom. Just playing in my room is all."

She made a face. "Well, if that's what it is, you still need to eat something. Even if it's just a little." I agreed to some oatmeal, and while I ate, Mom leaned on the kitchen counter and questioned me. "So, Mike, what are you playing with this morning that made you miss your cartoons?"

"I'm creating battle scenes with my army men."

Mother didn't like war stuff. She looked concerned and said, "Maybe you should find something else to do for a bit. It's a nice day. I want you outside for a while today."

"Sure, Mom," I told her, and after breakfast, I called a friend, Andrew Petrovski, who lived just one street over, almost in our backyard. I had always known he was Jewish from the different way his family celebrated things. And I knew he was Polish because that was fodder for teasing at school. But once, at a neighborhood party my parents hosted, I'd overheard some of the adults talking. I was supposed to have been in bed, but I was curious and sneaky and had sat under an open window, listening to them. A group of guests had circled Andrew's mother, who'd been dabbing her eyes with a tissue as she'd talked about her family and what they had gone through in the Holocaust.

Remembering this, I thought, *here's another angle of research for me.* When Andrew answered the phone, I asked what he was doing today.

"Nothing, really," he said.

I asked if I could come over.

He muffled the receiver and ask his mom if it was alright. "It's cool," he said. "What do you want to do?"

"I'll tell you when I get there," I said. "I'll be there in about ten minutes."

I grabbed a notebook and a pen, threw on my Minnesota Twins ball cap, and ran out the door before Mom could put me to work. I cut through our backyard, and when I rounded the side of his house, I noticed an extra car in his driveway. Hoping it wasn't visitors that would hinder me from asking Andrew questions, I rang their doorbell.

Andy answered and opened the door. "Let's go downstairs," he suggested. It was an unfinished basement and Andy's play space. As we navigated the open, wooden stairs, Andy asked, "So what's up, dude? And what's the notebook for?"

We plopped into beanbag chairs set out on a big carpet remnant over the cement floor. I told him about the things I found in my grandma's attic and that I had begun to research WWII, hoping to make sense of it. "I can't tell you everything, because I still don't know a lot, but I was wondering if I could ask you some stuff about when your grandparents were in the war. Or maybe your mom?"

Andy shook his head. "My mom doesn't talk about it. She says she's happy not remembering much. All I really know is what my grandma has told me. That she and my mom survived, my mom's little sister died there, and my grandfather went missing, and they never saw him again."

I was disappointed.

However, he went on. "Hey! My grandma is here! She's visiting today!" His eyes lit up. "You could be like an actual journalist and do like an 'interview' with her!"

He sounded almost as excited as I felt, but I didn't want to get my hopes up. "Do you think that would be too hard on her? Bad memories and stuff?"

"I dunno. I'll go ask her," and he bounded up the stairs.

Dang, I thought. I didn't want to be thought of as the troublesome neighborhood kid, but it was exciting to think I might be able to talk directly to someone who was actually there. I sat really quiet, trying to hear the conversation right above me.

I heard Andy's voice, "Grams, my friend, Mike, is here. He's doing some research on his family history and wants to ask you some questions about the Holocaust? Is that okay?"

There was a pause, and I heard her ask, "Is your friend Jewish?"

I gulped. *Oh crap*, I thought. *Here's where the dung pile hits the fan. She won't want to talk to me.*

"No, he's German," Andy answered, "but I don't know how much."

That liar, I thought to myself. *He knows exactly how much!* Then it dawned on me. He was probably trying to downplay the situation, so she would agree to talk to me. From above me, something was said that I couldn't make out, and I got nervous, thinking the answer would be "no."

That's when Andy flung the basement door open and yelled, "Mike, come on up."

Now, I was really nervous. I put together some questions in my head as I slowly climbed the stairs. Andy led me into their living room. Their house was always impeccable with white carpet, not a speck of dust anywhere, and the furniture looked like it came right from the department store catalog. I sat down on the couch across from Andy's grandma.

I nodded to her, and said, "Hello, Mrs...." and I held up my hands, gesturing that I didn't know how to address her.

"Mrs. Graham will do just fine, young man." She looked at me kindly.

"Thank you, Mrs. Graham," I said. "Are you sure it won't bother you to answer some questions for me?" She assured me she was fine, and I pulled the cap off my pen, ready to write.

Before I could begin, Mrs. Graham asked, "So, why is this of interest to you?"

I explained I was tracing my family heritage and was just trying to fill in some blanks.

"Okay," she said, "but what does that have to do with me, or the Holocaust?"

I told her the bare minimum. "My family fled Germany before the war, so I was just curious what people like you faced, being in the middle of a war, and how you made yourself keep going." I hoped I had spoken delicately enough not to offend her.

She nodded and said, "Okay, let's get started."

I noticed Andy was watching and listening intently. He would probably learn something too. Andy's mom was also looking on, holding her hands clasped in front of her mouth. Maybe she was the one I should have asked if this would be too hard. I looked at her questioningly and she seemed to know what I was asking.

She nodded at both of us. "It's okay. Go on."

I took a deep breath. "So, when did it start? How did it affect your family in the beginning?"

Mrs. Graham took a deep breath as well. "It was around 1942. I remember well. They cordoned off sections of Warsaw shortly after Germany defeated Poland. There was a section for Jews, a ghetto. We weren't allowed to travel outside the ghetto. Then, one night, German soldiers busted down our door and took us. We were only allowed one suitcase each, small ones. And we only had a couple minutes to gather what we could. They wouldn't tell us where we were going. We were marched off to a train station where we were separated from my husband. The men were loaded into their own box cars, women and children in another, and all our luggage was piled into a separate car."

I jotted stuff down like I was writing a book. She paused as if she was letting me catch up. When I looked up at her, she continued.

"It was a long and miserable train ride. A hundred people, maybe more, were all packed into this train car. There was nowhere to sit, no bathroom, and it was freezing cold."

I stopped her briefly. "So where did people go to do their business?"

She said, "You'd hold it as long as you could, then squat where you stood and went."

My eyes widened, and my nose wrinkled.

She nodded in confirmation. "The smell was terrible! And lots of people died before we ever got there."

"Where is 'there?'" I asked.

She paused and a tear began rolling down her cheek. "Treblinka," she said. "Long rows of wooden barracks stretched on as far as you could see with wire fencing surrounding it all. Our luggage never made it to us, so we had nothing but the clothes on our back. We had very little heat in the winter. Moldy bread and rotten meat were on the menu most days or slightly salty water they called soup. The only ones who were fed somewhat reasonably were those on work details. But even they soon wasted away to skin and bone."

"What kept you going?" I asked.

Another deep breath. "I was artistic and worked at a little shop designing porcelain figurines, dinnerware, and tea sets. This was high-end stuff, usually for the politicians and well-to-do aristocrats. The Allach Porcelain Company then sold these things under the SS designation. Everything was stamped on the bottom with the SS runes for authenticity. All the proceeds went to paying for war material, or parties for the Nazis."

"So, they fed you good then?" I asked. "Because you were working?"

"Better than most," she said, "but I tried to save what I could for my young daughter. She was about your age and only weighed about 35 pounds. She was so sick, and I would've done anything so that she could live." She paused again, and the tears rolled freely down her face. She looked off in the distance as if she could picture it like it was just yesterday. She shuddered and spoke again. "Often times, the meat would be covered with maggots. I'd scrape them off without her seeing if I could." She stopped a moment and looked over at Andy's mom. "Do you remember the maggots?"

Mrs. Petrovski just closed her eyes and nodded.

"I scraped the mold off the stale bread, too, if I could get it away from the rats. And if we caught the rats, we'd eat them too. They treated us like caged animals. But, that's pretty much how we survived for three years. Thousands from Treblinka never made it. Sometimes, the dead would lay where they fell for weeks or even months. We just didn't have the strength to move them or bury them ourselves. Eventually, they'd get stacked somewhere outside by the soldiers and then carted off and thrown in some pit outside the wire. They discarded them like trash. No prayer service or funeral, just a mass grave."

I had a lump in my throat and tears brimmed in my eyes. I got off the couch and sat on the floor in front of Mrs. Graham. I felt sorrow, but also admiration. "You were so brave," I whispered. "How come you don't just hate everybody after all of that?"

Her answer came quick and easy. "Because God wants us to love everyone," she said, "even our enemies. Don't get me wrong, Michael. For a long time, I hated Germans for what they did. They killed my husband, my youngest daughter, and took everything we owned for no other reason than who we were as a people. But, over the years, I've come to accept everything that happened, and I've forgiven. Besides, most of those people are dead now." She reached out and put her hand on top of my head. "How can I hold someone like you responsible when you weren't even born yet? What good would it do for me to hold a grudge that long?"

I simply shrugged. I thanked her for sharing and expressed my hope that this wasn't too hard on her.

She shook her head. "It's young people like you who need to learn this history... so it's never repeated. I think you're a fine young man, and your family should be proud of you for what you are doing and how you are doing it."

Hours had now passed, and I was ready to go home. Mentally exhausted, I stood up and thanked Mrs. Petrovski for letting me come over. I turned and held out my hand to Mrs. Graham, but instead of shaking it, she pulled me into a hug.

As I stepped outside, Andy followed me. He grabbed my arm, and in a hushed voice, he said, "Wow, that was intense! I've never even heard those stories before!"

I told him he should ask more questions about her life now because she wouldn't be around forever.

"I know. I will," he said.

Deciding to go the long way home so I could think, I strolled down the street, going around the randomly parked cars. I thought about everything I had just learned. I felt like a reporter, or investigator, digging up the truth and figuring out what happened after thirty plus years. There were two things that crossed my mind: how amazing it was that Andy's grandma was able to move on, and how incredibly cruel humans could be to their fellow humans.

I got back home just in time for dinner. Sitting at the table, I started asking my dad questions again. "How many brothers and sisters did Grandpa Heinz have?"

He smiled, happy to have another conversation about his father. "He had one other brother and two sisters."

"Are they still alive?"

"No, his brother died fighting in Stalingrad and his sisters and his parents all died when the Allies bombed Berlin one night."

"So, if Grandpa and Grandma moved here early on, he must have felt terrible when his whole family was killed over there." I was baiting him, but I was trying to root out the truth.

"Yes, I'm sure he did, especially because he tried to get them to leave and come to the States with him, and they refused."

I kept on, curious how deep the lies went. "How did they get here?"

My dad paused for a moment and removed his glasses. "They bought a cruise fare across the ocean to New York, but I'm not sure after that. I believe he sought asylum, but I don't know why they chose to move to Minnesota. I was born a few years later."

I was as convinced as a twelve-year-old could be that he wasn't lying intentionally.

After dinner, I went back to my books. I read more from the library book about D-Day. As I thought about how miserable it must have been and how awful it would feel to be scared all the time, I came to a conclusion. *I could never be a real soldier.*

Losing track of time was becoming a regular occurrence, and soon, I was told by my parents it was bedtime. I lay there, trying not to let my body toss and turn. I found myself genuinely excited about church the next day, although it wasn't really the church I was interested in as much as it was getting back to Grandma's house again. I wanted to go back up in that attic!

I awoke to Mom shaking me gently.

"It's time to get ready for church."

I stretched and yawned as Mom walked over to the closet door where my Sunday clothes were hanging.

"I'll need to iron this shirt before you put it on," she said. "Go get your brother out of his crib when you are dressed, would you please?"

I nodded.

Meandering downstairs, I went to Aaron's room and scooped him out of his bed. I got a big, drooling smile, and as I put him over my shoulder, I felt some slobbery wetness run down my shirtless back. I walked into the kitchen, where Mom had just finished ironing my shirt, and set the baby in his highchair.

Mom held out my shirt to me, but I grabbed a towel and handed it to her. "Aaron goobered on me. Will you wipe it off, please?"

Mom laughed and wiped my back.

As I slipped my shirt on, Dad came into the kitchen wearing his dark suit and sat down to put on his dress shoes.

"How are my boys today?" he asked.

Aaron sputtered and I just grinned.

"I'm going to pull the car out," Dad said, meaning we had better be ready to go in a few minutes.

I stepped outside and gasped. The air already felt heavy and humid. Big, white, puffy clouds stretched across the horizon. Mom came out behind me holding Aaron, her purse, and the diaper bag.

"The bags or the baby?" she asked, wanting me to take one or the other.

I reached for Aaron and put him in his car seat next to me. Mom checked that I had strapped him in correctly and got in herself.

We were soon pulling up in front of the church. Mom grabbed Aaron and told me to bring the diaper bag. With the warm weather, the church doors were left wide open, held by large door stops. The organ music emanating from inside was clearly audible from the street. As my father drove away to park the car, we walked up the steps to be met by an usher just inside the door, handing out programs. He was overweight, and I could tell he was uncomfortable in his ill-fitting suit; he was already beginning to sweat. The thinning hair on one side of his head was haphazardly combed over the top, attempting to cover the large bald spot.

"Good morning, folks," he said with a smile, and his hand extended with a program.

Another usher guided us to the pew where our family always sat. Grandma and a couple of uncles were already sitting in the first pew, and we slid in behind them. They turned around and said, "Good morning," in hushed voices. Dad scooted in just in time as the organ music got louder and the bells began to ring. Everyone rose to their feet, and the service began with a familiar hymn. The words came out of my mouth, but my mind had already wandered.

I thought of churches in 1940s Germany. I wondered how different, if at all, they would have been. Would families have come to church to pray for their loved ones only to find out hours later that they had been killed? Would soldiers come to church to ask for forgiveness for their sins and go right back out on the battlefield to kill again?

I also thought about Mrs. Graham and her daughter who was only thirty-five pounds. *About the size of a large bag of dog food,* I thought. Here I was, at almost eighty pounds, more than twice her weight. I couldn't even picture someone my age weighing only thirty-five pounds.

The service finished an hour later, and it was time for Sunday school. I was disappointed. "I thought there wasn't any Sunday school today," I whined. I begged to be able to skip it this week, but Mom told me how important it was. Dad chimed in, agreeing with Mom. Like most kids, I knew where the weak spots were with my mom or dad. So, looking right at my dad, I said, "But I have some questions about Grandpa Heinz that only Grandma can answer." Dad hesitated, and I gave him the "pretty please" face.

He said, "Alright, let's get going."

Mom dropped her shoulders in defeat. Smiling, I ran to the car and hopped in before he could change his mind.

Once at Grandma's, I dutifully carried in the diaper bag for Mom and dropped it on the floor just inside the door. I ran to Grandma and gave her a hug.

She caught me in her arms and said, "*Was hast du eilig?* What's your rush, Michael?"

I told her I was in a hurry to get the best piece of coffee cake. Before long, I had nothing but a pile of crumbs in front of me. I cleaned up my mess the best I could and threw my napkin in the trash. Nobody in the family was paying any attention to me by then, so I wandered upstairs. I waited at the top briefly, to see if I'd be called back down once they realized I was gone. Hearing lots of excited chatter as the family kept arriving, I felt like it was safe to keep going. I proceeded to the bedroom with the stairway to the attic. When I reached the attic door, I lifted it slightly, peering in as I always did, as if I was expecting some monster or intruder to be there. It was hot up there already, but I had only one goal, and then I'd leave.

I slowly walked to the trunk with the uniforms and medals in it. I felt apprehensive, even though I already knew what was inside. I placed a hand on each side and carefully lifted the lid, my eyes settling on the ring. I sat there staring at it, wanting to pick it up and look at it but fearing what I would see. Finally, I grabbed it and walked to the window where there was more light. It had a skull on top and five other symbols in a circle around the ring. On the inside, the name Heinz Dirden was inscribed, the date 20/05/43, and H. Himmler. This is it! I thought. *This is proof my grandpa served in the Wehrmacht, the SS!* On one hand, I felt a sense of shame, because of Mrs. Graham's revelations. But another part of me also thought it was cool and proud of him. After all, I hadn't seen anything, yet, that implicated him in any war crimes. And the uniform looked so amazing! I thought the Germans, and the SS in particular, had the best-looking uniforms of any country. Combat or dress uniform, it didn't matter. They were sharp!

Back on task, I slipped the ring on my finger. It was huge and spun around easily. I think I could've put both my thumbs in there and it would've still been loose. I was tempted to take it home but decided against it. I reasoned with myself that getting caught with letters, a journal, and pictures was one thing, but the ring would've been another matter entirely.

Lying just a few inches away, I saw a greenish brown book marked "*Soldbuch.*" I had seen that word in one of my books, although I couldn't remember exactly what it said about it. I picked it up and paged through it. My thoughts were interrupted by, "Michael, it's time to go!" being hollered at me from downstairs. I put the thin *Soldbuch* in my back pocket and quickly closed the lid to the trunk. I ran downstairs, out of breath, partially nervous, and partially from the physical nature of rushing.

When my mother saw me she asked if I felt okay. "You're sweating!"

"I was trying to hurry," I said. "And besides, it's getting hot." I said goodbye to Grandma and hurried out the front door before I could be asked any more pointed questions. In my rush, the screen door slammed behind me. I hunched, turned around, and yelled, "Sorry, Grandma!" She just shook her head at me with a smile. Grandmas know that twelve-year-old boys are always in a hurry.

At home, I went directly to my room and took the thin book from my back pocket. I sat at my desk, trying to decipher what was written inside. Some of the words were faded and some smudged, but I was able to piece things together. The medals that I had seen in the trunk and researched were written in it. Also, his pay schedule, and where he was stationed and with what unit, so, basically, it was his orders and a record of his service.

At dinner that night, after I finished eating, I asked to be excused. This time, I was questioned. "Why are you spending so much time in your room lately, Michael?" Mom asked, and both she and Dad looked intently at me.

I thought quickly. "I'm just having fun researching Grandpa's stories," I replied. I wasn't really lying, just not giving any extra details. Then I added, "Is it okay if I stay with Grandma again next weekend?"

Dad asked, "Again?"

"Yes, I was thinking I could meet up with Justin and do something together." I wasn't sure if I was lying this time or not.

"I'll call your grandma and we'll see."

It was my last week of school. Summer vacation started on Friday. Thankfully, my week flew by, full of tests, treats, and clean-up. I was able to put the whole journey out of my head, for the most part, for those few days and concentrate on wrapping up the school year. I was getting a bit overwhelmed by the depth of it all, anyway, so I figured a break would be good.

Now, Thursday, I was walking home, thankful the summer break was upon me, and I looked forward to Grandpa coming today. I was ready for more stories. I walked up the driveway but couldn't see his car. However, this time I wasn't worried.

Inside, Mom was doing the dishes with Aaron in his high chair next to her. "Hi, sweetie. How was your last day of school?"

"It was good," I said simply as I stopped to give Aaron a raspberry on his cheek and got a big grin. "Is Grandpa on his way?"

"Yes, don't worry, he should be here soon. You know, the grass needs to be cut."

"I know, but I thought I'd do that tomorrow since I don't have school."

"Okay, but at least take out the trash today, please."

I went to the back stoop where the trash was, and as I picked up the bag, I saw Grandpa's car around the corner. I hurried to the trashcan, dropped the bag inside, and it made a loud crash. A glass jar inside must have broken on impact. Grandpa rolled up the driveway, and I walked to his door, opening it for him. I reached in, pulling on his arm to hurry him along.

"C'mon, Grandpa!" I exclaimed.

He let out a hearty laugh, with the corners of his eyes crinkling. "Well, it looks like someone is happy to see me!"

"Yes! I can't wait to work on our project!"

"Me too," he said. "Hopefully, we'll get it done today, and we can fly it this weekend."

"That would be great!" I said, jumping a little like I was jumping rope.

"Well, let's go see where we're at, shall we?"

I nodded excitedly and led the way, opening the door for him.

Mom handed me a stack of old newspaper, and I spread them out on the table. Grandpa began spreading out the tools while I ran into the other room to get the plane. Walking carefully back to the kitchen, I placed the plane on the table and pulled my chair up right next to Grandpa's. I wanted to be sure I saw every detail of what he was doing.

Mom came back in the kitchen holding Aaron and said she was going to run some errands. She said, "I'll bring back dinner if you'll stay, Dad."

"That would be great, Sherry," Grandpa said. "We'll just be here building this old war bird."

Mom asked, "Chicken okay?"

"Sounds good!" Grandpa and I said in unison.

Mom laughed and headed out the door.

We were quiet for a few minutes until we heard the car engine fading off in the distance and then Grandpa said, "So... shall I continue the story where I left off?"

"That's what I was hoping for!" I grinned at him. "I think I'm more excited about that right now than the airplane!"

"Well, I think we can do both," he said. "Now, where did I leave off?"

"You were talking about England," I answered.

"That's right," he said. He squeezed some glue out onto the newspaper, handed me a toothpick, and pointed. "Put some glue here... and here." He leaned back in his chair slightly. "England is a lovely place. The weather, I didn't care for, but the beauty of the countryside is second to none." He continued talking, every so often giving me instructions on what to do with the plane. "We trained a lot, practicing putting in IVs under fire, stopping bleeding, and getting the wounded ready for transport. Several times, we boarded landing craft... do you know what those are?" he asked.

"Yes. The Higgins boats."

He looked impressed. "That's right. You're a pretty smart young man, I guess."

I enjoyed the compliment, but I tried to downplay it. "I just read about them, and they're on a lot of documentaries I've seen, too."

Grandpa directed me to sand a few pieces and continued. "So, we'd land on a beach somewhere in England with an infantry platoon, and the trainers would shoot over our heads and throw artillery simulators out among us. They would throw sand into the air around us to make it all seem very real. A trainer would walk up and point to some GI and say, 'You're hit, shot in the stomach.' Then a medic, like me, would run up and do what he needed to do to try and save him. The casualties would start adding up and we had to prioritize."

As he paused, I said, "Wow. That sounds really scary."

Grandpa nodded. "The days were long, but in the end, that training was worth it." Suddenly, he tucked his chin and chuckled. "Y'know, Mike, the civilians loved us, but the British soldiers... not so much."

"Why?" I was confused. "We were there to help them, after all, weren't we?"

"Yes, but they didn't like us chasing their girls and drinking all their beer!" he said with a twinkle in his eyes. "Speaking of girls, do you have a girlfriend yet?"

Blushing, I giggled and said, "No! Don't want one either!"

He tousled my hair and pinched my earlobe. "Take your time, young man. There will be plenty of opportunities as you get older. Just remember God and what He wants for us."

I nodded in acknowledgment and respect. "Yes, Sir."

Looking back at the plane instructions, he said, "Now, we need to find two of these little pieces next," and pointed to the page.

My head down, looking at the pieces on the table, I asked, "How long were you in England before D-Day?"

"I was there just short of a year. I arrived in August sometime and, as you know, the operation took place in June the next year. Actually, it was planned to happen a month or so earlier, but the weather was so bad they had to cancel it. Even the day we did go was a day later than it was supposed to be. It was raining, and the wind was incredible. The waves in the channel were huge. But we heard there was going to be an opening in the weather, so we boarded ships and headed to the launching point anyway."

"My book says over a million guys were in this operation. Is that true?"

"I'm sure that number includes everyone involved: British soldiers, Canadian soldiers, and the paratroopers."

"How come General Patton wasn't involved?" I asked. "Wasn't he the best commander we had?"

"Actually, he was involved."

I tipped my head in confusion. "Really? I haven't read about that yet."

"He was used as a diversion."

"Why would they do that?" I wondered.

Grandpa explained. "Because the Germans thought he was the best we had, too. They were sure that we would have him lead the invasion, so we put all kinds of inflatable trucks, jeeps, and tanks along several spots of the English east coast. We wanted their surveillance planes, or spies, to see them so they would think we'd land just across the English Channel in Calais."

Impressed, I said, "Ooh, that's tricky!"

Grandpa gave his head a little shake. "Well, Patton wasn't happy about it. He wanted on that beach in the worst way."

Taking my hands off our project for the moment, I leaned back, taking in all of it. I closed my eyes, envisioning what it was like.

CHAPTER EIGHT

The smell of glue was soon replaced with the scent of seawater as Grandpa's voice took me to the frontline. His voice lulled me, painting a vivid picture of scenes barely captured in documentaries or history books. But now, told to me firsthand, by a man who had been there, as an American, as an unarmed medic. And survived.

In June of 1944, my platoon and the rest of the company were marched to a rallying point where we loaded onto two and a half ton trucks. We hung our packs on the outside of the truck before jumping in the back. The olive-drab canvas kept the rain off our heads for now; a welcome blessing. Occasionally, the wind would pick up a bit, and the heavy cover would flap in spots where the fit was loose. The rain came down in torrents at times, making us think the invasion would again be canceled, and we'd be told to stand down. The idling diesel engine revved up, the whine of the turbo standing out over all the other noise. The truck jerked slightly, and we began to move, creeping along in a lengthy line of vehicles heading for the harbor. If all went according to plan, we'd be standing in France at this time tomorrow.

We crawled along agonizingly slow. It felt like an hour had gone by, and we'd only moved about a mile. "At this rate, we won't even be at the harbor by tomorrow night," someone said. Being fairly new to this platoon, it was impossible for me to know who said it.

Everyone laughed a little when the guy next to me pulled out a notebook. He said, "Okay, guys... bets on who gets it first." Guys started slapping down bets on who got KIA or just wounded. I sat back, astonished at the morbid gambling. The bookie looked at me while lighting a cigarette and said, "Doc? What do you say?" as he exhaled the smoke from the first drag.

I glanced at his collar. "Well, Corporal, how would it look if I bet on you dying first, then you get hit, and I let you bleed out?"

The smile instantly disappeared from his face. The group suddenly became so quiet you could've heard a mouse fart. He extended his hand and said, "Corporal Bill Dawson."

I shook his hand and said, "Corporal Dave Harper. Nice to meet you."

"Doc," he said, "please don't do that," unsure if I was serious.

I promised him I wouldn't and let go of his hand. "But that's why I don't bet. I wouldn't want anyone accusing me of playing God."

A couple other guys soon lit cigarettes as well and engaged in quiet small talk. It was now 1900 hours, and we were finally within sight of the harbor. The roads had been closed to civilians for the next twenty-four hours, so we could get to the harbor expeditiously. We had every type of military vehicle waiting in long lines for their turn to be loaded onto ships to take us across the channel. We had become tired of these "load up and wait" alerts, only for them to be canceled hours later. This was our third time doing this, but this was the farthest we'd ever gotten. Lately, the rain had been so heavy, we thought the island might sink.

I sat there, observing the guys. In a way, I wished I knew more about them, but I also realized I could do my job more effectively if I didn't get emotionally involved with them. There was nothing worse than seeing a close friend get splattered right in front of you. The non-commissioned officers were good, I thought, and I hoped everyone would make it through this. Realistically though, at least fifty percent would be dead before ever getting off the beach. I folded my hands and bowed my head, saying a little prayer, asking Jesus to protect these boys from harm so that they would see their families again. I thanked God for seeing us through this far and said, "Amen."

It was dark by the time the truck finally stopped, and we were told to get out. "Throw your packs inside the truck and form up." I grabbed my pack, checked that my name tag was still sewn on, and placed it in the back. Other bags were piled on top and pushed forward, making room for more. I stood at the back as the platoon came to attention, each squad becoming rigid, looking forward, head and eyes not moving. The rain beat down on the ponchos we were wearing, and it was distracting at times. My helmet kept my head dry, but my feet were soon soaked to the bone in my leather boots. My personal pack, with extra uniforms, socks and undergarments, was in the truck, but I still had a large medical pack on my back. The rain found a way into my poncho, and the wetness worked its way down my back, becoming trapped there under my pack.

The platoon sergeant began pacing in front of us, telling us this was the real deal. "Just do your job and let's all get through this safely. We'll most likely be in the first wave." He began handing out condoms, to be used later in waterproofing the gun muzzle, but without a rifle, he skipped by me. I went over things in my head one last time, trying to think of anything I was short of that I would need to get before we boarded. Of course, there was no way I'd know for sure until we hit the beach, but I did my best to anticipate the situations I might face.

The platoon leader called the sergeant over and they talked quietly. A few minutes later, the sergeant came back and told the platoon to get in single file. "Time to load up," he yelled. Then I heard, "Harper, get over here."

I hollered back, "Yes, Sergeant," and jumped out of line, walking swiftly toward him.

He said, "I know we haven't had much time to meet yet, but I want you to know these guys mean the world to me."

"Yes, Sergeant," I assured him, "I'll do my best."

"I'm looking to you for all the help you can give to protect them. Am I clear on that, Corporal?"

"Crystal, Sergeant Tillson."

"Alright then, get back in line, Corporal. You stick with the staff section until we hit the beach."

Again, I acknowledged his command and returned to the line.

It took a few more hours for all the troops to board the ship before it moved out of the harbor into the channel. We tried to remain on the leeward side of the island, but the waves here were still quite hefty. Occasionally, one would break over the bow, spraying cold salt water high up on the ship. I couldn't imagine trying to launch landing craft in this weather. We were surrounded by ships of all types; large warships like cruisers and even a couple of behemoth battleships. Destroyers patrolled around us, keeping any potential U-boats at a distance. Patrol boats ran up and down the harbor, keeping enemy submarines out. The anti-submarine nets and mines were not enough to guarantee our safety.

The ship bobbed and swayed, and guys weren't feeling well, especially ones who came from places like Iowa or Kansas and had little experience of the water. It was like a roller coaster that never ended. We changed into dry uniforms and tried to rest. Some troops played card games here and there. Eventually, the lights dimmed adequately to allow some sleep, but still glowed enough that if you had to get to the head, you could see where you were going. Guys stretched out wherever they could, and all the floor space was taken up by snoring men and their equipment.

I found Corporal Dawson sitting on a blanket near my own. He was reading a letter and looking at a black and white picture. When I sat next to him, he looked at me and said, "What will you do when this is all over, Dave?"

"I plan on getting a degree in medicine," I told him. "I'm not sure exactly what field yet. You?"

"My family owns this little restaurant in Texas," he said. "Really great food. I have big plans to turn it into several restaurants statewide, maybe even nationally one day."

"That's cool. What kind of restaurant is it?"

"Oh, your typical Texan thing—burgers, steaks, chicken, and pork. We do everything in-house from butchering our own cows, to making our own sauces."

"That sounds really unique," I said. "I'm sure it will be a great success." We talked a bit more before I said I needed to get some sleep. "Tomorrow is going to be hell on earth, you should get some rest, too."

He agreed, and we both lay down. He looked over at me and said, "Doc? I'm scared to death of drowning."

"Don't worry," I said, "they'll put us up high and dry, you watch."

With that, he rolled over and soon joined the chorus of snoring men.

I closed my eyes and prayed. "Dear Lord Jesus, hear my prayer. Please watch over all of us, but especially Bill. He needs your guiding hand. And please, Lord God, help me to perform the necessary tasks to help all those who may be injured. In our hour of need, we realize that only you can save us from the horrors that await us. In Jesus' name, I pray. Amen."

I took my Bible from a plastic bag in my medical pack, clicked on my flashlight, and read a few verses. It made me sleepy, so I turned off the flashlight and lay there with the Bible spread over my chest. The low rumble of the engines and vibrations of the propellers put me to sleep.

We were awakened by a 1st sergeant around 0300 who said, "Rise and shine, ladies!"

After a restless night, I felt extremely tired. I sat up, feeling the anxiety building as I stretched. I picked up my Bible and tucked it back in my medical pack, secured in its plastic bag.

The 1st sergeant yelled, "You have five minutes to get chow. Now move your asses!"

Groaning from the men ensued as he turned and left.

I said to Bill, "C'mon, I'll buy."

He laughed. "Very funny." After a pause, he went on. "Actually, Dave, I feel pretty good about today. I don't think it'll be easy, by any means, but I think we're all going to be just fine. You know, they always hype these things up, and it never turns out as bad as they say."

"Let's hope that's the case this time," I said.

Bill and I got into the line moving slowly toward the mess area. Most guys were pretty quiet, contemplating what the future may hold. I grabbed a metal tray and, looking at the food, I couldn't believe our luck. Real steak, real eggs, with bacon and sausage! I looked at Bill and said, "Probably not as good as you make it, but this looks decent."

"Yeah," he said, "the last meal, right?"

Nudging him with my elbow, I said, "Stop it! You just got done saying everyone would be fine. Believe in that."

He shrugged. "You're right, I will."

We ate quickly and got back to our packs. As we were gathering our stuff, Sergeant Tillson came over to us. "Boys," he said. "I want you to gather over there in fifteen minutes." He pointed to a bare spot along a wall.

"Roger that, Sergeant," I said.

As he went to round up the rest of the platoon, I went through my pack one last time, making sure I knew where everything was for easy access. Morphine syrettes were all in place, sterile gauze bandages, medical tape, a couple pairs of scissors, a dozen scalpels, clamps, needles and thread for sutures, limited IV supplies, about fifty packets of sulfa powder, and other assorted pills like aspirin and antibiotics.

Bill looked at me and said, "I'm glad you're so organized."

"Makes me feel better," I said, "but I won't need all this, remember?"

He smiled slightly and said, "Yeah, right."

"C'mon, let's get going."

The platoon huddled together for the sergeant's address. "Okay, guys, remember, we hit the beach and get to the first berm. From there, we'll see what's going on. Either we make a hole in the wire or form up and assault the cliffs. Private Dickerson, your flamethrower ready to go?"

"Yes, Sergeant," he answered.

"Good. Now, every third man carries one section of Bangalore torpedo." That was a six-foot-long pipe that could be connected to other pipes and carried an explosive charge. It was used for removing obstacles such as barbed wire. "They'll be on deck, so grab one if there are two guys in front of you without it. We should have eight for our platoon. I'll have a satchel charge if we need it. We don't anticipate armor, yet. That might come tomorrow, providing we gain a foothold." He turned his head around and pointed. "Private Jepsen, you and Smith load heavy for the BARs." Those were the Browning automatic rifles we carried.

Jepsen and Smith sounded off together, "Already done, Sergeant."

"Good. And make sure everyone has at least three grenades. Okay, let's meet up on deck. Grab your equipment, weapons and the ammo should be top side. Let's do this, ladies!"

I got in line behind everyone else, up the grated stairs to the deck. Just then, there were huge explosions as the battleships and cruisers opened fire in an attempt to soften up the beach. This was the first time I had seen a battlewagon in action, and I stood there in awe. The guns recoiled, pushing the ship to the side as if they were trying to roll the whole ship over. Fire belched from the muzzle, like an angry dragon from the days of kings and castles, culminating in a huge smoke ring, as the fire extinguished and turned into a dirty, gray cloud rising above the sea. All nine sixteen-inch guns going off almost simultaneously was an unreal sight.

"Glad I wasn't on the receiving end of that," I said to Bill.

"Let's hope they actually hit something," he said.

I stood looking toward shore when we saw this monstrous explosion—a huge fireball reaching skyward, rolling and boiling like some evil entity. Then we heard it. A loud thunderous roll that you could feel in your bones.

My God! I thought. *How could anyone live through that?* Gradually, it became non-stop with the cruisers firing and even the destroyers moving in close and firing. Tugging on Bill's sleeve, I pointed skyward. "Look!"

A wave of B-17s was headed for the coast. They dropped bombs on the coastal defenses as their ordnance mixed in with the naval gunfire. It was only now that I noticed the sun lightening up the eastern horizon.

"No beautiful sunrise today," I said under my breath. It was no longer raining, but the clouds were thick, and the wind was chilly. Life belts were handed to us in case the landing craft capsized. I slipped mine on, thinking, *this thing is useless! With all the weight we're carrying, we'd surely go right to the bottom!*

Guys drew their ammo and stored their reserve in canvas pouches on their web gear. They drew their grenades and hung them carefully on their gear by sticking the grenade's spoon handle in their belt. Just as instructed, every third man picked up a Bangalore torpedo. Those holding the unwieldy weapon, couldn't wait to use it or lose it. Now, everyone started taking out gum and popping it in their mouth, chewing vigorously. They looked like little kids stuffing stick after stick in their mouths until they could hardly chew it. This gum would soon play a major part in helping them survive the trip.

Seconds later, Sergeant Tillson yelled, "Platoon, over the side!"

Men started climbing over the side of the ship, carefully navigating down the cargo nets hanging from the rail, the ship bobbing, the landing craft below trying to hold steady to allow the men to enter safely with all their gear. It was not an easy task for either of them. Once inside, they bunched up together, taking out the condoms and unrolling them, stretching them over the muzzles of their rifles and fastening them in place with a wad of gum. Some guys crammed gum into their ears, while others kept chewing as long as they could to help with the pressure in their ears from all the explosions and shock waves constantly bombarding us.

We pulled away from the ship once we were fully loaded. Each Higgins boat was designed to hold a platoon worth of men with very little extra room. They were like giant bathtubs with an extended steel ramp in front that would drop down once on the beach, allowing the men to rush out. The driver sat high at the back, the walls extending roughly seven or eight feet high. Larger landing craft were also available, but those were meant for bringing tanks and other vehicles to the beach, and some were used as a weapons platform.

There was a deafening roar as rockets sped off over the top of us. I grabbed the starboard edge and lifted myself up. A couple of guys locked hands so I could use it as a step to see. The rockets kept going, one after another, like flaming arrows only moving at the speed of a bullet. Hundreds, even thousands were launched, arching up into the sky then pummeling the surrounding cliffs. Like a shotgun, but instead of pellets, little explosions saturated the landscape. Certainly, anyone not in a bunker was going to be in a world of hurt.

I stepped down and said, "I think the Navy is giving them hell, boys!"

The shells from the battleships passing overhead sounded like locomotives that couldn't be seen. The explosions became more deafening with every minute that passed. A detonation on the port side lifted a geyser of water high into the air, fifty maybe even sixty feet. We all ducked as the water returned to earth, showering us in cold, salt water. Bullets began zipping over the top of us periodically, then *ping, ping* when a couple hit the front ramp.

A man in front began to panic, "SHIT!" he yelled, "they're zeroing in on us!"

The wind had made the sea rough, and the explosions also whipped up the water, making the boat moving wildly in all directions. Several men began vomiting, both from fear and motion sickness. The wind swirled around us, bringing a mix of smells: body odor, vomit from the heavy breakfast most were now rethinking, and the diesel exhaust from the landing craft's engines.

I looked down just as another wave slammed against the tiny craft and splashed us. The salt water mixed with the contents of the men's stomachs and sloshed around the floor, now ankle deep. The driver yelled at us, "Two minutes!" We readied ourselves as more bullets bounced off the front ramp, some leaving indentations in the wall, right where a moment ago there had been a soldier's head. This was rather unnerving if you were in front. We knew we were surrounded by hundreds of other landing craft, the object being to overwhelm them with numbers.

Suddenly, we hit something, and the boat lurched to the port side and almost rolled before righting itself, causing guys to fall to their knees, cussing in the slurry they found themselves in. They were forced to regain their footing and composure, as the engines slowed and the driver yelled, "Ready!" With that, the craft ground to a halt, stopping with a jerk and challenging the men's balance again. The ramp crashed down with a splash.

Several bullets ripped into the Higgins boat, killing two instantly. They fell where they stood as the rest of us rushed to get off, jumping into waist-deep, cold seawater, and trying to run forward. It was as if we were running in quicksand, barely moving, while more bullets slammed into the water all around us. A guy right next to me was hit in the chest and fell backward, a red cloud instantly forming around him. I stopped to grab him, but Sergeant Tillson yanked on my arm.

"Leave him," he yelled. "He's already dead! We need to get out of this damn water, NOW! Assholes and elbows everyone! Get to that berm!" He pointed ahead of us.

As I struggled to get out of the water, I felt like I was in a dream. Littering the beach and heading into the surf were metal tripods. These stuck out of the water and were designed to rip the bottoms out of our landing craft. Also, there were wooden poles, like telephone poles, that were designed to capsize boats. A short one stuck in the sand and a much longer one sat on top and angled into the sea.

I thought to myself, *I bet that's what we hit earlier but it was too deep to capsize us.*

There were other wooden poles stuck in the sand too, topped with mines. Finally, reaching the shore, I dove behind a piece of steel to catch my breath, removing the worthless life belt and tossing it aside. As it landed in the water, I noticed the first three or four feet of surf was red with blood, the foam a pale pink.

I looked back toward the sea at the landing craft and the explosions that lifted water high into the air above them before it crashed back down. It was chaos. One boat suddenly vaporized, exploding into jagged pieces as bodies were flung in all directions. I sat stunned by what was happening. Another boat stopped short, and the driver, most likely terrified, dropped the ramp. Guys jumped out, never to be seen again, sinking in ten or fifteen feet of water, their heavy equipment pulling them to the bottom. Occasionally, one would strip everything off and bob to the surface, swimming to the beach if he was lucky, with nothing more than the clothes on his back with no weapon, no boots, not even his helmet. Another boat swerved into the path of some other landing craft, either by a mechanical malfunction or because the driver had been killed. They collided, and one capsized, flinging everyone into the sea.

We're doomed! I thought to myself. *I just witnessed almost a hundred soldiers die in just a few seconds. How can we ever gain a foothold on this beach and succeed in our mission?*

"Harper! Get your ass moving!" the sergeant yelled, waving me up to the berm.

I stood, and bullets instantly clanged off the steel I was hiding behind. Crouching low, I ran forward, the bullets following me, drilling into the sand all around me. Thirty yards from me, a man was sent flying about six feet in the air. I watched him somersault, thinking something looked odd about it. That's when I caught sight of one of his legs flying in my direction. I ducked as it flew over my head and landed fifteen feet behind me. The soldier landed on his back, screaming in agony and holding the stump where his leg had been just seconds ago. I quickly changed course, running to him. Blood squirted from an artery like a pulsating garden hose. I instinctively tore off my pack and grabbed for a clamp first, thinking I would try to clamp the artery closed. Noticing another toe popper (a German box mine) just inches from us, I grabbed the man's arm and pulled him away. As I took hold of his mangled leg, machine gun bullets stitched him at an angle from shoulder to hip. "Damn!" I screamed. Dropping the man's leg, I grabbed my pack and ran for the berm. Out of breath, I looked back. Bodies littered the beach in every direction as far as one could see.

Just up from the water's edge, another man lifted his arm, begging for help. I wanted to go retrieve him, but the sergeant held me back.

"Saving people is noble, Doc, but you gotta be smart about it or you'll end up just like them."

All of a sudden, I noticed my armpit stung. I stuck my hand under my arm and pulled it out, expecting to see blood. Instead, I had a hand full of sand. The grit had found its way into vulnerable spots, in between legs and armpits, making things very uncomfortable. It was like sandpaper anytime I moved, tearing at flesh and rubbing everything raw. The saltwater touching it stung like an angry beehive was in my clothes.

I caught movement out of the corner of my eye and noticed a couple of men connecting several Bangalore torpedoes together and pushing them forward to where the concertina wire was preventing our advance. Someone yelled, "Fire in the hole!" as they pulled the cord, igniting the fuse. It hissed and promptly exploded, throwing sand over us, leaving a huge hole in the wire. One guy stood to run through and was immediately cut down. I crawled over to him and checked for a pulse. Nothing! *Why am I even here?* I wondered. *Everyone dies before I can ever help!*

I looked up to the cliffs in front of us. What an intimidating sight! Large concrete bunkers stretched for miles in each direction, pockmarked from the naval gunfire. Some of the chunks taken out of the cement were the size of cars, but the bunkers were left unaffected. The reinforced concrete looked to be at least ten feet thick.

The MG 42 in the bunker above us had command of the beach. We couldn't hit anything with a rifle from our angle, out of range for a flamethrower, and no one could throw a grenade that far. That left very few options.

Sergeant Tillson yelled, "Dawson, go find me a bazooka team! On the double!"

Dawson crouched and ran down the line to our right. Sergeant Tillson took the radio receiver from his radio telephone operator's hand and called for gunnery support from a nearby destroyer. He pulled the map from his shirt pocket and began sending the coordinates.

I looked out to sea and saw another wave of landing craft inbound. Pretty soon, we were going to be stacked up like cordwood if we didn't advance.

Private Jepson, overwhelmed and in a state of shock, panicked and stood suddenly, firing his BAR from the hip and ran toward the hole in the wire. Several bullets came zipping his way, one finding his right shoulder. He spun around and fell to the sand, grasping his shoulder and screaming in pain. Two men grabbed his ankles and pulled him back hollering, "Medic!" I scrambled on my hands and feet to him. I ripped his shirt open and saw the bullet had gone clean through, so I tried to calm him down, telling him he'd be fine if he could just relax a bit. I grabbed a sulfa packet, ripped it open and dumped it on his wound, then, with two compression bandages, I wrapped his shoulder and told him to lie on his back and apply pressure to it. I grabbed a morphine syrette and jabbed it into his right arm, counted to ten and removed it, pitching the empty vial into the sand ahead of us.

Corporal Dawson arrived with a bazooka team from the 4th Platoon. Lying behind the berm, the gunner pointed the six-foot bazooka tube toward the bunker. Sergeant Tillson shouted, "Put a couple rounds in that aperture," pointing to where the firing was coming from the machine gun. The loader took a cardboard tube from a canvas satchel and removed the top, tipping it upside down, sliding the round into his hand. He placed the round in the back of the stove pipe, removed its safety, slid the round all the way in, unwound and connected a wire from the round to the tube, completing the connection. He jumped out of the way and tapped the gunner on his helmet, signaling he was clear to fire.

The gunner took careful aim and squeezed the trigger. *Whoosh!* The rocket blasted, fire spitting out of the back of the tube several feet. A smoke trail followed the round as it streaked to its target. *Boom!* A huge explosion. Fire, sparks, and chunks of concrete flew into the air. When the smoke cloud was whisked away by the wind off the ocean, a slight hole or piece of cement missing from the opening is all that could be seen, and the MG 42 kept targeting our position with relentless conviction.

The loader, while lying there, again inserted another round, tapped the gunner on his helmet and rolled over. When the enemy fire ceased momentarily, the gunner rose to his knees, took aim and again squeezed the trigger. *Whoosh!* The rocket sped out of the tube and Boom! The round struck just below the opening, fire and smoke reaching skyward. Bullets ripped through the air, the machine gunner just hoping to hit something, striking the sand all around us, bouncing off stones and discarded equipment. But one lone bullet found the front of the gunner's helmet, piercing the thin steel. It entered the man's head just above his right eye and exited out the back. It removed most of the back of his skull and knocked the helmet off his head. The interior was covered in bloody brain matter. The gunner hunched over and fell to his right, the dark red blood pooling in the sand around him.

I never moved. *What was the point? He's surely dead,* I justified to myself.

Just as the next wave of landing craft hit the beach, the destroyer began firing from about a thousand yards away. Initially, the rounds went long, but they adjusted their fire and soon were hitting their targets. Five-inch shells pummeled the pillbox to no avail. It was like trying to destroy a house with a sprinkler.

Several men used the distraction to get up and burst through the hole in the wire. The machine gun again fired incessantly, but he wasn't shooting at us. I turned my head and saw one Higgins boat drop its ramp; the men cut down in no time flat as they rushed out as if they'd run into some deadly invisible wall. They dropped instantly as they were hit, flailing their arms as miniature pink clouds surrounded each one. Twenty-five men lost their lives in an instant. *This is insane!* I thought.

The progress of each wave seemed painstakingly slow. As more boats landed, men rushed out toward our line. We cheered them on, willing them to run faster to the relative safety at the berm but so many didn't make it there, artillery raining down on the advancing force.

One man was flung five feet in the air, separated from his legs as an S-mine found a victim. Another man vaporized in an instant, the only thing left of him being his mangled helmet that tumbled back to earth. A soldier struggled out of the surf and burst into flames when the flamethrower tanks on his back were punctured and set ablaze by a bullet or shrapnel. Swinging his arms wildly, he tried to extinguish himself by dropping to the sand and rolling, but his body continued to burn. He rose to his knees, pleading for help, and collapsed face first in the sand. Thick, oily, black smoke ascended from his body until the fuel burned up, his corpse smoking long after. The stench of burning flesh and blood was everywhere.

Seeing one man fall about twenty yards from me, I jumped and ran to him. He'd been hit in the leg, so I helped him to his feet, and we half-ran, half-hopped back to the berm. Tearing open his pants, I examined the wound, the man screaming in pain. The bullet was still in his leg but had not hit the artery. I washed the wound and applied a compression bandage. The gauze immediately became soaked in blood and I realized the bullet had been so close to the femoral artery that when I moved his leg to wrap the bandage around it, the bullet had cut the artery. Quickly, I loosened the bandage, sliding it up his leg. Grabbing his bayonet, I wrapped the cloth tails from the bandage around the knife and twisted it several times, cutting off the blood flow. As per the standard operating procedures (SOP), I marked his forehead with a T, using his own blood, to convey to whoever cared for him next that he had a tourniquet applied.

I glanced toward the channel again. Men and equipment lay everywhere, and I decided not to sit here any longer when hundreds of soldiers needed my help. Telling the man with the tourniquet that he needed to loosen it every twenty minutes and tighten it again, I stood and raced to another wounded man. Shrapnel had ripped his stomach open, and he was holding his intestines. He was a mess; sand and seaweed mixed with his guts was a recipe for problems. Right now, though, I just wanted to extend his life as long as possible. I grabbed a piece of nearby canvas from the beach and placed it over his stomach. Corporal Dawson came running out at that time, and we pulled him to the berm. Removing the canvas, I dumped a packet of sulfa over his wound, took a large pressure bandage, and tucking his bowels under it, secured it, hoping to keep everything in place, and gave him morphine.

I was hurting from physical exhaustion, the sand had got into several delicate places, I was hungry, thirsty, and mentally tired, but I wasn't about to quit. Another wave was headed our way. The death and destruction were unimaginable without seeing it firsthand. Empty brass bullet casings lay everywhere. The beach was cratered from north to south, like the surface of the moon. Landing craft dotted the beach, burning or capsized. Rifles, machine guns, and life belts were discarded haphazardly. A few bodies rolled gently in the ever-expanding red surf. Here and there lay body parts without an owner; an arm, or leg, and sitting near a shell hole was a foot still inside a boot. I continued to do my job the best I could with the chaos that surrounded me. The whistling got louder as artillery began hitting the beach again to keep the men landing from reaching the cliffs ahead.

Seeing more wounded men, I grabbed my pack, took a swig of water from my canteen and placed it back in its canvas pouch. I took a deep breath and ran toward the water. As I knelt by one soldier, Corporal Dawson came right behind me. "Damn you, Harper!" he said. "You keep doing this and we'll both end up dead."

"Get outta here!" I barked.

He shook his head. "Somebody's gotta protect your dumb ass, so I'm staying!"

The downed soldier had been shot through the hip, so I grabbed one arm and Dawson the other, and we dragged him to safety as artillery shells and machine gun bullets landed all around us. I felt like we were in a protective bubble. Suddenly, Dawson screeched in a hair raising, high-pitched scream. He dropped the man's arm, causing me to lose my balance. I fell to the beach and reached back to grab hold again and saw Dawson, holding his throat with both hands, blood gurgling between his fingers.

The dilemma I now faced was one I'd feared: wanting desperately to save Corporal Dawson while knowing he didn't have a great chance and trying to save the man I didn't know, who had a better chance of survival. It was tearing at my heart. I yanked a compression bandage from my pack and placed it on his throat. I told him to run for the berm, and I'd help him soon. I grabbed the other wounded man, and alone, began pulling him toward safety again as Dawson stumbled forward. Watching Dawson fall and struggle to his feet again was hard to take.

Without ever hearing the warning, a shell landed just in front of me, throwing me ten feet backward. My face burned like it was on fire. I tried to open my eyes but couldn't. I put my hands to my face, and blood filled them. I felt pieces of metal sticking in my skin like a pincushion. Everything became quiet in my head, except for the ringing in my ears and my throbbing head. I rose to my feet, unseeing, and hobbled toward what I thought was the berm, tripping over bodies and who knows what else, I was suddenly punched in the arm. The stinging that instantly ensued told me I was shot. Falling to my knees, I wanted to give up. I quietly asked God for help and groped forward on my hands and knees. Two men soon grabbed my arms, dragging me ahead. I was injected with morphine and became oblivious to my surroundings.

I woke up briefly on an operating table hours later. The doctors, working quickly to treat my wounds, asked me to close my eyes and keep them that way for the time being. They finished by wrapping my head in a bandage and pumped me full of antibiotics and painkillers.

That's all I remember of the next two days, not being able to see and wondering if I'd be blind forever. A few days later, they removed the bandage from my head. I could still see, but everything was cloudy. The doctors told me they hoped my vision would clear, but they'd had to leave some pieces behind that were too risky to remove and advised if it bothered me later, to seek medical attention.

A couple weeks later, my Battalion commander came to the hospital and issued me the purple heart.

"That's the one you have right now, Mike," Grandpa said.

CHAPTER NINE

1978

I opened my eyes. "That's amazing, Grandpa!"

Grandpa and I had just finished with the plane.

"Yeah, it looks pretty good, huh? Let's hope it flies."

"No, I meant your story! I mean, the plane is really cool too, but the story is crazy. Weren't you scared?"

"Heck yes, I was! The whole time!"

I was awestruck. His story made the medal even more impressive to me now. We were picking up the scraps from the plane when I asked, "So, whatever happened to Corporal Dawson?"

Grandpa answered, "Well, he survived! I heard he was evacuated to England for further medical treatment, but after he fully recovered, he was shipped home to the States. I think he sold war bonds for a while. After I recovered, I went back to my unit. I guess my injuries weren't severe enough to warrant being sent home. So, in January 1945, back I went."

"So at least you missed the Battle of the Bulge, right?"

"Yes, I missed it. I was lucky."

By the time Mom came home from her errands, we had cleaned up our mess, and by the time Dad came home from work, we had the plane prominently displayed on the coffee table in the living room. When Dad came in, the first thing he said was, "Nice Mustang!" He and

Grandpa talked about when and where to fly it, and Dad said he'd like to come along when we took it out. I was very excited about this prospect. He rarely had time for activities with me, much less joining an activity with me and Grandpa. I looked up at Grandpa with expectant eyes, knowing my dad wasn't his favorite person in the world but hoping he'd say yes anyway. He nodded his consent with a smile, and I was sure he was allowing it just for my sake, knowing it would mean so much to me to do this together with all three of us.

After our take-out chicken meal, Dad and Grandpa sat outside. Dad cracked open a beer and lit a cigarette, and Grandpa sat in the rocking lawn chair with baby Aaron on his lap. Mom told me I could go out with them instead of helping her clean up the kitchen, which was my usual chore. I sat on the grass in front of Grandpa. I asked him to tell me more about General Patton, and he smiled, very willing to share. As Grandpa spoke, I felt like if it wasn't for the casual and familial atmosphere, it would feel like history class. He would have made a wonderful teacher.

He told me about how General Patton was a secret weapon of sorts for the Allied armies, although he didn't really have an army at the time. The Germans thought the initial landings in Normandy were a ruse and that the true invasion, led by Patton, would follow later, at Pas-de-Calais. When that didn't happen, there was a report intentionally leaked that Patton was being disciplined for earlier behavior but would soon enter the fight. That delayed the Nazi's plan for a counterattack. When he finally did land in France, he took command of the U.S. Third army.

The sunshine began to fade into dusk and the mosquitoes came alive. We swatted at them and Aaron began to fuss.

"I guess that's my cue to leave," Grandpa laughed. "I'll see you in two weeks for our maiden voyage, Mike."

Since it was summer vacation now, I was allowed to stay up an extra hour. With my head filled with new knowledge, I capitalized on that and went straight to my room. I needed to figure out where Grandpa Heinz was on D-Day, this day being my latest obsession. I picked up the journal and started flipping through pages, looking at the dates. I noticed an entry that looked different, so I read.

September 13, 1943
PROMOTION!
    Received my captain's rank today! I'm finally getting my own company. Sad I'll leave my guys behind for now, but God willing, we'll see each other again. Being shipped soon to a new division. Captain Kinsler is trying to have it postponed for now as the need here is too great.

Unfortunately, there isn't a company here available for me, so it would most likely be temporary.

I found another interesting one.

November 8, 1943
Arrived at my new unit today. A ceremony I've never had before with the changing of command. I think it's a good unit, but I'm a bit unnerved. These are just boys for Christ's sake. Fifteen to seventeen-year-olds. The 12th SS Panzer division, "Hitler Jugend" are all boys brought up through Hitler's youth program. I pray I never have to send them to their death! Getting seventeen-year-olds driving forty-ton tanks is ludicrous!

I was appalled at the thought of kids not much older than myself killing people and being killed themselves. They never had a childhood. I kept reading.

December 24, 1943
The Atlantic wall is an impressive sight. We schedule work around the clock, knowing the Allies will come at some point, we just don't know when. So, until they do, we work hard. Four million mines planted so far with another seven million to go. Thousands of metal tripods line the beach and surf depending on the tide. Poles are struck in the sand, some with ramps. Concrete dragons' teeth in a few vulnerable spots, but concrete is becoming scarce, so it is

needed for the bunkers mostly. Quality has been degraded as we've had to resort to using sand and seashells from the beach to help finish the project. Doesn't seem much like Christmas. Wish we could call a truce and go home.

And a couple pages later:

December 27, 1943
Flooded fields and pastures will occur in spring. All in an attempt to keep airborne landings from taking place. Telephone poles will be planted randomly in fields that can't be flooded to keep glider-borne troops out. More mines will be planted, along with anti-aircraft in key positions. Thousands of miles of concertina wire are being laid daily. Ammo stockpiled in bunkers. We cannot allow the Allies to gain ground. We will throw them back into the sea.

I couldn't believe my eyes! Both my grandfathers had fought in the same region for the opposing sides! I skipped ahead to June.

June 7, 1944
They finally landed yesterday. I had never seen so much equipment in my life! Ships as far as you can see. And yet the planners think this isn't the real invasion. Supposedly, that's yet to come in the north, so the reserves are being withheld. We ended up having to evacuate and pull back.

The American soldiers are brave and relentless, just the opposite of what we've been told about them. Gotta write Stella and let her know I'm okay.

I grabbed the letters, searching for the one to Stella just indicated in the journal. Dang, it was not there! I was disappointed. My hour was up so I said goodnight to my parents and lay in bed thinking. Why wasn't it in there? My brain was in overdrive, thinking what my options were at this point. I figured if I had to, I'd ask Grandma if she had any D-Day letters. But that would be a last resort. I couldn't take the curiosity any longer and got out of bed. Turning on my flashlight, I examined the letters again. Nothing. Rummaging through the pictures, I noticed a letter stuck to the back of one of them. Carefully peeling it off the back, I opened it and looked at the date: June 8th. Relieved, with my heart racing, I crawled back into bed and read.

June 8, 1944
My dear Stella,
This war is not going well for us. The Allies landed in Normandy the other day. Thousands of ships landed with thousands of more troops. I must tell you of something I witnessed that day before we evacuated, something strange. An Allied medic kept running back and forth on the beach, saving men. I kept directing the machine gunner to hit him, and he couldn't do it. It was like this guy had an

angel with him. Another man came out to help at one point and he was taken down. So, I directed an artillery barrage and finally, he was knocked down when a shell landed just in front of him. But the funny thing was, he kept getting up. My gunner kept trying to hit him though, letting loose one last volley before I told him to forget it and we evacuated. I can't seem to get this guy out of my head.

I love you, darling and I can't wait to be back in your arms again.

Heinz

I lay there thinking, I wonder if it was my American grandpa he's talking about! I'd already uncovered some strange things, so this wasn't exactly out of the question. I figured there was no way I could prove this, but my suspicions were that this was an account of them facing each other, even if they didn't know it then. If this was, in fact, true, it would be so... I couldn't think of a word. Interesting? Yes. Coincidental? Yes. Creepy? Yep. Dramatic? Absolutely!

I put the letter back with the stack of other letters and climbed back into bed. Turning off my flashlight, I rolled over and hugged my belly, trying to stop the butterflies, and forced myself to let sleep come.

CHAPTER TEN

Early November 1943

I was on a train returning from leave after the battle for Kursk. Two small red flags with black swastikas flapped wildly at the front of the engine, and thick, black smoke emitted from the top. The train was a heavy one, delivering new Panthers to units that had lost so many, though I doubted they would ever reach full strength again. Two cars were filled with troops, mostly green replacements, and another two with sandbagged anti-aircraft guns for air defense.

The sound of the cars running over the track joints and the slight sway of the cars was relaxing. I sat next to a couple of young lieutenants who chatted excitedly about finally seeing combat. Finally, I chimed in, "Combat isn't all glory." I shared my experience at Kursk with them, told them how worn down a man could get after just one week of fighting, and that they would lose friends. "And if that isn't enough, the weather on the Eastern front is miserable." They listened intently to every word I said and maybe were in shock, which wasn't my intent. I just wanted them to sober up and realize how serious things were about to get for them. I asked where they were headed. They both had been assigned to the 4th Panzer Army under General Hoth. I nodded, "Yes, the looming battle for Kiev. Well, you guys have a good commander in General Hoth." With that, I turned back toward the window, staring at the expansive Russian steppe, happy to be leaving it behind.

I woke up an hour later, the train jerking as it came to a gradual stop. The whistle blew and white steam jetted out of the vents on each side of the engine. The men all stood, gathered their belongings, and began to file out of the train car. I made sure I was the last one to exit. On the track next to us was another black steam engine, heating water for the boiler before getting underway. I boarded and handed my orders to the lieutenant in charge. He looked them over and claimed we'd be in France in a few days. "Make yourself comfortable, Captain. It'll be a long ride." I found an empty window seat, stowed my duffel bag in the rack overhead, and sat down.

The boarding officer stopped at my aisle and told me that in about forty-eight hours, we would be laying over in Berlin. He leaned over toward me, "Just in case you want to get off for a bite of real food." He straightened and said, "We'll be serving meals in a couple hours."

"Thank you, Lieutenant." I turned back toward the window. The sky was darkening in the west, and it looked like there would be more snow. It was only about fifteen degrees, and I felt sorry for the poor souls I was leaving behind. Winter out here was brutal.

It was almost evening when the locomotive blew its whistle with several long blasts. The engine's drive wheels spun around once, grabbed for a second, jerked us forward, and spun again several times before taking hold and slowly pulled us forward, gathering momentum. The black smoke drifted past my window. I noticed snow flurries beginning to fall and was glad to be on our way.

Dinner was served soon after, the chow marginally better than from the mess tent, but I was hungry, so I ate everything and even contemplated ingesting the napkin. As I tried to get comfortable enough to sleep, I gazed out the window. An occasional flash could be seen in the darkness on the distant horizon; explosions from some far-off battle.

I awoke the next morning as the train slowed to a stop for a refill of water, wood, and coal. I went to the bathroom to wash up, and as I splashed cold water on my face, I looked in the mirror at my reflection and thought, *That's a soldier.* I couldn't wait for the day I could see the same reflection and think, *that's just a man—a husband and a father.* I just wanted life to return to normal.

Breakfast was served when I got back to my seat, and I ate the sausage and toast, leaving everything else. The train began to move again, chugging and struggling to get back up to reasonable speed. I turned to the window, the scenery sufficient entertainment for me. A few small farms dotted the landscape. Here and there was a burnt skeleton of a farm building, a chimney standing alone, old, dilapidated barns falling in on themselves, or a house, its inhabitants long ago removed.

The next day, we arrived in Berlin. Pulling into the station, I noticed soldiers waiting to board. I placed my duffel in my seat before getting off the train and walked about a half block to a little cafe. I ordered a couple of cold cut sandwiches to go and a bratwurst sausage for the walk back. The fraülein behind the counter wrapped the sandwiches in butcher paper and served up the brat. It smelled heavenly and tasted just as good as it smelled. I walked slowly back to the train to finish it before I boarded. Walking to my seat, I noticed my duffel in the next aisle. Four junior grade Wehrmacht officers sat in what had been my aisle. I stopped, looking at them as they talked excitedly about going to France. I cleared my throat loudly and they looked up. The realization of what was happening quickly entered their feeble brains. They instantly stood, came to attention and saluted.

I said, "I don't believe I heard a 'Heil Hitler!'" They promptly raised their right arms, fingers extending out and very loudly proclaimed, "Heil Hitler!" Returning the salute, I told them all to remove themselves from my aisle before I had them sent to the Russian front. I chuckled to myself as I watched them scramble to gather their things. They were so nervous, stumbling over each other and knocking one another down. Falling into my now vacated seat, I thought, *Rank sure has its privileges!*

The train began to move again. Next stop, for me anyway, was the western coast of France. I pulled out my book about the French Revolution and determined to finish it before getting there. I read until my eyes wouldn't stay open any longer and gave in to sleep.

The next day was a bright sunny one. The lieutenant stood at the front of the car and announced we'd make Caen in roughly four hours. I removed my book again and swore to finish it once more. The miles clicked by as I turned the pages, a race to see who was faster, the train, or my reading. Thirty minutes outside Caen, I closed the book for good. I reflected on what I'd read as I stared out the window. Like Napoleon, I felt we, as an army, made too many mistakes. Yes, the times were different. We had more new modern equipment, and we had gone further into Russia than any army ever had. But Russia was so expansive that conquering her was almost impossible. They had the luxury of giving up space for time. Most countries couldn't afford that. They used winter to the fullest advantage, while we just tried to survive it. Fighting a war on two fronts couldn't be done, at least not without disastrous results.

As we reached the outskirts of Caen, the increased military activity was obvious. The number of anti-aircraft guns was phenomenal with all types from 88s to 20mm available. Work crews, local civilians, and prisoners were used to constantly improve positions and perform back-breaking labor. Stepping off the train, I noticed a few soldiers supervising some workers and approached them, asking where I would find Colonel Zoeller of the 12th SS. Right away, they called up a car and driver to take me there. A Volkswagen convertible pulled up, and the driver hurried over to open my door and take my duffel.

"Reporting to Colonel Zoeller, Sir?"

"Yes," I said, "are you familiar with the area?"

"Yes, Captain," he replied. "I've been stationed here for over a year now."

We pulled up in front of a large bunker complex, and I told the private to wait for me. I looked down, straightened my uniform as best I could and hoped the colonel would forgive my unkempt appearance. Inside the bunker, a half dozen officers milled about, and I stopped one lieutenant, asking where I might find Colonel Zoeller. He led me to a door in the rear of the room and knocked. A voice said, "Enter." The lieutenant swung the door open and stepped aside.

Entering the room, I didn't know what to expect, so I came to attention, arm extended and said, "Heil Hitler."

The colonel, waving his arm in a lazy fashion said, "Relax, Captain. We're not real formal around here. You'll find a lot of second and third-rate soldiers here, and if we held them all to such high standards, you and I would be the only ones remaining."

I relaxed a bit. "Yes, Sir."

"I understand you were with the 2nd SS for Operation Citadel. That must've been amazing! Wish I had been there."

"It was tough going, Sir."

"Have you met your company yet?"

"No, Sir," I said. "I just arrived and came straight here. I have a driver outside waiting."

"You go to your company CP and get settled. Come by here tomorrow around 1500." He paused and looked at me thoughtfully. "You'll fit in well here, Captain."

Thinking of my company that I had left behind, I hoped that would be the case. "That will be my aim, Sir," I said, and with that, I came to attention and saluted.

The colonel said, "Captain, informal unless we're in front of the troops, remember?"

"Yes, Sir. I apologize. Old habits die hard, I guess." I walked out to my car and found the driver sitting in the front seat, head tilted back, snoring. I quietly opened the door, slid in, and slammed the door closed.

The private bolted upright and began stammering. "I'm sorry, Sir! I didn't intend to fall asleep."

Thinking about what the colonel had said about the soldiers here, I said, "Don't worry about it, Private. Take me to the 4th Company CP."

Driving along the cliffs, I saw a lot of construction underway. At one point, I hollered for the driver to stop, and slamming on the brakes, the car skidded to a halt, sending a cloud of dust forward. I walked a few feet to the edge and looked below. From this vantage point, I could see the work being done on the beach. It looked like a colony of ants, building in the sand, a constant flurry of motion. *Good*, I thought. *They're working like the Allies could invade any day now.* Satisfied, I walked back to the car. My new CP was only about a half mile further, so in just a few minutes, we were in front of another large concrete bunker.

I thanked the young private and said, "I never did get your name."

"Sir," he said, "I'm Private Brashears."

Inside the bunker, a lieutenant came over and with the obligatory salute said, "You must be Captain Dirden."

I had to smile. I still wasn't used to being called Captain, but admittedly, I liked the sound. "Yes, I am."

"Very good, Sir. We've been awaiting your arrival. Let me help you with your bag, Sir." He reached over, taking the straps from my hand. "Follow me, and I'll show you to your quarters."

Most bunkers were of the cookie cutter variety, so I had a good idea where it was already but humored the officer anyway. This particular class of bunker had a large room where operations took place and another large room for crew quarters attached to the back with a separate latrine and utility room. Pipes for ventilation and wires for the lights were affixed to the inside walls. The doors all around were an inch and a quarter of solid steel with steel hinges. The outside of the bunker was painted a camouflage pattern and covered in camo netting. Real vegetation was planted around and even on top of the bunker to conceal what was underneath. Outside the main entry door was a separate room, like a mud room, and another steel door. This was so the enemy wouldn't have unfettered access to the interior if the outer door was breached. The outer door was also set back, and the walls on either side were angled in with narrow slit openings for machine guns to defend the entry. A U-shaped trench system was dug in front of the bunker so the main entry couldn't be seen straight on, making it impossible to target with a bazooka. The cement on the roof of this bunker was over fifteen feet thick. The walls were much less as they were partially protected by earth and rock.

Inside my quarters, the lieutenant placed my duffel on the bed. "I'm Lieutenant Schwartz," he said, "your intelligence officer."

"Nice to meet you," I said. "Where's my first sergeant?"

"I'll have him notified you're here, Sir. I believe he's out looking over the defenses for our sector."

"Very good. I'm going to get situated here. Bring him in when he arrives, please."

"Yes, Sir. Will there be anything else I can get for you right now?"

"Just some water, please. Preferably with ice if it's available. And a small fan, if you can find one."

"The mess area will have ice. I'll have it brought over, Sir. I'll look for a fan." With that, he left and carefully closed the heavy door.

I looked around the room. A simple desk sat along the back wall with a picture of the Führer hanging over it.

The usual items adorned the desktop: a black phone, a small goose-neck lamp, a tin cup holding a handful of pencils, and the newly issued ballpoint pens, so much nicer than using an ink well. There was a small dresser at the end of my bunk and a little closet built into the wall, with no door, for hanging my uniforms and jacket. There were a couple of steel chairs with thin seat cushions built for working, not for comfort.

I unpacked my things and placed a photo of Stella, Karl, and little Arnold on my desk. I was admiring them when the door opened slightly, and a head poked in. "Yes, come in," I said to the head, and a mountain of a man entered, carrying a pail of ice. Setting it down, he came to attention and saluted.

"Sir, Master Sergeant Kaeppler, here."

"Sergeant, have a seat." I sat back in my chair and waved to the chair across from me. "What can you tell me about our current situation?"

Kaeppler didn't sugar-coat it. "Well, Sir, we are so far behind schedule, it's ridiculous. We need to plant more mines and more obstacles along our sector. We've requested the supplies, but they're slow in coming, and when we do get them, we don't have the manpower to put them in."

"That's going to change tomorrow," I assured him. "We'll commandeer it from somewhere else if we have to. Now, I want a detailed report by 1400 on what's needed."

"Yes, Sir." The sergeant looked both relieved and hopeful

"I want to meet with the men in a couple of days. Figure out a good time when it won't be much disruption to the work schedule."

"Will do, Sir."

"For now, tell me a bit about yourself and the unit."

We talked for about half an hour. It was getting late, and I wanted a shower after my days on the train. The bathroom that was attached to my room was tiny; a sink, a toilet and a shower no bigger than a phone booth were crammed into a room the size of a small closet.

Glad I'm not the famous Field Marshall Herman Goering, with his whiskey barrel belly, I thought. *He'd never fit in here without applying axle grease first.* I turned on the hot water and waited, and waited, and waited some more. Concluding that hot water was a luxury I wouldn't find here, I gave up and jumped in. I convinced myself that the forty-degree water was "refreshing" as I quickly washed and rinsed. I had to admit, I felt like a new man when I stepped out. I put on a robe, went to operations, and called Lieutenant Schwartz over to tell him I was going to bed.

"Unless the Allies invade before 0500, I don't want to be disturbed."

Back in my room, I closed the door slowly but, even though I was gentle, there was still an audible clang as the heavy steel slammed shut. Even though the bunk was a bit lumpy, it was the first time I was able to get horizontal in a week, so it felt good. It was pitch black and so still, it was deafening.

The next morning, I stepped into operations and got the report from Lieutenant Schwartz that all was quiet. I asked him to have someone fetch me breakfast, as I intended to work while I ate. I felt so good! There was nothing quite like being clean and getting a good night's sleep. The bunker was great for that. No disturbance at all.

As I waited for my breakfast, I examined unit supplies and general health reports. Most were several months old and likely changed by now. My door opened and a private entered, carrying a tray of eggs and sausage with black bread and jam which he placed on my desk along with a carafe of coffee. Another private followed right behind, carrying a small fan and asked where I wanted it. With a mouthful of eggs, I pointed to the filing cabinet. I swallowed and said, "Low," as he plugged it in and turned it on, sending cool air in my direction. More importantly, though, the slight hum of the motor would be a comforting sound.

The master sergeant poked his head in. "Sir, is this a good time?"

"Yes, come in." I waved him in and dismissed the privates.

Kaeppler, holding a stack of papers in his hand, said, "I've prepared that report you asked for."

"Wow! That was quick."

"You ask, and I deliver, Sir."

As I finished my breakfast, he went over what was still needed, and it was a lot—troop strength, ammo, food stores, fresh water and filtration, and even the available vehicles in the motor pool were low. Things looked bleak. I didn't see any way we'd get all or even most of what we needed, but I'd give it my best effort. The room was quiet as I stared at the pages, only the hum of the fan could be heard. I looked up at Kaeppler, then back to the pages, sorting through them. I sat back and rubbed my temples.

"This is unacceptable," I said.

"I know," he said, "but there's nothing I can do about it."

"I'm not blaming you, but things around here will change. Get the men working and I'll work on a plan."

He opened the door to leave but turned his head around to face me again. "Sir, do you like jokes?"

I said, "Sure, I could use one right now."

"How many Frenchmen does it take to defend Paris?" he asked.

"I give up. How many?"

"Nobody knows because it's never been done, Sir." With a smirk, he left the room.

I was glad for the moment of levity before getting back to business. I called out to Lieutenant Schwartz to get my driver. I made a few minor additions to the report, placed the file in my briefcase, and stopped to talk to the lieutenant. "Can you see about getting Private Brashears as my driver? I can't remember where he was from."

Schwartz said, "I'll get on it, Sir, but if he's Wehrmacht it may be a problem."

I tilted my head, "Lieutenant, you'll find that with me, any problem can be overcome. Now make it happen." I walked out without waiting for any further reply. The driver was waiting by the car with the passenger door open. Getting in, I said, "Take me to Colonel Zoeller's CP."

Arriving at the command post, the driver scurried around to open my door. I adjusted my uniform before going into the bunker.

Colonel Zoeller saw me walk in and waved me over. "Ah, Dirden, come on in."

"I know I'm a bit early, but—"

"It's fine," he said, cutting me off. "Before we get too busy and I forget, I want to let you know we're going to have a change of command ceremony for you tomorrow."

"Just a small one, please," I replied. "My men are really behind schedule and I don't want to stop their work just for my command ceremony."

"Very well. Make it just your headquarters and intelligence staff then."

I thanked him and opened my briefcase. "Now, Sir, I have a brief report on what I'll need ASAP," I said, removing the file. Handing it to him, I felt nervous, like asking a parent for money.

When he finally looked up from the report, the expression on his face wasn't what I was expecting. "Captain, is this for the whole German army?"

"Sir," I said, "we're desperately low on everything. If the Allies attack tomorrow, we won't last no matter how thick the cement is."

He looked at the pages again. "I understand, Dirden, but the resources just aren't there." Handing it back to me, he said, "Narrow it down and resubmit it."

Reluctantly, I agreed. "I'll have a new request on your desk by tonight."

Back at my CP, I contemplated ways I might side-step this request process. I called Schwarz into my room. "Shut the door and sit down." He gingerly sat into a chair, and I had to smile. "Relax, Lieutenant, you're not in trouble." The tension released from his body as he sat back. I said, "We must find a way to get what we need. I want you to visit local units and ask if they'd be willing to barter for ammo." I handed him a list of things we were well stocked with. "I figure if we don't have enough ammunition, it won't matter how much food we have, so let's key on that first. Offer them fuel, sandbags, or anything else on the list, but get that ammo!" I told him to take my driver and get moving. I spent the rest of my day modifying my request for Colonel Zoeller and sent it via messenger to him.

The next day, there was a ceremony for the change of command. I was glad I had asked for it to stay small. This was the first ceremony I had attended where I was the man in the spotlight. I felt a bit overwhelmed and was relieved when it was over.

I asked to be taken to the beach where work was progressing. I walked among the troops, asking where they were from, or other short-answer questions, so as not to disrupt their work for too long. I made a few little speeches to address larger groups, then moved on to the next bunker. It was 2100 before I called it quits and headed back. I was exhausted and fell into my bunk without even removing my uniform.

The next few weeks were a blur of activity. The work progressed on the beaches with concrete bunkers built or expanded. We began using sand from the beach for the cement. The debris like seashells and weeds that got missed made for an inferior product, but we had little choice. Trucks began arriving with ammo, and soon, our storage bunkers were overflowing, so we utilized the extra ammo to barter for food now. After that, we'd go on to the next most important supply.

Months went by, and the work never ceased. It was beginning to look like a formidable defensive network, finally. Every week, I toured the sector. I was so proud of these boys. They were young kids being asked to do the unthinkable, and they never complained, always wanting to do more. They were the future pride of the German race.

It was now April 1944. The High Commanders thought the Allies would attack sometime in the next three months, likely at Pas-de-Calais, and if the attack did come anywhere but on our doorstep, we'd either become a reserve force or guard the left flank. We worked at a furious pace anyway, determined to succeed in our mission. No matter what happened, we had an important role to play, and it was my job to keep these kids safe while defending against the Allies' onslaught.

In my room, the phone rang. It was Colonel Zoeller.

"Dirden, I don't know how you did it, but it appears your sector is the model for all." He spoke excitedly. "Field Marshall Erwin Rommel and Hitler himself want a tour of our sector, so be ready. Your life is about to get a whole lot more complicated, Captain."

"Just what I needed, Sir," I said, trying to see this for a positive thing. "Thank you, Colonel."

"No, thank you! You've made me look good too, but this is all you, Captain. After their visit, I'll recommend you for a Knight's Cross. Keep up the good work!"

I hung up the phone, nervous like never before. Two men were coming in a week's time that could make or break my career, my life, and even the life of my family. I had to get this right. I called out to Schwartz, telling him to get my driver. I sat looking at the picture of Stella when I heard a young voice.

"Sir, you called for me?"

I looked up, pleased at the sight. "Private Brashears! Nice to see you, finally."

"Yes, Sir. I came as soon as the orders came through."

"Fine. Now let's get to work. I need to find Master Sergeant Kaeppler."

After a few stops along the beach, we found Kaeppler in a huddle with a few platoon sergeants, discussing where to place some new machine guns we'd received. I called him aside and we walked several steps, out of earshot, before I turned to him with my announcement.

"Master Sergeant, Rommel and Hitler are coming here next week."

His jaw dropped.

"Make sure this place is fit for a king. I don't know any details yet, but have the mess tent plan some kind of elaborate dinner in case they stay. Make sure these kids have their best uniforms on, boots shining, and weapons clean."

"Yes, Sir," he said, excited and nervous.

"Pass it along."

From there, Brashears took me to each platoon. Upon hearing the news, their reaction was all the same: shock, followed by a mix of honor and fear.

The days went by faster than I wanted. We often worked late into the night, planning, getting everything ready. This had to go well. So much could ride on this one visit from the Supreme Commander. There was frustration, however, that with these dignitaries coming, it was taking men away from important tasks, work that may prevent an Allied landing. Instead, we were trying to impress a few big shots.

The day before their arrival, I checked on the progress again, calling on Private Brashears to drive me around. At the mess tent, the cook assured me he had a great meal planned for a hundred officers. A rack of lamb, baked potatoes, a fresh mix of vegetables, and six cases of a reserve cabernet had been procured for the event.

"It'd better be good, or you may find yourself on the Eastern front, Sergeant," I said with a smile.

He nodded. "It'll be top notch, Sir, you have my word."

From there, we toured the defenses one last time. I found Kaeppler, and we went over the itinerary again.

"They'll arrive at the Caen airfield around 1100. We'll have the band play while they disembark. After that, there'll be a review of the available troops and then a tour of the defensive positions. Some Q&A will happen somewhere along the way, I'm sure. Dinner in the mess tent at 1700, another formation of troops for their send-off, at which time, we'll present the Führer with a gift from the unit."

"What did we get him, Sir?" he asked.

"I'm not even sure. That was Colonel Zoeller's idea." Confident that we were as ready as we could be, I told Kaeppler to be at my CP at 0700 tomorrow and left.

That night, lying in my cot, my mind swirled with thoughts of all the things that could go wrong. I woke up being shaken gently by Lieutenant Schwartz.

"Sir, it's 0500."

"I'm up," I said, "you can stop now." It was dark, and the hum of the fan was comforting. Suddenly, I was being shaken again.

"Sir, it's 0530. Are you getting up?"

"Damn." I sat up. "Yes, Lieutenant, thank you." I flipped on the light, temporarily blinding myself. Despite the nervousness that had been building in me since I learned of this visit, I tried to convince myself this was nothing to fear. I had done everything I could to ensure success. I got in the shower, the cold water instantly waking me up. Grabbing a fresh, clean, and crisply pressed uniform, I put it on and got out the boots I kept just for parades or inspection that were deep black with a mirror-like shine. Lastly, I checked that my medals were in their proper place. I knew that looking tidy might not make much of an impression but looking sloppy surely would be a bad one.

I stepped into operations and looked around. "Schwartz, where is everyone?"

"Oh, they're getting breakfast, Sir. They should be back any minute."

"Send Private Brashears to see me."

"Of course, Sir."

I stepped outside. The eastern horizon was lightening up. I inhaled deeply, hoping the fresh air would calm my nerves. *God, I can't wait till this is over,* I thought, and I paced in front of the bunker until Brashears walked up and came to attention.

"Sir, you wanted to see me?"

"Yes. You will be my personal assistant from now on."

"Yes, Sir!" he said, smiling as if I had just given him keys to a brand-new car.

"I want you within earshot always, unless I send you somewhere. For right now, I want you to go get me something from the mess area. Keep it light, though."

"On it, Sir," as he ran off, still grinning.

Damn, I like that kid, I thought. I hoped to keep him close and help him survive this horrible campaign. I went back to my office, endeavoring to keep my mind off the impending visit and its potential ramifications.

Brashears came in with a bagel and cream cheese and some juice.

"Thank you, Brashears. Now, make sure the staff car is clean. We'll be leaving soon."

Kaeppler walked in as I finished eating, carrying two cups of coffee. It smelled heavenly, but I knew the taste wasn't going to match the aroma. I took a sip, almost burning my tongue. "Damn, Sergeant! Did you brew this with a flamethrower?"

"No, Sir, but I didn't think you'd want to start this day with a cold cup of coffee," he said and smiled sideways at me.

I sipped some more as we discussed the preparations. "Is everyone ready?" I asked.

"Sir, you keep asking that. Have some faith in me. It will all be good, trust me."

"Okay, Master Sergeant, but if it's not, I'm bringing you with me to the gulag!"

On our way to the airfield, we made one more round of the positions. As we made each stop, I would pick out some little thing to accomplish before we came back. In some instances, it was applying better camouflage or straightening up an improved position, more sandbags, or maybe just tidying up a fox hole. Schwartz was already at the airfield when we arrived, and Colonel Zoeller showed up soon after. The drivers parked the cars in neat formation behind us, their black paint glistening in the sunlight.

"Captain Dirden," Colonel Zoeller addressed me.

Saluting, I said, "Sir!"

Returning my salute, and everyone else, with a quick wave of his hand, he said, "This is going to be a bigger deal than I thought."

"Oh? Why is that?"

"You'll see, Captain."

At 1100, right on schedule, we heard the rumble of aircraft engines in the distance.

The master sergeant yelled, "Okay, this is it! Everyone in formation!"

The men all scrambled to line up properly. Two Bf 109s flew overhead, making sure the landing strip was clear. The Ju 52 was on approach. Two more Bf 109s were behind and above it, plus one on each side, protecting its occupants. The plane landed gracefully and taxied in front of us, the bare corrugated aluminum reflecting the sunlight, there was no mistaking the large swastika painted on the tail. Pulling even with us, the plane's tri motors slowed down until the propellers came to an abrupt stop.

The band started playing the national anthem, and the troops came to full attention. The door swung open with someone lowering a set of stairs to the ground. The first to step out was General Kurt (Panzer) Meyer, Commander of the 12th SS. Next off was General Alfred Jodl, Commander of the OberKommando der Wehrmacht. Then came Field Marshall Erwin Rommel, Commander of Army Group B, Field Marshall Gerd von Rundstedt, Armed Forces Commander in Chief, followed by Heinrich Himmler, Reichsführer of the SS, and finally, the Supreme Commander Adolf Hitler. They formed a circle, talking momentarily, before Colonel Zoeller made his way to them. He came to attention and snapped his right arm out. "Heil Hitler!" he said with authority. The Führer raised his arm, returning the gesture. A few words were exchanged, and the colonel led them toward me, stopping right in front of me. I stood there stiff as steel. Without hesitation, I jabbed my right arm out and up, "Heil Hitler!" The Führer raised his arm again and repeated the phrase.

Looking at me, he said, "Captain, I understand you're responsible for the defenses in this sector."

"Yes, Sir," I replied, "but I couldn't have done any of this without a lot of great men, including Master Sergeant Kaeppler and Lieutenant Schwartz, Sir." I spoke quickly, not wanting to be interrupted before I got those names out.

"Well, I can't wait to see what you've accomplished here," he said.

The colonel chimed in. "Sir, Captain Dirden has scheduled a tour of the defenses if you'd care to see them."

"Yes, yes, very well. Shall we go?" not really asking the question, but proposing we go directly. "Captain," the Führer said, "you and Rommel ride with me."

"Yes, Sir. The car is right over here, Sir," I said as I led him to it. Private Brashears was holding the passenger doors open, and I could see his pant legs shaking as we got closer. As I stepped into the back seat, I looked Brashears in the eye and whispered, "Relax, Private."

He nodded, still trembling. Rommel got in beside me and the Führer got in the front passenger seat, Brashears closing the door behind him and rushing around to the driver's side. As we drove, the Führer began asking

Brashears questions. The young private stammered and stuttered with each answer.

At one point, Hitler leaned over and said, "You're fine, son. The future of the Fatherland relies on good boys like yourself. Your duty to country is the single most important thing you can do with your life. Fight hard and make lots of babies. Our most important resource is children!"

I felt my stomach turn, knowing he was talking about military service and children as if they were cattle, or produce.

We parked behind the first bunker, Brashears hurrying around to open the passenger door. Once our other guests joined us, I led the group to the door, the guard saluting as he ushered us inside. Hitler walked to the machine gun position, and judging from the glee written on his face, he was fascinated by the magnitude of everything. Like a kid with a shiny new bicycle, he marveled at everything from the thickness of the cement to the work on the beach. Each stop we made, he had a similar reaction. He asked about ammo, troop strength, food stores, and whether we needed more weapons. I spoke honestly and told him we could use more of everything. When asked how much more, I shot him a number off the top of my head.

"Another 10,000 men would be great, along with another battalion of artillery, anti-aircraft batteries, and a million more mines would be helpful. The Allied fighters come by day and knock out bridges, rail lines, communications, radar facilities, and strafe the beaches, causing delays in what needs to be done."

The Führer said, "Alright, Captain, you shall have it."

"But sir," I said, "each sector of the Atlantic wall needs it, not just mine."

Looking me in the eyes, he said, "Captain, we'll start with your sector and expand." Still looking into my soul, he said, "I understand that is how you built up your sector, isn't it? One piece at a time, starting with what was most important?"

"Yes, Sir, but we don't have the luxury of time anymore, Sir. The Allies will be here within a few months."

Patting me on the shoulder a bit condescendingly he said, "You let me worry about that, Captain."

After the last stop, we proceeded to the field kitchen. The chefs, if you could call them that, were lined up outside the doorway in spotless white aprons and chef hats. Hitler greeted each one and shook their hand. Inside, we divided up into groups of about twenty-five, sitting at long tables. I was seated next to the Führer. The food was brought out, and I had to admit, it looked, smelled, and tasted like perfection. The wine flowed, and the conversation turned to family. I told him I'd just recently had a new son, Arnold.

He congratulated me, and said, "Captain, have you ever considered a job in headquarters? Maybe an adjutant to Himmler? Then you could spend more time with your young family."

Cringing inside, I said politely, "Thank you, Sir, but that's not really a job for me. I feel like I can make a bigger contribution out here with the men."

Upon finishing our meal, we drove back to the airfield where the troops were already in formation.

Hitler's staff lined up, and Himmler called out, "Captain Dirden, front and center."

I walked swiftly to him and saluted. In his hand, was a small jewelry box. Inside was a silver ring with the death's head top center.

Himmler spoke, "Captain, I present this Totenkopfring to you for your steadfast commitment to the defense of the Fatherland. Your sacrifice, duty, and honor are an example to be followed by all." He removed the ring from the box and slipped it on my ring finger. It was a perfect fit. He shook my hand and said, "Congratulations, Captain."

I made my way down the line, saluting and shaking hands with everyone, and lastly, the Führer. He told me if I needed anything at all, not to hesitate to call on him, although I suspected this was just polite talk. I thanked him for taking the time to come to visit the men. "It's a big morale booster," I said.

Colonel Zoeller walked up and handed Hitler a wooden box. Another officer grabbed the box, opened it, and looked over everything rigorously, inspecting for explosives. Once satisfied it was harmless, he handed it back to the Führer. Inside was a bottle of the cabernet we'd just had with dinner, some fine French cheese, and some chocolate. The Führer shook hands with the colonel, and the band began to play Hitler's favorite song while he ascended the steps to the aircraft, disappearing inside. The motors of the Ju 52 started to crank, drowning out the music. The transport took off first and the rest of the aircraft followed, fading into the evening sky.

Dismissing everyone, the colonel came over to me and said, "Great job, Dirden!"

"Thank you, Sir, but I'm glad it's over."

"So am I!" he said. "What do you think of your ring?"

"I'm a little shocked, Sir. I didn't know I was getting one."

"That will wear off. Just make sure the Russians don't capture you with it. They'll torture you just for having it, or so I hear." He took a step toward his car, but stopped short and added, "Oh, I almost forgot. They want to pull your unit back to Carentan for rest."

I asked when this would happen.

"Sometime next month. You'll be a reserve element for the summer."

I cringed inside. "I'm not sure what to think of that, Sir. I built this up," I said gesturing toward the beach. "Now I have to turn it over to someone else?"

"It'll be fine, Dirden. Take some time to relax a bit. You and your boys have been working hard."

"Sir, with all due respect, we don't have time to relax."

"I don't even know when it'll come through, so until then, just keep doing what you have been doing."

With that, I knew it was pointless to continue and replied, "Yes, sir," saluted, and turned toward my staff car. "Brashears, take me to the CP."

In my room, I closed the door and lay on the bunk, twisting the ring around my finger, wondering how this would all play out. I removed the ring and looked closely at it. My name was engraved on the inside with the date 14/05/44 and Himmler's signature. I once thought these rings were just a worthless trinket, but now that I genuinely owned one, it felt like I had done something really special, something worthwhile for the Fatherland.

CHAPTER ELEVEN

June 1944

"Lieutenant Schwartz!" I hollered. The lieutenant rushed into my office. "Is everything ready to pack tomorrow?" I asked.

"Yes, Sir."

"Good. We assume our new role on June 7, so I want everything in place the day before to minimize any confusion."

The phone rang, and as I reached for it, I told the lieutenant to get me Master Sergeant Kaeppler. The call was from Colonel Zoeller.

"Dirden, your orders to move have been delayed a week. Some issue with the weather has slowed things at the top, I guess."

"Damn," I said, "I'm half packed already!"

"Well, unpack! Think of this as a proficiency test."

"Yes, that's funny, Sir. I'll get it done, Sir."

"Alright, Captain, I'll keep you informed."

He hung up before I could respond. I placed the receiver back in its cradle, frustrated and happy at the same time. Frustrated at packing and unpacking when there were more important things to be done, happy that we were staying put a while longer.

Moments later, Kaeppler poked his head in the door. "Sir?"

"Come in, Master Sergeant," I said, "and bring Schwartz with you."

He turned and motioned to the lieutenant, and they both entered the room.

"I just got off the phone with Colonel Zoeller. Our move has been delayed for at least another week." I saw the confusion on their faces. "Something with the weather, I don't really know. Just get unpacked for now, and I'll let you know when there's a change."

Lieutenant Schwartz said, "This will be good. This storm isn't supposed to let up for three or four days, so we know the Allies won't attempt a landing until next week at the earliest."

"Don't be so sure of yourself, Lieutenant," I said. "The aerial bombings of critical infrastructure have picked up over the last few days, so stay on your toes." I looked at Kaeppler. "Master Sergeant, get to the platoons and tell them to stay vigilant. I want observations doubled over the next forty-eight hours."

"Yes, Sir."

"Alright, make it happen!"

They left the room, and I began making corrections to a stack of requests I had made, working late into the night. I looked at the picture of Stella and the boys again and decided to write a letter.

June 5, 1944
My dear Stella,

How are you, darling? How are the boys? I can't wait to come home. We're staying here another week before transferring to Carentan. All is well here, although I'm getting rather tired of all the rain we've had lately. With a little luck, I may be able to come to visit next month. I'll try for a week, but I may only get a couple of days, darling. No matter what, I need to see you. I miss you tremendously!

Heinz

I walked into operations, told Schwartz I was going to bed and said he should do the same. I asked him to wake me at 0500. He assured me he would do both.

In my room, after saying goodnight to the picture of my little family on my desk, I turned off the lamp on the dresser and fell into bed. The hum of the fan was all I could hear in the pitch-black room. Like the light, I was out almost at once.

Later that night, the door flew open with a loud *bang*! It was Lieutenant Schwartz. "Sir! You gotta get up! There have been reports of Allied airborne landings all up and down the coast!" In a panic, his voice was almost shrill. "This is it, Sir! They're coming!"

I sat up quickly, still groggy. "Calm down, Lieutenant," I said. "Turn on the light, and tell me what's going on."

He lunged toward the dresser and flipped on the lamp. "Sir, I've just received reports of the 101st and 82nd Airborne landings all over!"

"Schwartz, are you sure it's not just a report from a jumpy guard somewhere?"

"No, Sir, there were multiple reports from different units that came in almost simultaneously."

I stood up and the cold cement on my feet was just the shocker I needed. "Okay. Get Kaeppler and Brashears in here."

"Yes, Sir!" he said as he bolted out of the room.

I went to the restroom and looked in the mirror. I said to the man staring back at me, "Are you ready for this, Captain?" Splashing some water on my face, I wasn't even sure of my answer. I put on my only available uniform since everything else had already been packed for the move.

Brashears walked in as I was buttoning up, saying, "Sir, you called for me?"

"Yes. Get the car, and make sure it's topped off. This could be a long day."

"Already done, Sir," he said, "last night before I hit the sack."

"Okay, wait for me outside."

He turned to leave and almost collided with Kaeppler rushing into the room. They sidestepped each other, and Brashears paused a moment with a confused look on his face but continued out of the room. Kaeppler was holding a three-and-a-half-foot dummy soldier with a small parachute attached.

"Sir—" he started, but I cut him off.

"What the hell is that thing, Master Sergeant? Tell me you're not playing with dolls!"

He didn't see the humor. "No, Sir, these were dropped all around the northern sector, Sir."

"Schwartz just said he had reports of the American 101st and 82nd being air dropped. I suppose they are a diversion to keep us away from the real landing. I'll call Colonel Zoeller and see what he knows." I picked up the phone. Nothing. I tapped the disconnect button several times. Still nothing. "Phones are dead. Schwartz, get me a runner!" I hollered out the door. I turned back to face Kaeppler. "Master Sergeant, I want you to go to Fourth platoon. Make sure they have their shit together. We can't afford to lose the right flank. That's our key to survival. Without a connection there, we lose artillery support and command of the battlefield. I'm going to head to 2nd platoon and see what's going on there. Follow me." I stepped into operations. "If we can't connect or have to pull back, we'll meet here," I said, pointing to a spot on the map. "It's about a mile behind the beach and it'll give us good fields of fire from the high ground. Now, go!"

"Yes, Sir!" He left with an urgent step.

The runner came in as I was jotting down some things for the colonel.

Reports of airborne landings close by. Toy soldiers also dropped.
Heading to 2nd platoon now.

Will pull back to rally point (Alpha) if overrun.
Phones down. Will radio from 2nd platoon bunker.

I placed the paper in an envelope and handed it to the private. "Take this to Colonel Zoeller on the double."

"Yes, Sir," he said, his hand a bit shaky as he took the envelope from me. I was sure he could feel how tense the situation was.

I finished readying myself. I checked the Luger to make sure it was loaded and placed it in the leather holster, then grabbed my MP 40. I slapped a magazine in and cycled the bolt as I started out. The guards closed the door behind me. All doors were to remain closed at all times with this heightened threat. Brashears already had the car running.

"Take me to 2nd Platoon." I could hear the constant chatter of machine guns all around me. Tracers leaped into the overcast night sky, winding like a snake, eventually disappearing into the clouds. Shells burst with a sudden flash and trailing sparks would fall toward earth. Here and there, I could see a plane hurtling toward the ground, trailing fire and smoke. Parachutes dotted the sky and could only be seen when backlit by an exploding shell or airplane. I felt surrounded, chaos everywhere.

We pulled up in front of the bunker, and I stepped from the car just as a 20mm gun opened fire on a C-47 transport caught in a spotlight. Catching me by surprise, I ducked at first, and looked skyward. The tracers from the

20mm looked like flares racing toward its target, the long line snaking and curving until it caught up to its unfortunate victim. The gun kept firing while men continuously loaded clips of ammo into its open magazine. *Boom... Boom... Boom.* It didn't stop until the plane burst into flames. It flew straight for several hundred yards and gradually went into a nosedive, plummeting to earth at a couple hundred miles per hour. A huge fireball ensued, rising into the night sky, lighting up everything for miles. A second or two later, we heard the explosion as it shook the ground we stood on. It was hard not to watch, imagining the horror its occupants were going through, the fear and pain endured until the abrupt end of its death ride.

The guards opened the door, and I walked in, the door closing behind me with a loud bang. Two men at the front of the bunker with field glasses looked out its opening, scanning the horizon for threats. From inside the bunker, all seemed normal, the terrifying sounds from outside kept at bay by the bunker's thick walls. An occasional muffled explosion could be heard if one really listened for it. I looked seaward where white caps were breaking on the sandy beach. It didn't seem possible that this could all be unrecognizable in just a few hours.

I walked over to the radio operator and asked, "Who's in charge here, Private?"

"Sergeant Wolf," he said, pointing toward another room.

"Okay, get me Colonel Zoeller." I stood there anxiously waiting. I began to pace, wondering if there was anything else I could do.

It seemed like hours, but in just a few minutes, the radio operator said, "Sir, Colonel Zoeller is on. What would you like me to—"

Before he could finish, I clutched the receiver from his hands. "Sir, we have reports of airborne units dropping all over, and dummy soldiers being dropped in the north. Do you have any word yet?"

"Nothing I can tell you over the radio, Captain," he said. "Stay observant. They think this is the diversion and the landing will be at Calais this morning sometime. Be ready to pull out at a moment's notice if you're needed."

"Yes, Sir," I said, handing the receiver back to the operator.

Sergeant Wolf was making sure everyone had ammo when I walked in.

"Sergeant," I said, "is there enough food and water in case we're here a for a few days?"

"Yes, Sir," he replied.

"Good. Now, would it be possible for me to get a cup of coffee?"

"There's a pot near the radio, Sir," he said, pointing with his thumb. "We keep one on all the time."

I saw the pot on a table in the direction he indicated, walked over and lifted it. It was light, so I would likely be taking the last available cup. I took a tin cup from the table and blew the dust out of it. I poured the thick, black liquid and told one of the door guards to start a fresh pot. The guard nodded and leaned his rifle against the wall. As he performed his new task, I walked over to the front of the bunker, looking seaward. The eastern sky was just beginning to lighten up.

I sat in a chair, lost in thoughts of home. Sipping my cup of black tar, the percolating coffee pot brought back memories of Stella and me on a Sunday morning. Usually, we'd sit and chat, watching the birds from the porch of our modest villa. She would have on her favorite dirndl and smell of some delicious perfume. I knew how lucky I was to have the most beautiful woman in all of Germany.

Suddenly, I detected the front observers moving differently. The one on the right muttered, "Holy shit!" and let his binoculars drop. They fell, the strap around his neck keeping them from smashing on the floor. The other man stood there, bracing himself against the parapet in front.

"What is it?" I asked, standing up as I said it. The sky was considerably lighter now, and I could see thousands of small dots just with my naked eye. "Give me those!" I barked, holding out my hand, moving my fingers in a "hurry up" fashion.

The soldier, shaking, removed the binoculars from around his neck and passed them to me. I put down my cup and brought the field glasses up with both hands, adjusting the eyecups and the focus. Scanning the horizon, I couldn't believe my eyes! Ships, as far as I could see. I knew we were in trouble.

"Send a message!" I hollered to the radio operator.

To Colonel Zoeller.
Warships by the hundreds.
Cargo ships also in the hundreds.
Believe the landing is here, not Calais.
Have reserves in standby, please.
Captain Dirden, out.

"Okay, men, you know what you need to do. Have faith and do your job to the best of your ability. Smoke 'em now and save the butts for your ears. When the shelling begins, you'll want them, trust me."

Everyone lit up, even the men who didn't smoke. I handed the binoculars back and told them to get confirmation on which warships were out there. Stepping outside, I told Brashears to move inside and get comfortable, for now. Fifteen minutes later, I saw the first white puffs of smoke as the battleships began to fire at us.

I yelled to everyone in earshot, "Put your earplugs in and get ready. Here they come!"

Men scrambled to get their ears stuffed, some using cotton balls from the first aid kit, others with partial cigarettes sticking from their ears. If it weren't so serious, the sight of this would have been funny. Moments later, up and down the coast, shells landed in the water, their first salvo falling well short. The bigger ones were so obvious, they'd explode and throw a geyser of water a hundred feet into the air. The shock wave hit immediately, and the ground shook. They fired again, and again, we waited, counting the seconds to impact. The next salvo went long, the *whoosh* of the large shells passing overhead left us thankful they'd missed again. Knowing this was about to end, I told the men the next salvo would hit us. "They're walking the rounds in."

Looking out toward the enemy, it appeared that every gun had fired. The ships were blocked from view by a massive smoke screen. I was hoping they had all sunk in one massive blow, or maybe I was dreaming. I blinked, and the smoke began to lift on the slight breeze. The ships started to become visible once again, the smoke drifting over them. They emerged from out of the fog like ghosts from a bad nightmare.

The shells began bursting on the beach and among the cliffs, throwing sand and water high in the air. A shell from one of the big battleships must've hit our bunker. Everyone dropped to the floor as the world around us shook violently. Dust fell from the ceiling. The lights flickered, then the bulbs just burst, showering us in thin shards of glass. I got to my feet only to be knocked down again by more hits.

We'll see just how strong this concrete really is, I thought.

Like in an earthquake, things that weren't bolted down were thrown about the room. The radio had fallen off the table, the coffee pot spilled its contents all over the floor, cups rattled as they fell, and small chairs bounced and finally tipped over. The world was crashing down on us, and I expected to be buried under tons of concrete any minute. One guard lost his mind in the turmoil. Screaming, he dropped his rifle and bolted for the door. There was no chance for anyone to stop him. After he left, the other guard slammed the heavy steel door shut again.

At one point, it let up a little, and I stood up. Peering out, I saw the bunker next to us was scarred beyond recognition, large chunks missing from its roof and sides, some the size of small cars. The beach was now littered with craters as far as you could see. Dead fish floated in with the tide, rolling up on the beach in the light surf. I could see the enemy landing craft circling out in the channel, waiting for the rest of their formation before storming ashore. Like vultures, they'd circle, looking for an opportunity to come and peck away at our flesh.

There was smoke everywhere, and in the blink of an eye, another salvo rained down on us, the shaking so violent, my teeth rattled, and a filling popped out! A couple of the younger men curled up in a ball, crying for their mothers. There was no time to console them, they'd have to gut it out. Looking at my watch, I noticed the crystal had cracked and it had stopped working, the shaking and vibrations obviously too much for it to take.

Small pieces of cement started to fall from the ceiling, and I noticed small stress cracks forming in the walls and floor. How long we could withstand this brutal pounding was just a gamble. It seemed to go on for hours.

When it let up again, I stood and was shocked to see the landing craft were only about a thousand yards out. I yelled out again, "Man your positions! They're about to hit the beach!" Several of the men rushed out with their MG 42s, headed to their fighting positions. The low rumble of the landing craft engines could be heard faintly. I shouted at the radio operator, "Get the artillery, NOW!" He scrambled for the receiver and cranked to charge the system. While he jabbered in the mic, I handed him a set of coordinates. "When you get them, tell them to send everything they have."

It wasn't long before our shells started to rain down among the American soldiers. I watched as shells hit the water, sending a fountain high into the air that came back down on the enemy. Occasionally, a craft would get hit, the destruction complete and catastrophic. The left-hand gunner started to fire. I yelled, "Ceasefire!" He stopped and looked questioningly at me. I said, "Wait till they land and lower the ramps, then fire into the boat and take them all out." He nodded his understanding. Our men with rifles fired at the stragglers wading ashore when their boats let them out too early.

In a way, I felt bad for them. They didn't stand much of a chance. There was nothing to hide behind and no way to fight back; we picked them off one by one, the lead bullets tearing through wet clothing, flesh, and internal organs alike. If they weren't dead already, they'd die shortly from drowning. They just kept coming, wave after wave. Our machine guns opened up, killing men by the twenties and thirties. It was a grisly sight indeed. One I was sure would stick with me if I survived this war.

As more and more men made their way to the berm, it became increasingly difficult to direct fire on them, so I now called up an additional two riflemen, armed with the Kar98k, the standard German bolt action rifle. Using a 7.92 x 57mm Mauser, this rifle had excellent action with a great cartridge, plenty of knock down power, and amazing accuracy.

One American attempted to move and when he got to his feet, the soldier on my right fired. *Bang!* The sound echoed and reverberated through the bunker. I watched as the bullet flew straight and true to its destiny, piercing the side of the man's helmet and knocking it off. As he fell face first into the sand, his body lifeless, a pink cloud dissipated into the air. His helmet tumbled, rolling four or five times down the beach before coming to a rest upside down. I couldn't stop watching it, as if everything was in slow motion.

I yelled at the radio operator, "Call for artillery now!"

All the artillery in our vicinity were pre-zeroed on several locations in our sector. This saved time giving coordinates and coming up with the firing solution, potentially saving minutes and many lives. Soon, the shells began pounding the sand. More than once, I watched as bodies were flung into the air, limbs were torn apart, clothing and equipment shredded, turning them into an unrecognizable mess. This was worse than anything I'd ever witnessed on the eastern front. The experience of this war would leave a scar on my heart and mind that would never heal.

The beach became red with the blood of the Americans. They would pay dearly for every inch of sand they took. Equipment and bodies littered the entire length. The wounded lay where they fell, crying out for help. Although we could neither hear them nor understand them, the cries of the wounded were universal; men, reduced to infants when on a deathbed of agony, desperately wanting the torture to end but not wanting to die. Men, lying with their intestines spread out before them, or walking in shock as blood spewed from torn and absent arms or legs, like a pulsating fountain, blood pumping out with each beat of the heart.

Everything slowed down as I took it all in. I felt sick and disgusted that mankind could do this to one another. Is this really the answer to our problems? I wondered. *Is this what God intended for us?* Wars were fought every other decade and decimated people by the millions. Was there not a better way? I hung my head for a minute, tears filling my eyes, not just for the Americans, but for my own countrymen as well. *This is insane.*

I was shaken back to reality when I felt the heat. The bunker to my right had burst into a flaming inferno. Most likely an American flamethrower had gotten to it and unleashed a jet of flaming fuel. Anything flammable inside would catch fire instantly. Clothing, tables, and leather all burned. The concrete walls acted like a pressure cooker, and things inside would be blown from any openings, men included. They screamed as their skin melted and literally fell off their bodies, the jellied gasoline refusing to relent. They flailed their arms wildly, in fact fanning the flames and making it burn more intensely. No longer able to bear the burden of living, they gave up and fell, but the flesh would continue to burn until all that was left was a black crust of a human.

I was about to pull the plug on our location when I saw an American medic bolt from his cover. He ran toward the surf, obviously on a mission of compassion, picking up a wounded man. I instructed my machine guns to take him out. They both fired, bullets striking all around him. Even the soldiers with rifles joined in, and still, they couldn't hit him. The machine gunner on my left called for a new barrel as his gun overheated, a common problem with the MG 42. As the barrel was removed, it popped and crackled as it cooled, smoke emanating from its exterior. The other gunner also stopped, calling for more ammo.

Another American soldier ran out to help the medic and as they hauled the wounded man back, the second soldier was hit. They both fell when he let go. Stumbling on alone, the medic continued to drag the other wounded man. I yelled at the radio operator again. "Send more artillery! Tell them to put it on our location! Do it now or we'll all die!" Knowing the bunker would protect us from the shelling, I waited and watched as this medic continued to work, seemingly untouchable. The rounds began impacting the beach, one eventually landing just in front of the blessed medic, throwing him backward. After thirty seconds or so, the shelling stopped, but I had no time to determine if the medic had finally met his end. American GIs, using a Bangalore torpedo, had cleared a hole in our concertina wire and were rushing through, headed our way.

I yelled to cease fire and told Sergeant Wolf to pull his troops back to rally point Alfa. I looked at Brashears. "Get the car. I'll be right there."

Quickly, the soldiers filed out of the bunker. Making sure all were out, I made my way to the door. I turned to take one last look when I saw the grenade come in and bounce off the south wall. I slammed the steel door closed just as the explosion happened, throwing the door wide open and forcing me against the far side of the trench wall. Mostly uninjured, I felt a tingle in my left wrist.

Hopefully, just a sprain, I thought.

I rounded the corner of the bunker and saw Brashears standing there, staring. The car, once a nice, shiny black, was now a mangled chunk of metal. The previously round tires were a melted puddle of rubber, still burning, the flames gently licking at the charcoal black fenders. The inside was nothing but ash. The seats were still there, but only the springs outlined a once plush interior. The glass was all missing, and only the frame of the convertible's top stood defiant. A skeleton, just like the burning soldiers.

I looked Brashears in the eye and said, "Okay, Private, let's move. No amount of looking will bring it back."

An explosion within the bunker behind us made me realize how close the enemy was. The Americans most likely had thrown in a satchel charge, which consisted of about ten pounds of dynamite.

"C'mon, Private. We need to hurry up."

We jogged for a couple hundred yards before slowing down. Walking briskly, with the sounds of war all around us, we made it to the rally point in two hours. Kaeppler and Schwartz were already there with what remained of the company in defensive positions. Pre-dug foxholes and log and barbed wire barricades covered the roads.

Stepping away from the men, I called Kaeppler over. "What's the casualty situation, Master Sergeant?"

He said he had been informed that 1st Platoon was completely destroyed.

I looked at the ground. *Forty-five kids who will never experience life again,* I thought. "What else?" I asked.

"Fourth Platoon is about half strength, and Third is about three-quarters."

"Okay. Get me a motorcycle driver. I need to find Colonel Zoeller." I needed answers before I could plan a counter attack. I paced as I waited, searching for a solution. Nothing came to me. The motorcycle pulled up and I got in the sidecar. "Do you know where Colonel Zoeller is, Private?"

He replied, "I believe so, Sir."

"Then take me there."

We drove cautiously, navigating several checkpoints. Driving up to a group that appeared to be looking at a map spread out on the hood of a staff car, I recognized the colonel. He spotted me getting out and rushed over to me.

"Dirden!" he said, "How's your unit?"

"Sir, we're not good. We took a bad pounding. I figure the company is about half strength, Sir."

"Damn!"

"I had to pull back to Alpha, Sir. If I hadn't, we'd be in a lot worse shape."

"I understand, Captain. Things are bad everywhere."

"Where are the reserves, Sir?"

The colonel shook his head in disgust. "Still sitting where they were yesterday."

"What?" I exclaimed. "Why?"

"Because the Führer is still asleep, and everyone is too afraid to wake him! Only he can control the reserves."

"And Rommel?" I asked.

"He figured with the weather being so bad, the Allies wouldn't land, so he left for Germany to celebrate his wife's birthday! He's on his way back now but won't be here till tomorrow."

Keeping my thoughts to myself, I couldn't believe the war was being run this way. How could we realistically expect to win when so many men were only concerned with their own power?

"Dirden, you need to do what you can to hold the line at Alpha. I'll send word about what the next plan is when we figure one out."

I could say nothing more than, "Yes, Sir." I ran back to the motorcycle and we sped back to my company.

Nightfall was fast approaching, and we finally felt like we could afford to take a breath. The boys ate and rested in between the guard's rotation. Things didn't look good. Food, water, and ammo were all in short supply.

By the time I took care of business, it was well past midnight. I found a piece of paper, pulled a blanket over my head and with the aid of a flashlight, began to write. Stella needed to know I was okay. She would hear the news soon, and I didn't want her to worry needlessly. After carefully composing my letter, I folded it and placed it in a makeshift envelope, addressing the outside. I handed it to a messenger, telling him to send it off right away. I just hoped that when she got it, I would still be alive.

Curling up next to a tree, exhaustion taking over, I was asleep before my eyes closed.

CHAPTER TWELVE

1978

I awoke to the telephone ringing downstairs. I looked at the clock and was shocked: 10:30! *I never sleep this late,* I thought. But even now, I still felt tired. I rolled over, watching the shadows of the trees dancing on my shade, hinting at the wind outside. My mind was tossing around just like those leaves, my head wandering all over about my dreams. *Do they mean something?* I wondered. *Or is it just my imagination running wild?*

I heard the door open and Mom came slowly up the steps. Coming over to my bed and sitting beside me, she asked, "Mike, are you feeling okay today?"

"Yes, Mom," I said. "I just didn't sleep all that great."

She touched my cheek and brushed my hair from my forehead. "Okay, well, your friend Andy just called. He wants you to call him back when you get up."

"I will," I said.

Mom got up and started down the stairs. She told me she'd have cereal waiting for me when I was dressed. I waited until the door closed at the bottom of the stairs, then I pushed the covers down and sat up. I pulled the shade up and was greeted by a bright, sunny day, although the wind was howling. I watched through the window for a minute as dead leaves were swept across the yard. Occasionally, the wind would come through a small opening in the window frame and make an eerie sound, like a ghost was there. It used to scare me when I was younger, but now I knew better.

In the kitchen, as I poured milk in my cereal, I was suddenly curious if they had milk and cereal for the soldiers in WWII. *It would be a shame if they didn't*, I thought. I wondered how they kept things like milk cold. It wasn't like they could make ice. Another thing for me to research sometime. I finished eating, put my dishes in the sink, and grabbed the phone. Dialing Andy's number, my fingers slipped in the rotary holes and I had to start over twice. When I finally got through, Mrs. Petrovski answered in a somber tone, and I said, "Hello, is Andy there?"

She knew my voice and said, "Hold on a minute, Mike. I'll get him."

I heard her set the phone down.

A moment later Andy picked up. "Hey, dude. Can we meet at the pond?" he asked.

"Sure, what's going on?"

"I'll tell you when we meet up."

"Okay, I'll be there in ten minutes."

Andy seemed different, and I wondered what was going on. I put on my Twins hat and told Mom I was going to meet up with Andy. "I'll be back later, Okay?"

"Alright," she said. "Just make sure you're back by dinner time."

It was the standard answer when I went somewhere else to play.

As I walked down the street, the wind almost took my hat. I grabbed it and had to hold one hand on it for the rest of the way to the pond. I felt like I was walking in a tornado. I had to literally lean into it to keep upright.

The pond was a little water hole about an acre in size. The street wound around the south and east side, a couple of homes stood on the north shore, and on the west side, there was a large hill that connected to a state forest. This was a popular place for the neighborhood kids. In the winter, we would clear off an ice rink and play hockey almost every weekend. During the warmer months, there was a large oak tree on the bank, complete with a tire swing. Kids would swoop out over the water, although I don't think anyone was ever brave enough to jump in. The water was always a muddy brown and the muck on the bottom could swallow up a small body easily. Local legend had it that a boy named Jarvis drowned in the pond years ago when he couldn't break free of the mud. That was enough to keep me on land! Sometimes, we'd attach a kite string to toy boats and set them to sail. When they were out far enough, we'd throw rocks at them, pretending it was artillery. When they sank, we'd haul them back in and repeat. Occasionally, one neighborhood kid would bring down a canoe or inflatable raft and we'd try to catch turtles or frogs on top of the water. It was a fun place for young boys if you didn't end up in the water. We all worried that the ghost of Jarvis would take us into the depths if we fell in.

Our meeting place was always at our bus stop on the southeast corner, and as I approached, I swore I saw white caps on the little pond. I spied Andy, sitting on a slab of cement that jutted out from shore a couple feet where the storm drains flowed into the pond. He was picking up stones and flinging them into the water. I walked up and sat beside him.

"What's up, dude?" I asked casually and realized he'd been crying. The only other time I'd seen him cry was when he'd broken his ankle sliding into second base in Little League three years ago. "Andy, what's going on?"

"My grandma died two days ago, Mike."

"Holy crap!" It was my gut reaction, even if it wasn't the most appropriate thing to say. "I'm so sorry, bud!" With that, I reached over and gave him a hug. "What happened?"

"Mom and Dad think it was a stroke or something. She was in bed, so they think it happened while she was sleeping."

"Dang, Andy, I don't know what to say!"

"It's okay, Mike." He pulled out a few old black and white pictures and handed them to me. "Mom said there was an old photo album on her nightstand. I guess in light of recent events with your interview, she wanted to go back and look. She talked with Mom the night before, and they planned to give these to you."

I looked closely at them. You couldn't really see any distinguishable faces, but it looked to me like the pictures were taken from inside a concentration camp. A couple of pictures had long buildings all in a neat row. The guard towers could be seen in the distance and a few people standing behind barbed wire fencing in striped clothing. "Why did they want me to have them?" I asked.

"She liked you, Mike. Grandma thought you were an honest, good kid, and she wanted the past remembered by someone who would respect it, so it would never be repeated."

We sat and talked for hours, throwing stones in the water. He recounted stories of his grandma while I sat and listened. The pain in his voice was real. I could tell he had a deep bond with her, and I had nothing but respect and admiration for both of them. I wished I could do more to help him, but I knew inside I was doing what he needed me to do. Just listen. He was my friend, and that day, we both needed each other.

When he finally ran out of tears, he asked, "So, have you learned anything new?"

"Oh yeah! Where do I start?" I began telling him everything I had learned from the books and journal. "There's so much I still haven't figured out. I'm convinced that the man writing the letters and journal is my grandfather, but everything from the trunk calls him 'Heinz Dirden' when our name is 'Schmidt.' I wonder what that's about?"

"Was that his middle name maybe?"

"I don't think so," I said. "That doesn't make sense either."

Andy suggested that maybe this whole thing wasn't the big family mystery I thought it was and it was all just a fluke.

"That would be an easier answer," I said, "but I think I'm onto something here. There's just a connection I'm missing somewhere."

When we said goodbye a while later, I told him to hang in there and we gave each other a friendly "see you later" push on the shoulder. Walking home, I thought of Andy's grandma. I hoped that my interview wasn't what had indirectly caused her death. I was glad to have gotten her story, but right now, I didn't feel very good about it. At dinner that night, I only picked at my food, moving it around on my plate with my fork.

Of course, Mom noticed, and asked, "Why aren't you hungry, Michael?"

"Andy's grandma just died," I said.

"Oh, that's too bad! How old was she?"

"I don't know exactly, but she survived the Holocaust."

Dad said, "Well, she's in a better place now."

I just stared at my plate. I couldn't let myself cry in front of my dad. Boys just don't do that, according to him. I had never seen him cry in my life.

Mom could tell I was trying not to break down. "Don't let it bother you," she said.

"I can't help it, Mom. A couple weeks ago, I was asking her questions about her life, kind of like an interview. She told me about what it was like during the Holocaust. I guess she took out an old photo album the night before she died. I feel responsible! I'm the one who brought up those memories for her. What if the stress was just too much for her?"

My dad said, "If she hadn't wanted to talk about it, she wouldn't have. She would have told you to get lost. Stop worrying about it."

Just then, baby Aaron let out a squeal, letting us know he wanted more food. We all looked at him, and I was thankful for the distraction. I asked Mom if I could go to my room, my eyes pleading with her not to make me stay.

She nodded. "I'll give your chicken to Aaron."

I ran upstairs before my dad could protest. I flopped on my bed and let myself cry. I prayed for Andy's family. When my tears subsided, I got the photos that Andy had given me. I was glad I hadn't mentioned them at dinner. Using a handful of thumbtacks, I pinned the pictures above my desk.

The next Friday, I headed to Grandma's again. I was looking forward to spending more time in the attic. I was both excited and apprehensive, wondering if I'd find any more clues. At Grandma's, Dad and I went straight to the kitchen. She spent most of her time there, so it was a calculated guess. I hugged her "hello" and ran upstairs to put my stuff in my room. Dad and Grandma were chatting at the kitchen table, and I interrupted to ask for a Popsicle. I heard, "You know where they are. Go ahead."

I opened the freezer and eyed the new half-gallon of chocolate chip ice cream. I muttered, "Ooh, ice cream!" and was reminded that was for after dinner, so, taking my Popsicle, I went to the screen porch to sit in an old wooden rocking chair while I licked my treat. Dad came out to say goodbye and told me to behave.

Grandma said, "He always does, Arnold. He's my little angel," as she smiled at me.

I smiled back, feeling a little like I was getting away with something.

With Dad driving away and Grandma back in the house, I sat alone on the porch, resisting every urge to go straight to the attic. *I'd better at least wait until after dinner,* I thought. Grandma had said she was making one of my favorites, spaghetti. So, instead, I walked out to the garage next to the house and opened the door. The paint was peeling from the exterior panels and the lone window rattled slightly. I turned on the light to reveal the usual cluttered mess. A lawn mower and old rusty tools lined a workbench along the wall. Mason jars full of screws and nails sat on top. Other odds and ends filled old coffee cans. *Grandma probably hasn't been in here in at least twenty years,* I thought. My uncles would come in here when they took care of her yard or other household repairs. Inside had a peculiar smell, musty and damp, as moisture crept in from under the rotting garage door.

I grabbed the purple banana seat bike that Grandma kept for when the grandkids came over. After giving the tires a quick squeeze to verify they had air in them, I walked the bike out the entrance door and got on. Pedaling down the alley, I avoided the occasional broken glass and steel beer can. I rode around the block several times, dodging potholes and large cracks. Figuring it had to be close to dinner time, I rode back and parked the bike by the garage.

I came in through the back door and Grandma said, "You're just in time," as she set the table.

I washed up and we sat down, folding our hands and bowing our heads as Grandma said the Lord's Prayer.

Our father, who art in heaven,
Hallowed be thy name.
Thy kingdom come,
Thy will be done,
On earth as it is in heaven.
Give us this day our daily bread
And forgive us our trespasses
As we forgive those
Who trespass against us.
And lead us not into temptation
But deliver us from evil.

For thine is the kingdom,
And the power, and the glory,
Forever and ever.
Amen.

I piled the noodles on and topped it off with the best sauce I'd ever tasted. I shoveled it in, realizing just how hungry I was. But even the delicious food could not distract my mind from the attic. I could almost hear it calling my name. As soon as I finished my last bite, I asked to be excused.

Grandma said, "What? No dessert? *Was ist den los?*"

I said, "I'm pretty full."

"Okay, you may be excused."

"Thank you for dinner," I said and ran upstairs. Stopping at the top, I listened for a minute. Not hearing anything unusual, I went to the other bedroom, right to the closet, carefully picked my way up the stairs, opened the attic doors, and stepped in. Turning to the trunk, I saw it right away. My heart fell into my belly. They had been moved! Maybe not much, but enough that it was obvious to me. I opened the first one that had held the uniforms, and it was now full of clothes! I quickly opened the other one to find the very same thing! *What the hell?* I thought. Strange as it was, I felt like there had been an intruder in my space. Was Grandma onto me? Was everything just a dream? I suddenly felt uneasy about even being up here. I went back down the stairs, through the closet and closed the door behind me. Every move I made now made me nervous.

I needed to think! I flopped down on my bed, breathing heavily as if I had just crossed the finish line of a race. I consoled myself that I still had the letters and the journal. Too restless to lie there, I went out to the little deck outside my room. The neighbor was cutting the grass, and I let myself be distracted to calm myself. Mesmerized, I watched the grass clippings coming off the old push mower. I was thankful I didn't have to use one of those contraptions to cut our lawn.

When my breathing returned to normal, I parked my butt in a chair and began to consider my options. Should I say something to Grandma? Come clean with what I knew and see what happened? Or should I play it cool? Maybe she didn't even remember what was in the trunks. Maybe this was all just a coincidence. The family was always coming over here: her kids, their spouses, and other grandchildren. If she did know someone was in there, she may not know who, so why incriminate myself? Not that I had really done anything all that bad. I hadn't broken anything. I hadn't stolen anything either, not technically anyway. So how bad could it be, right?

I put on my pajamas and went downstairs, knowing I couldn't avoid Grandma and hoping I could keep up an innocent look. She was watching a movie, so I sat in the recliner and looked at the TV, not really paying attention, my head swirling, wondering what might have been done with the things in the trunks. I didn't even notice Grandma get up and go to the kitchen, coming back with a bowl of ice cream, drizzled with butterscotch and chocolate syrup, with a couple of cherries added for good measure. In that moment, I knew I was still loved. With Grandma, food equaled love. I thanked her and with that first bite of the cold, creamy sweetness, I thought about the soldiers again, surmising that they would never get a treat like this. I couldn't imagine going months or even years without ice cream! I scraped the bottom of the bowl, trying to get every drop out. I wanted to stick my head in the bowl and lick it out like a dog, but I knew I'd be scolded if I did, so I made do with my spoon.

That night, I tossed and turned for hours, just as I thought I would, even past when Grandma went to bed. I couldn't stop worrying about the trunks, wondering what had gone wrong and what was going to happen now. Not knowing was killing me. I just knew that somehow, I would get in trouble for finding the attic secrets.

I awoke at seven am and decided to just get up instead of trying to sleep any more. Grandma was sitting in the screen porch with her cup of coffee. The porch lined the entire front of the house. A half dozen chairs sat in a line, none matching, and all had seen better days. I sat in an old, yellow, metal one next to Grandma. The metal was cold, and I recoiled at the first touch. I rocked slowly, watching the hummingbirds sip from the feeders that hung from the eave on the front of the porch.

"How did you sleep, *meine liebe*?"

"Okay, I guess," I replied, not wanting to lead on to something bothering me. "I'm still tired, though," I said as I yawned.

"Then let's go in and get you some breakfast. That will wake you up. I have some peaches that have been known to wake the sleepiest of boys, and I think they have your name on them."

My face brightened. I loved Grandma's canned peaches and cream. It was a taste of heaven in every bite! I hopped off my chair and followed her into the kitchen. She set the bowl of venerable sweetness in front of me, along with another bowl of cold cereal and set about preparing her Saturday coffee cake ritual. I watched her as I ate, amazed at the amount of work she put into this, week after week. The trunks kept popping into my head. Grandma acted like there was nothing out of the ordinary, but I was still uncertain of what she knew and if I was in trouble.

Her voice broke my thinking with, "What will you do today?"

"I thought I'd ride to the park this morning," I said.

"Okay, but keep an eye on the weather, they're talking storms later."

"I will," I assured her, placing my empty bowls in the sink, and giving her a quick hug from behind so as not to disturb her busy hands. I ran upstairs, grabbed my hat, and went out the front door. I wiped the dew off the bike seat with my hand, wiped my hand on my shorts, hopped on, and pedaled down the alley, making it to the park in no time. Getting on the swing, I began to think of what options I had regarding the trunk. *Maybe I should look around the attic,* I thought. *It could be the stuff was just moved to a cardboard box.* Reasoning with myself that she wouldn't put it in her dresser or closet, I figured it had to be up there still. If not, I decided I would check the basement, although I was almost certain it wouldn't be down there. The basement was damp and musty, used for a fruit cellar and a storm shelter, but not dry storage.

After almost two hours thinking of very little else, I decided to head back. I rode slowly to the front of the house and parked my bike on the side, out of view if Grandma were to look out a window. I opened the front screen door, very slowly, knowing exactly at what point the door would squeak, or the spring would creak. Inside, I picked the spots where I would step, carefully avoiding the noisy main walkway of the steps. Grandma was still busy in the kitchen, and I was almost home free when I took an errant step. I missed the edge and slipped. Grabbing the railing to keep from falling down the stairs, my right knee hit with a loud thump! I winced in pain as Grandma rushed to the landing.

"Are you okay, Mike?" she asked.

"Yes, Grandma, I just missed a step."

"I didn't even hear you come in."

"I had to use the bathroom," I said quickly, thinking on my feet.

"Slow down and be careful! I don't want you falling down the stairs!"

Getting up, I nodded at her and limped up the stairs.

At the top and out of sight, I swung my fist through the air. "Way to go, moron!" I said to myself. I waited for a minute and flushed the toilet. I turned on the water for another minute and moved the hand towel in the squeaky brass ring to simulate drying my hands, just in case she was listening. Exaggerating my departure, I went down the stairs a bit louder than usual, wanting her to hear me.

"I'm going back to the park for a bit, Grandma. Be back soon."

"That's fine, Mike," she said, "but the weatherman was just on and said we're in a storm watch, so be back in an hour."

"Okay," I said, rushing out, the screen door slamming as it closed. I got on the bike and rode around the corner, stopping as soon as I was out of sight. I sat on the curb, picking dandelions from the yard behind me and popping the flower off into the street. When I thought enough time had passed, I got back on the bike and returned to the house.

I parked in the same hiding spot and again tried to enter without a sound. Confirming the coast was clear, I went in just as I had before, only this time I concentrated on every step until I was at the top. I opened the closet door, turned on the light to the attic, and closed the door behind me just in case Grandma came upstairs. I didn't want her seeing the door open. Entering the attic, I went to the trunks. I covered my eyes as I opened the first one, hoping I was imagining things the last time. I counted to three and slowly peeked through the fingers of my hand. Dang! I wasn't dreaming. The clothes were still there.

I looked around to see if there were any new boxes. Nothing. I looked for boxes that had the dust on the top disturbed. Again, my search revealed nothing. Out of options, I began opening a few boxes I thought were large enough to hold all the items from the trunk. I even looked under the first couple layers in each box, being careful not to drop anything on the floor and alert Grandma to my presence. Getting hot and beginning to sweat, I went to open the window. Halfway across the floor, I heard the first rumble of thunder. I stood still, hoping it was something else I heard. I heard it again, a little louder, and there was no mistaking the sound. I rushed to the window and pulled the shade back. Just my luck. The clouds were building to the west in a dark purplish color that was turning to a dark black. *How ominous*, I thought. One of my friend's dad was a pilot, and one day, a thunderstorm had threatened our flight, and he'd taught us a little about storms. Guessing from that conversation, these thunderheads had to be approaching 25,000 feet! The air was still, and the light was taking on a funny green color. I needed to get out of here before the storm hit. I packed stuff back in the boxes and headed downstairs. In the closet, I cracked the door slightly to make sure I was alone before stepping out and closing it behind me.

CRAP!

The TV was on. The meteorologist was giving updates, and our county was now in a tornado warning. I needed to get downstairs before Grandma came looking for me. I went to the edge of the stairs to peer around the wall and down into the living room. I was in deep! Grandma was standing in front of the window, keeping an eye on the storm and watching for me. The weatherman talked excitedly about winds reaching sixty-five miles an hour with large hail and heavy rainfall, and warning people to seek shelter immediately! I went to my room, wondering how I was going to explain this. Maybe I should just go downstairs. I talked myself out of it, though. Grandma would surely be onto me if I showed up in the house when she thought I was outside for a second time today. I went to the balcony and looked over. It was a long way down.

I had seen one of my older cousins do something before, something I was about to try. I figured this was my only option. The floor of the deck I was standing on was the roof over the back door. This deck wasn't big, maybe 6' x 8'. Slightly below and to the right was a small section of roof that was the pantry off the kitchen. It extended out from the house about ten feet or so. Still too far to drop. There was an eye bolt stuck into the corner of the eave that ran a cable to the T-shaped clothesline pole twenty feet away. From there, six ropes ran to a twin T-shaped pole another twenty feet away. An additional cable was attached to that pole and bolted into the back of the garage.

I crawled over the railing and stretched out toward the roof over the pantry. A loud crack of thunder close by made me realize time was of the essence. I sat on the edge of the roof, straddling the cable. I placed both hands on the cable and leaned forward. I swung around without hesitation and wrapped both legs around the wire. The cable was old and had broken strands that poked and cut at my skin. I hadn't even crawled halfway, when a flash of lightning rapidly followed by window-rattling thunder caused my now bloody hands to lose their grip. The cable slipped between my feet and I fell eight feet directly onto my back. The wind knocked out of me, I writhed in pain on the ground, unable to breathe. Finally, I gasped and inhaled deeply. My back was killing me, but I managed to get to my feet. I got to the bike and brought it back to the garage. On my way to the back door, Grandma came out.

"Where have you been?" she asked. "I was worried about you!"

Unable to walk normal, and holding my hands up, it was obvious I was hurt.

"What happened?"

"I crashed the bike, Grandma," I cried, tears streaming down my cheeks. The first raindrops were beginning to fall, large enough to drench a car in one drop.

Grandma took me upstairs to the bathroom. She soaked a few cotton balls in hydrogen peroxide and dabbed it on my hands. It started to pour outside, and the wind surged to a light gale. She started to question me. "So how did this happen? It doesn't look like a scrape. And how did your knees survive this fall?"

I was still sobbing, unable to speak, when the tornado siren sounded.

Grandma said, "Okay, Mike, get to the basement. I'll be there in a minute."

The wind was screaming at this point. I glanced out the window on my way to the basement. The trees were bending almost horizontally. Leaves were whipping across the yard, the rain coming down so hard, I couldn't see across the street. And the street didn't even look like a street, more like a river, as the storm drains couldn't handle the sudden influx of water. Then came the hail. Large chunks of ice the size of golf balls bounced off cars and roofs, smashing anything in its path. The ground soon looked as if someone had opened up bags of ice and dumped them in the yard. Huge ice cubes floated down the street. The siren wailed as I ran to the basement. I hated it down there where it was dark, damp, and creepy! Grandma came down the steps and closed the door behind her. The thunder was constant. This was a nasty one, by the look on Grandma's face.

We listened to the radio Grandma brought downstairs with us, and it reported devastation everywhere. Tornado sightings were listed in several places, one not far from us. There would be six tornadoes that day, the largest an F4. After almost an hour, Grandma went upstairs to check on things. A few minutes later, she hollered down that I could come upstairs. The rain was now nothing more than a light sprinkle, and clear skies could be seen heading our way. I went outside. The ice lay thick like snow on the grass. The air must've been at least twenty degrees cooler now. Branches lay scattered about, and two doors down, a tree had fallen on a car parked in the street. The power was out, and people gradually came out to survey the damage. The telephone rang, and Grandma picked it up. Not really paying attention to it, I wandered down the street. There were garbage cans and other debris everywhere I looked. I had never experienced anything this violent. I overheard the neighbors saying a tornado had touched down less than a mile away. I wanted to go see, but knew I'd never be allowed.

I felt guilty, like this was all my fault for not telling the truth about the trunks. I thought God was unhappy with me and taken out His wrath on the community. I had to fess up, but how? Was there a way I could do this with minimal impact? I walked back and sat on the screened porch.

Grandma came out and sat next to me. "You never did tell me how you fell off the bike, Michael," she asked.

Darn! I was really hoping she'd forget. I had to change the subject, and fast. So, I just blurted it out before I could think of the consequences. "Why was Grandpa called Dirden?" If I could have gotten away with swearing at that moment, I would have. *SHIT!* I thought. I looked at Grandma. The color had drained from her face as if she had just seen a ghost!

It took her a moment to find words. "Where did you hear that?" she demanded.

I sat looking at the floor, not sure how I should answer. I was paralyzed.

Grandma got up and walked in the house, returning moments later with Grandpa's picture. "So, it was you who took the letters and journal from the trunk, Michael?"

"Yes, Grandma," I admitted. "But I was going to put them back, I promise. I just found them one day and wanted to know more. I didn't steal them, Grandma."

"I knew that stuff should've been destroyed long ago," she said, hanging her head. "I begged your grandpa to get rid of it all, but he thought the truth should come out someday when people could forgive. But that day has not yet arrived!" She sank into the chair next to me, as if her legs could no longer hold her. "When your grandpa passed away, I was going to get rid of it. But looking at the letters made me rethink it. Those are words written to me! Written in the hand of my husband. And besides being history, there are words of love written there that I just couldn't destroy." She straightened her shoulders and smoothed her skirt. "And so, it never got done. Now, you've found out more than I hoped would come out."

I felt ashamed to have brought this distress to her, and now more confused than ever. "But why, Grandma? I don't understand. How did you know?" I asked.

"Your dad mentioned your sudden interest in your grandfather and that you had been doing some research on WWII." She tipped her head as she looked straight at me. "He also said you wanted to come to play with Justin this weekend."

"Yes, I did," I said, wondering how that could be a clue.

"But your cousin is in Indiana this weekend, Mike. On top of that, your interest in coming over so much this summer made me wonder." She shook her head. "I love having you, but I didn't think you came just for my cooking. I didn't raise nine children without learning a few things along the way. Especially boys! They are sneaky and always finding something to get into. Eventually, I put two and two together and went to the attic. I saw the trunks had been opened, and there were little fingerprints all over them. And that day your shirt was so dirty, and you'd said your ball had gone under the bed? I knew my floors weren't that dirty, so I figured it was my little Michael. I've been waiting for you to come clean with me."

Although I understood now how I had been caught, I still didn't understand why the things I found were such a big deal to keep hidden. "But, why all the secrets?" I asked.

"I'll tell the family after church tomorrow," she said. "Then you'll know the whole story." She took hold of my hand and continued. "Michael, you know you shouldn't be going through stuff that doesn't belong to you, right?"

My heart was heavy with guilt now. "Yes, Grandma."

"You also know that you had no right to just help yourself to those things, right?"

"Yes, Grandma." Thinking this was my opportunity to at least figure out where the stuff had gone to, I said, "Would you like me to return them now, Grandma?"

"No, you may keep them, since you are so interested in them." Grandma stood, indicating the conversation was over.

I was relieved.

She must have been relieved too. She took a deep breath and sighed. "Okay, get ready for dinner, please. It'll be done soon." And with that, she walked in the house.

Taking my time going upstairs, I wondered what the rest of the story could be and if she would reveal more than I had even discovered. When I came back down, Grandma was sitting at the table with her head in her hands. She just sat there. I sat in my usual chair, and she didn't look up. After a minute or two of no movement, I finally asked, "Are you alright, Grandma?"

She looked up. "Yes, I'm fine," she said. Getting up and moving to the stove, she put the finishing touches on her macaroni and cheese.

She looked really tired, and I thought about how much stress I had put on her. I could see the concern on her face each time she looked at me. I almost wished I had never gone to the attic. I felt responsible for all of this.

She placed the bowl in front of me and sat with me while I ate.

"You're not hungry?" I asked. This wasn't like her.

"No, I think I snacked too much today. I'll be alright. You just eat up, please."

It was a somber mood. When I finished eating, she checked my bandages and sent me off to take my bath. My hands stung badly as I got in the water, but I realized I probably deserved it and the sore, achy body as well. I soaked until the water was almost cold, reliving the events of the day with sorrow and wondering how Grandma would fill in the blanks of the story I already knew.

I got my pajamas on and headed downstairs. I usually sat in the recliner facing the TV, but now, I snuggled up beside Grandma on the couch. Whether it was trying to show my remorse or trying to comfort her, I didn't know. Maybe both. We watched a little TV, and I got my usual bowl of ice cream, always a treat at Grandma's house, and today was no different, despite the turmoil.

When my ice cream bowl was empty, Grandma suggested an early bedtime, and I was more than willing to comply. My body and my mind were exhausted.

She patted me on the cheek and said, "*Gute nacht,* sweet dreams, Michael."

"Sweet dreams to you, *Oma,*" I said, and wandered upstairs.

CHAPTER THIRTEEN

October 1944

I had just taken over command of my new unit, the same company Captain Kinsler had commanded, the 2nd SS. He had been promoted and was now Colonel Kinsler. My unit was a mere skeleton of itself. Being surrounded at Roncey, France, we had lost most of our equipment. We were left with only a couple Panthers, a few field guns, and about half my compliment of soldiers. Moving during the day was becoming increasingly dangerous. American P-51 Mustangs and P-47 Thunderbolts roamed the skies overhead. They had complete air superiority, and they pounced on anything that moved.

"Sergeant Hummel, get Corporal Brashears, please. Tell him to get my car ready." I needed to get to the maintenance crew and talk to them in person. The few tanks I had needed to be operational, and I didn't want the Allies to know my strength, or lack thereof, if they were listening in.

I heard Brashears pull up outside the tent. I walked out and got in the car before he could come around to open my door.

I said, shortly, "To the maintenance A.O."

As we drove, I thought about the crimes that had been committed recently by this unit. Ninety-nine people had been hung in Tulle, France on 9 June. Another 642 men, women, and children had been locked in a church and burned alive on 10 June at Oradour-sur-Glane. I knew that the orders for these attacks had not come from Captain Kinsler, but any number of commanders above him. When I was in this unit, we were honorable. It disgusted me that it had digressed into murderers.

I was relieved that at least a handful of guys from my original unit were still around. And I had brought the kid with me, promoting him to corporal, although I was afraid his next promotion to sergeant would put him in the thick of the fighting.

We arrived at the maintenance facility, and I jumped out, saying to Brashears, "I won't be long. Stay alert." As I walked into the tent, men scurried about doing odd jobs. I went to the lieutenant behind the desk and asked if my tanks were ready.

He looked up from his paperwork and, seeing my rank, dropped everything, jumped to his feet and saluted. "You must be Captain Dirden."

I returned his salute and confirmed my identity.

"You can pick them up when you are ready, Sir. They're ready to go."

I thanked him, turned, and left the tent, keeping things short and simple. Getting back in the car, I asked Brashears, "Have you ever driven a tank before?"

"No, Sir," he replied.

As we drove away, I said, "You may need to learn how to drive one soon."

***

We were a few miles away when bullets suddenly impacted the road in front of us. Brashears swerved and lost control. The car slammed into a ditch and came to an abrupt stop.

"Get out!" I yelled.

I opened the door and ran to the tree line in front of me. A pair of Mustangs raced overhead. Their Merlin Rolls Royce engine made a unique sound. I got to the first tree and turned around to look. Brashears slipped as he came around the front of the car, fell, and stumbled to his feet. The Mustangs were now gaining some altitude before turning as thin, white vapor trails came off the edge of their wings. The four-bladed propeller bit the air, screaming as the aircraft made its turn even tighter, like wheels losing traction on pavement.

After leveling off, they opened up again, the six .50 caliber machine guns sending lead to its target. Brashears jerked violently and fell to the ground again. The Volkswagen was riddled, big holes drilled from bumper to bumper. The glass shattered, the tires burst, and just before they passed over us again, the once pristine car exploded into flames.

Damn. This is my second car that has burned up, I thought. *I think I need a fireproof car.* I watched the car billow black smoke and yelled, "C'mon, Brashears, let's move!" I turned to head further into the woods and after a few steps looked behind me. Brashears was still laying there. "No, God! Please no!" I turned back, running to him, yelling, "No, no, no!"

The Mustangs were making another turn and heading toward us. Expecting them to fire any second, I pulled out my Luger. They were coming right at us, but surprisingly, they never fired, apparently pleased with their work. I started shooting, not expecting to cause any damage, it was purely out of frustration and anger. I emptied the small magazine and watched as they flew off.

Once I got to Brashears, I saw the three large holes in his back. Horrified, I rolled him over. He blinked a couple times as bloody bubbles came from his mouth and bright red blood oozed from his chest. His stomach was split wide open. "God!" I screamed. "Why the fucking kid?" A tear formed in the corner of his eye and slowly rolled past his ears. He made an effort to speak, but I stopped him. "Shh," I said, "it'll be okay, Corporal. Just hang on." I held his head in my lap, trying to comfort him. A few more ragged, gasping breaths and he was gone. I just sat there rocking him. "Damn this war!" I cried. "I just can't take this anymore!"

I lost track of time, but sometime later, a half-track pulled up and stopped. I lay Brashears' head gently on the ground and rose to my feet. A few soldiers rushed out of the APC and came over to me. "Take him back to my CP," I said. "I'll walk back." It was only a mile or so away, and I needed some time to think.

"Yes, Sir," the Sergeant said, and with that, they loaded Brashears inside and drove away.

My walk did nothing to quell the ache in my heart. I went directly to my tent and sat down. Paper and pen in hand, I began to write.

October 23, 1944
Dear Mr. and Mrs. Brashears,

I'm writing to inform you of the passing of your beloved son. I was with him in the end and want you to know that as his commander, I was very proud of him. As parents, you too should be proud. He always performed his job well. Unfortunately, a recent air raid found him in the wrong spot at the wrong time. I am recommending him, posthumously, for the Knights Cross. I know this doesn't do much to relieve the pain of losing your son.

Please know he will live in my heart for eternity.
Respectfully yours,
Captain Heinz Dirden, Commanding Officer

I stuffed it in an envelope, took it to the mail facility and told the private to get it out straight away.

The following weeks went by quickly, and although we continued to be pushed back, I was somewhat excited. The end of the war was fast approaching, and this meant I could finally get home to my family. On the other hand,

Germany was being crushed in a vice. Soon, there wouldn't be much left. Surviving was the key to success.

When Italy capitulated in 1943, Germany began losing its allies one by one. Romania was the latest victim to fall and switch sides in August 1944. It was now December, and Operation Mist was about to begin. We were standing alone, and the writing was on the wall. We fought on proudly, but the end would be devastating. We had seventeen divisions, all under-strength. There were only around 800,000 men and most were old men and very young boys. The battle-hardened soldiers were either dead or prisoners of war or out on the Eastern front. The objective was to drive through the Ardennes to the port of Antwerp, split the Allies in half and sue for peace.

We had just received a new allotment of Panthers to our inventory. Fuel was becoming scarce and more precious than gold. We had to use it wisely. Every soldier in charge of a vehicle, whether it be a tank or a truck, also carried a four-foot piece of flexible rubber hose. This was to siphon fuel from abandoned American vehicles or our own disabled ones. As it was, we didn't have enough to get to Antwerp, and resupply wasn't an option.

It was around 0500 when I made my way out to my command tank. The rear echelon detachment would pack up the tent and non-essential supplies and follow behind us. It was cold and snowing, which was both a blessing and a curse. It would prevent the Americans from having air cover and conceal our advance, but on the other hand, we couldn't see targets of opportunity until we were practically on top of them.

With the Panther now covered in six inches of new snow, I struggled momentarily to get a good hold and hoist myself up to the turret. The gunner removed the barrel shroud and clamored up the tank as well, almost beating me. I allowed him in first, then told Williams to start it and warm it up. The engine cranked slowly, stopped, and cranked again. I thought it wasn't going to start, but it finally caught. The engine groaned a bit until the oil was pumped up to the top of the bearings. As the whining faded, the idle became smoother, and the exhaust was a rich, almost intoxicating smell. Other tanks were now running, and the forest came to life.

At least this isn't the Eastern front, I thought to myself, thinking back to the winter of '42. That year, it had been so cold we'd had to run the tanks and other vehicles every couple of hours or they'd never start in the morning, and the engine oil became so thick, it was like molasses. The coolant would gel and even freeze, splitting radiators and hoses so that the engines would overheat and seize up. Even gear oil would become so thick that the tires would not turn and lock up like the brakes had been applied. If any of this happened, the only way to fix it was to get a pan of hot coals from a fire and place it under the affected area, cover it with a blanket to keep the heat in, and wait. Or have maintenance pick it up and tow it out. However, these options weren't always available, so the vehicle would be destroyed and abandoned. Life in Russia was a constant challenge. If it wasn't the snow and cold, it was mosquitoes and the hordes of black flies. *Why did we want that land again?* I wondered now, thinking back on it. To hell with it all. I just wanted to go home to Stella!

I looked back at Sergeant Hummel, and he gave the thumbs up that everyone was ready. I radioed to tell Battalion we were moving out and hollered below, "Forward, slow." The tank lurched ahead, the vibrations now disturbing the once pristine snow that covered us. Cracks formed from the vibrations, sending icy chunks sliding off the steel exterior. The tracks and road wheels were already packed with snow and ice. Icicles that once hung from the top of the stationary track now broke off and shattered like fine crystal.

We made our way to the main road that cut through the Ardennes, making our own trail through the field. The scene was pretty with the trees covered in fresh snowfall; the evergreens' branches coated in white. We drove over small saplings and hidden objects like stumps and rocks. The ride was not smooth but expedient. We were not the hammer on this day, but the following force or reserves. We were the ones who could provide that little extra oomph or firepower to get through a troublesome defense. Speed, again, was key. We had to achieve our goals before the weather broke and the Allies could again control the skies with their suffocating air cover.

Arriving just outside Bastogne, traffic started to back up. Bastogne needed to fall soon or this whole mission would be jeopardized. It was a hub, with roads going in and out like spokes on a bicycle. Going around it would cause delays we could ill afford. Although it was surrounded, the Americans fought valiantly. The 101st Screaming Eagles, as they were fond of calling themselves, were a thorn in our side. They were the one unit none of us wanted to fight. They would dig in like ticks on a hound. They'd fight in the worst possible conditions and always come out smiling. They took great pride in making things miserable for us.

I was about to ask Colonel Kinsler if my assistance was needed in Bastogne when the radio operator said we had received a message to go around. This was my answer. Over the intercom, I told Williams to stop. I removed the map from my satchel and unfolded it, spreading it out. I called Sergeant Hummel over and told him the route I thought we should take. I was sure it would add several hours, but what choice did we have? I asked if he had any input, and he pointed out a slightly different route.

"It's probably going to add some miles, but it might be quicker," he said.

The dilemma now was: should we move fast to the objective or burn more fuel? Neither choice was ideal. I chose my route, thinking if we ran out of fuel before getting there, it wouldn't matter how fast we were.

The sergeant headed back to his tank, and we continued our advance. Leaving the road behind now, we would travel cross country. Cutting through fields and forests was hard on machinery and man alike. It was slow going, and fuel was consumed at an alarming rate. At 1300, I called over the intercom again to stop. I ordered everyone into a defensive posture and called Sergeant Hummel over.

"Sergeant," I said, "we need fuel soon. I think we should send a scout team to that farm over there." I pointed to a set of buildings visible about a mile away.

The sergeant formed a team of four and sent them in an armored scout car toward the farm. The rest of the men took this opportunity to sleep, eat, or both. I again stared at the map, desperately trying to find a better way.

"Sergeant Hummel," I called.

"Yes, Sir," he answered, and as he walked toward me, we heard gunshots.

It had been about a half hour since the scout team left. Looking toward the farm, I brought my binoculars up. Our men were running for cover and shooting back at enemy troops in the farm buildings.

"Mount up!" I yelled. "Williams, to that farm! On the double!"

The metal giant jumped forward, and soon we were bouncing across the open field to help. The rest of the company followed behind us slightly. I motioned for Hummel to approach from the rear while I took the front. The Americans, preoccupied with the initial soldiers, never saw us coming. We surrounded the small house and pumped in a few hundred rounds from the mounted MG. I knew we had their attention, so I yelled at them to surrender. I told my men I thought it was better to keep them alive than waste another HE round. Realizing they had no way out, a white flag jutted from a window. They came out empty-handed, and I had them sit abreast, facing away from the farm. There were eleven of them, not counting their seven wounded. They were a platoon from the 1st Infantry Division.

These are the same guys I faced in Normandy! I thought. I wondered to myself if any of these men were the medic on the beach, that man still haunted my memories. Not seeing a medic, I quickly put the thought out of my head. I picked five guys to search the building while the Americans were held at gunpoint. I went over to my tank and asked Hoffman to get me Colonel Kinsler on the radio.

"Sir," I said, "I have eleven American prisoners. What do you want to do with them? Where shall I take them?" When the reply came back, I asked for him to repeat it as I could not believe my ears.

"Captain Dirden, we cannot take prisoners currently. You'll need to liquidate them. Am I clear, Captain?"

"Sir," I said again, "they're disarmed, and they surrendered."

"I understand, but you can't watch them, I have no one you can turn them over to, and we certainly can't let them go. Now get moving, Captain!"

Ordering them on their feet, I had the prisoners line up against the wall of the barn. They knew what was coming. The younger ones became almost hysterical, crying and pleading for their lives. I couldn't understand what they were saying, but their distraught faces and actions made it pretty clear what they were asking. Not wanting to see their faces anymore, I made them turn around and face the wall. I pulled out my Luger and pressed it to the first man's head. "Please forgive me, Lord," I said, as I squeezed the trigger. *Bang!* The pistol recoiled when the bullet left the barrel. It entered the back of the man's head and exited his forehead. Blood and brains splattered against the wall. Blood blew backward against my face, and I never blinked. The man's now lifeless body slumped to the ground. I took a step to my left and repeated my actions with the same devastating result. I tried to be a robot, just a machine with a single mission, with no feelings, but nevertheless, the tears flowed from my eyes as I took the lives of these men for no good reason. I took another step to my left and again repeated my crime. Three bodies lay at my feet, kids not much younger than myself. I turned and saw the looks on my men's faces. Some were shocked, while others looked delighted. It was the latter I worried about.

I faced the next man and pulled the trigger—*bang!*—only he jerked just as the pistol fired, the bullet removing the top of his head like a scalp. Still alive when he hit the ground, he tried to crawl away. I watched the disgusting scene, his brain bulging from the now boneless section of skull. I holstered my Luger and watched, expecting him to die any second. But instead, he kept crawling, moaning as he moved. Hummel came over, grabbed a private's rifle, and smashed the buttstock into the man's head three times until the contents of his head now covered the rifle stock, Hummel's boots, and the ground. The snow was stained red everywhere I looked.

The next American in line started to run and was promptly shot about a hundred times from half the company.

I stood there in a daze, the robot inside surfacing.

Hummel came over to me and, in a whisper, said, "Sir. This isn't you! Let these men go. They've got no weapons, and they're surrounded by the entire German army. What harm can they do?"

I looked him in the face and said, "Sergeant, get back to your tank!"

He replied smartly, "Yes Sir!" and turned. He left without looking back.

As I faced the Americans again, the robot melted, and I knew the Sergeant was right. This wasn't me. What the hell was I doing? Without further thought, I grabbed the next American by his shirt collar, pulled him back, and shoved him in the direction I wanted him to run. He halted, looking back, confused, and hesitantly ran away, looking over his shoulder. I grabbed the next guy and shoved him in a different direction. I did this with each man until they were all out of sight. I had done it. What I just did would change the direction of my life and the lives of my men forever. There was no going back. I was done with this war. I wasn't going to take any more of these gutless, illegal orders.

I walked back to my Panther, not looking at anyone. I could not deal with the looks on the faces of my men. Without saying another word, I got in my turret and told Williams to move west again. Moving cross country used more fuel, and it wasn't long before I had vehicles running out.

Halting for a brief rest, I called Colonel Kinsler. "Sir, I need resupply. I need fuel badly. Tomorrow, I'll have no armor by 0900 if I don't get it."

He said, "Captain, there is no resupply right now. You'll need to make do or find some from somewhere else."

I found Sergeant Hummel and said, "Put a team together and go find us some damn gas."

I decided to shut it down for the night, and with all engines silenced, the quiet of the night rang in my ears. With temperatures in the teens, it was going to be a long, cold night. I decided if the team didn't come back with gas, or at least know where we could get it, I was going to turn this company around and head back. I knew I'd be imprisoned or executed for it, but I wouldn't squander my men's lives on this joke of an operation.

For the next two hours, I sat with my canteen and a handkerchief, trying to remove the blood from my hands and face. I couldn't see myself, but I knew I was covered in blood. I could taste the metallic on my tongue whenever I licked my lips, and there was blood crusted in my eyelashes that I could feel every time I blinked. And all the while, I thought about those I had executed. I was mad at myself for caving into pressure. Although I would eventually be able to remove the blood, the memory would never be erased.

The scout team arrived and said they had found a couple of American Jeeps about two miles away. They had gas, but how much was just a guess. I told them to get a little rest as we'd be leaving soon. I went back to my tank and woke my crew up.

"Get ready to move," I told them.

They stirred and groaned.

I said, "You have five minutes. Williams, warm this pig up. And one of you, discreetly grab a Panzerfaust. The heavy weapons platoon should have plenty. Actually, get two and store them inside the tank for now." I went over to Sergeant Hummel and woke him up next. "Sergeant, get up."

"Yes, Sir," he said, sitting up right away.

"In an hour, I want you to go drain the gas from those Jeeps the scouts found."

"Yes, Sir, but where will you be, Sir?" he asked.

"I'm going to go see Colonel Kinsler." I took a step closer to him and lowered my voice. "Don't expect me back, Sergeant." He looked at me with a strange combination of shock and understanding. "You know how this works, Hummel. If I'm not arrested and shot on the spot, I'm sure I will, at the very least, be relieved of command."

He straightened up, as if coming to attention, but not saluting. "It was good knowing you, Sir." He relaxed his stance a bit, and asked, "Are you sure you want to do this?"

"Yes, I'm very sure. I'm tired of killing. You said it yourself, this isn't me." I gave him a reassuring, sly smile. "I may need you at my trial, though, if I make it that far," I said.

"I'll be there, Sir," he said.

I knew he was sincere. Before we finished talking, my tank started up. I said goodbye and crawled in the hatch. "Okay, Williams," I said, "to Battalion Command."

The left track kept stationary while the right one rotated forward, turning the tank on a dime. We had traveled about a mile, when I yelled down to Williams, "Change of plans. There's a road up ahead, take a left and head east." I was met with a sea of confused faces, but I did not elaborate. I stood back up in the turret, watching ahead for any threats.

We got to the road, and Williams did as he was instructed. We went another ten miles east before I told him to stop, which he did, and I told him to turn off the engine. I needed to conserve every drop of fuel I could, knowing we were already below a quarter tank. Now that the engine was no longer running, I didn't need to yell. "Everyone out," I said, crawling out myself. It was still dark, and the sun wouldn't rise for a couple hours yet. My plan was to be as far away from here as possible by that time. I felt a sense of guilt for leaving Hummel behind with the other men, but right now, I had to think of my own survival for the sake of my family. I felt fairly confident that the men with me had morals like mine and would accompany me in my plan.

Everyone gathered around, and I looked into each of their eyes and studied their facial expressions. I said, "Men, I've had my limit with this war and orders that are illegal and immoral. I'm done, and I need to know who wants to come with me."

They were shocked. They searched each other's faces for answers, clues of what to do, but were completely quiet.

I said, "Look, you can walk back now if you want. We're not too far away. I only ask that you don't say anything about me or those joining me. I'll have no ill feelings toward you, but you need to understand what you're getting yourself into if you come with me. You'll be considered deserters. If caught, we'll be put in front of a firing squad, most likely without a trial. If the Russians catch you, you'll be executed anyway just because we're SS. If we stay and fight, we have a 50/50 chance. Our country is being decimated left and right. We have no more allies to count on, and we cannot possibly win. The Allies want unconditional surrender and Hitler will never go for that. So, it's win or die! We can't win, and I am not throwing my life away or the lives of my company because of some third-rate neophyte!"

Corporal Helmut said, "What's your plan, Sir?"

"Well, I was going to drive east until this thing runs out of gas," I said. "It should still be dark. If we can find more gas, great. If not, that's fine too. I'll reveal more of my plan to those who want to come. Otherwise, I'm not divulging information to someone who can jeopardize our goals. So, who's with me?"

One by one, all four men raised their hands saying they were in.

"Okay, once the tank is unusable, we split into two groups. My mission is to get back to my wife and get her out of Germany. Once that's done, I'll try to get out myself, or surrender to the Americans or the Brits. What you guys decide to do is up to you." I could see doubt on their faces now. "C'mon," I said, "let's get moving. We'll discuss this more later."

We got back into our positions and brought the engine to life.

"Just follow this road, Williams."

Once again, we were heading into danger. With each rotation of our track, things would get harder to explain if we were picked up by the Gestapo. An hour or so passed while we delicately picked our way to the rear. Suddenly, the tank jerked violently, hesitated and went on again, then jerked a few more times before it sputtered and died. Private Williams attempted to restart the engine several times. It would crank and briefly start, only to die again a second later.

"Well, that's that," I said. "Grab your gear. It's time to walk."

Exiting the tank, I gave instructions to take the usable gear. I told Private Rundle to leave the magazine doors open and partially pull out a few HE rounds. This way, the door wouldn't accidentally close, and it would make the rounds in the magazine more susceptible to the next part of my plan. After everyone was out, I grabbed the two anti-tank weapons and told everyone to follow me to the rear of the tank, about forty yards away. I removed the safety and aimed the weapon at the engine compartment. I pulled the trigger and *whoosh!* The rocket struck dead center and exploded in a blinding flash. One was all it needed; the engine now a blazing inferno.

"C'mon, let's go," I said, "before someone comes to investigate."

We continued to head east. The snow seemed to be letting up a bit, which could be bad news as it would be harder to cover our tracks. A couple of miles down the road, we came to a crossroad.

"Okay, we need to split up," I said. "One person with me, and I'll go left. The other three take the right."

Corporal Hoffman said he'd go with me.

"Just remember, guys, if you get caught, things are likely to get very unpleasant. So, keep low and move only at night if possible."

With that, we wished each other well and went our separate ways. Looking back, I could see the light of the burning tank, two miles away, reflecting off the clouds. I wondered if anyone had shown up to check it out. Not waiting around, I turned back south and began to walk.

It was almost 0700 when I mentioned to my traveling companion that there should be a farm place up ahead. "We'll stay there until dark." We each had personal weapons and ammo, a few small cans of meat, and a canteen of water. This wouldn't last long, so we needed to do our best to conserve.

Within thirty minutes, we saw the barn. Luckily, it appeared the farm had been deserted long ago. There was no foot traffic in the snow and no signs of life. This was good in the sense that we didn't need to worry about civilians, bad because it likely meant we wouldn't find any food. I decided we would take refuge in the barn instead of the farmhouse, thinking it would be easier to keep watch, and easier to escape if need be. We made our way to the loft and made a nest of the available hay. It would be good to sleep on and keep us warm, so I wasn't about to complain. I figured by now, they had to know we were missing. I hoped they thought we were killed. The destroyed tank would help to some degree, but the absence of bodies might be a giveaway. I got as comfortable as I could in the hay and prayed God would keep us safe. And as always, I prayed for the safety of my precious Stella and my boys.

I lay there for some time, thinking. I knew that as soon as the skies cleared, the Allies would have their airpower back, and it would all be over. I considered just staying here, letting the German army pass me up when they retreated. There were two problems with that, though. One, I didn't know when that would be. It could be two days, two weeks, or two months, for all I knew. Secondly, if I was captured, how would I ever get Stella to safety? I had to get her out of Germany! I considered that my only mission. My eyelids began to feel heavy, and out of sheer exhaustion, I fell asleep.

I woke sometime later to the sound of approaching vehicles. "SHIT!" I said. "Get up!" I nudged Hoffman. "We have company." Looking out the upper door, I saw a truck approaching. "At least this isn't the Einsatzgruppen," I said aloud of the paramilitary force responsible for most mass executions. "I think these are just regular Wehrmacht soldiers."

I handed our last Panzerfaust to Hoffman. "Use this on that truck, only if I say," I told him. "With any luck, they'll keep going." Only that wasn't our luck. "Mess up that hay so it doesn't look like we were lying there and get in the corner to hide!" I took one more look out the door and realized our footprints could still be seen faintly where we hadn't completely covered them up. I suspected they'd seen them. I made sure my MP 40 was loaded and crawled behind another pile of hay in the other corner.

It wasn't a big truck, so I figured it was only a squad. *Could be big trouble just the same,* I thought. I heard the truck brakes squeak as it came to a stop and the sergeant hollering to his men to dismount. He split them into two groups, sending one group to search the farmhouse and the other one to search the barn. Spurring them to hustle, I heard the lower barn doors slam open, the men yelling to come out. We stayed put and quiet. I made a small hole in the hay, so I could see if anyone came up the ladder. I heard things being moved around as they searched for us. I saw a head poke up above the floor, but he stayed there just looking around. Then he descended and said it was empty. They left the barn, and all the troops gathered around the sergeant. I went back to the upper door and slowly peeked out again. He said something I couldn't understand, and a private went to the rear of the truck and came back dragging Williams and Rundle at gunpoint.

"Captain Dirden, come out with your hands up!" he hollered. "We have your other men here."

I sat there watching as the sergeant put his sub-machine gun to the back of Williams' head.

"Come out or I shoot this traitor!" he growled.

"Damn!" I said under my breath. *Please don't do it!* I thought. There was no way I could give myself up now! My wife and children were more important to me. I would have to deal with the guilt of having this man's death on my conscience later. Right now, my own survival was paramount for the safety of my family.

The sergeant chambered a round and counted aloud. On three, he pulled the trigger and the gun fired past Williams' head and struck the wall of the farmhouse. Williams jerked and started sobbing loudly. The sergeant, not happy he hadn't found us, loaded his men and prisoners back into the truck and turned around, slowly driving away. When they were out of sight and the engine faded, I finally breathed a sigh of relief.

I lay back down, my heart pounding. I called Hoffman to come out. When he had crawled out of his corner toward me, I asked him, "What time is it?"

"It's 1600, Sir," he replied.

"Okay, I'm going to try and rest for another two hours," I told him, sure I wouldn't sleep after the turmoil of the last few minutes. "Keep watch and alert me if anything comes up." I curled up in the hay again, and just before I closed my eyes, I said, "Be ready to move at 1900."

CHAPTER FOURTEEN

1978

I dressed in my nice clothes and made my way downstairs. I saw Grandma standing by the front door like usual, waiting for my uncle. She wore a dark dress this morning. *That's unlike her,* I thought to myself. She usually wore bright, cheery dresses with a floral pattern since flowers were her favorite thing, next to the grandkids, of course. Although, right now, I didn't feel like a favorite. I knew today would be hard on her.

We arrived at the church, and everyone seemed to look at her differently, like they could tell something wasn't quite right. Occasionally, she was asked if she was feeling okay. She nodded and quickly changed the subject.

The organ began to play, and the first hymn was sung. I drifted off into daydreams, so much on my mind. I thought about everything, from hoping Grandma didn't destroy or get rid of Grandpa Heinz's stuff, to wondering what had happened when the war ended for them. What had happened with my American grandpa, and how did that tie in? Or was that chapter over now?

Before I knew it, the service was over, and everyone was waiting for the cue from the ushers to leave. I ran out, jumping in the caddy, while Grandma talked with the pastor for a couple of minutes and got in the front seat. I stared out the window on the short drive back, wondering how things might change after today. When we pulled up to the house, I jumped out so I could hold the front door open for Grandma. She didn't say anything to me, but she gave me a weak smile and patted my cheek. Once inside, she put her purse down, went to the kitchen, and set about taking out the coffee cake and butter. The family started to arrive, and I was surprised to see my parents already.

It's awfully soon for them to be here, I thought.

Grandma must have asked them to come early so everyone would be together for her announcement.

Mom pulled me aside. "Did you get in trouble, Mike?"

I shrugged my shoulders, knowing this was my doing, but not really sure if I was in trouble for it.

Before she could ask more, Grandma raised her voice and said, "Will everyone have a seat in the dining room, *bitte*?"

One by one, everyone found a seat, asking one another in hushed voices if they knew what this was about. Everyone was clueless. Everyone but me, that was. Nobody asked me, so I kept my mouth shut. I sat on the floor in a corner, hoping to be overlooked and forgotten.

Grandma stood in front of everyone and waited until the room grew extremely quiet. Even then, she stood there watching everyone. Eventually, she looked toward the ceiling, and a tear rolled down her cheek. My dad began to get up to comfort her, but she held her hand up, signaling him to sit back down. After a couple minutes of dead silence, she spoke.

"This is hard for me, so everyone, please, be patient. Let me tell the story before asking questions," she said, with pleading in her voice. "All of you know this family moved here from Germany in 1938 with the name Schmidt." A long pause ensued. Then, she said, "But... that's a lie."

A few gasps were heard at the word "lie" and some looked to their spouses, questions already swirling around the room.

Grandma held up a hand, and again, the room fell silent. "Our family name is actually Dirden," she said, "and we didn't come to America until 1946. Heinz, the father and grandfather to many of you in this room, was actually involved in the war." She looked out into a sea of questioning faces. "It's true what you've been told, that his brother was killed at Stalingrad, and his parents were killed during a bombing raid over Berlin one night in 1943."

Taking a deep breath, knowing her next words would be difficult to hear, she said, "But Heinz fought in WWII too. He was a member of the 2nd SS Division, Das Reich." Grandma noted the wide eyes and open mouths of her family, and knowing they understood the reputation of the SS, she spoke quickly to reassure them. "He was not proud of some of the things he did during the war. He tried to atone for those sins every day of his life. He deserted his unit even and came to get me safely out of Germany. He got in touch with an elderly friend of his father's, who was a fisherman, and arranged for me and Karl and you, Arnold," nodding toward my father, "to travel on his fishing trawler, bound for the coast of Spain. From there, your aunt Nora and uncle Juan came and got us, and we stayed with them, hoping your father would make it back to us."

Grandma paused a bit to catch her breath and let her words sink in before going on. "In 1945, Heinz was captured and taken prisoner." She paused again, this time for effect. "But God must have had a plan for him, I guess, because a week after his capture, a young, sympathetic, American soldier helped him escape."

I closed my eyes, picturing what Grandma was saying.

Late April 1945

I sat on my bunk, awaiting my next round of questioning. I had already been hauled into this sparsely lit room three times and asked questions by two army intelligence officers. They asked about my unit, operations that we partook in, and so on. Suddenly, the door opened, and an MP told me to get up. I was led out of the cell into another room. A GI signed something and told me to get moving, motioning me toward the door. I walked out into the courtyard where a Jeep was parked and was told to get in. I figured I must not be considered much of a threat as I had no other guard and no handcuffs.

We sat in the Jeep while the American spoke in German. He told me he was with intelligence, and a board of officers had decided my punishment. I was to go before a military tribunal where a sentence would be handed down. I thought this was odd to happen so quickly, but as I had no idea how the American military worked, I accepted my fate. I was just happy this would be over soon, and I could get to my family.

We drove out the gate and down the dirt road about five miles or so before the Jeep slowed and came to a stop. We were surrounded by forest, and I suddenly felt uneasy. *So, this is where it will all end,* I assumed. I figured this soldier had a score to settle. He'd execute me in these woods and claim I tried to escape, and he had to shoot me. I was resigned that if this was God's plan, I would accept it. After all, I reasoned with myself, I did get Stella and the boys out of Germany, and this would be just punishment for what I had done in this war. The soldier had an M1911 on his hip, and I thought about making a move for it, but ultimately, I decided against it. He shut off the engine and turned to face me. I stared out the front windshield, waiting.

He spoke again in German. "Heinz, you have one shot at this. You will get out and run that way," he pointed east. "When you get to the river, there will be a tree half laying in the water. Near the base of that tree is a burlap bag with some presents in it, including a change of clothes. You are to change and place the clothes you're wearing in the bag. Weight it down, tie it up, and pitch it in the river. There will be dogs here looking for you within the hour, so don't screw around. From there, you do what you want. But I'll warn you, all trains and highways will be closely guarded."

I looked at him intently to see if he was serious. Or was this just an excuse for me to run so he could shoot me in the back. "Why are you doing this?" I asked.

"Because I was asked to by a friend who I owe a favor to. Apparently, you've made an impression on someone who wants to see you free. Now, get out of here!" The soldier got out and pulled a knife from his pocket, walked to the rear of the Jeep, and stabbed the spare tire. Air hissed violently from the large gash in the tread. "Go!" he yelled.

I jumped from the Jeep and began to run. I didn't look back. I didn't want to see him pointing that .45 at me. I waited for the searing pain I knew was coming any minute. I just hoped he wasn't a good shot. I was halfway to the first tree. *Almost there,* I said to myself. *Bang, bang, bang!* I heard the shots. The bullets struck a large pine tree beside me, showering me with splinters. Instinctively, I ducked but continued to run. After about fifty yards, I stopped to see if I was being chased. After ten seconds or so I determined there was nobody pursuing me, so I kept heading toward the river.

It didn't take long and I was there. I looked in both directions. Upriver from me, I saw a tree hanging over the bank with several branches hanging in the water. *Is that the one he was referring to?* I asked myself. Jogging over to it, I followed the trunk through a tangle of underbrush to the base. The soft earth was easy to dig into, and within seconds I pulled a large burlap bag from the ground. It was tied with a short piece of twine, which I fumbled with, my hands shaky, and finally got it open. A plastic bag was inside, and I ripped it open. I pulled out a pair of slacks, a button-down shirt, socks, and a slightly used pair of dress shoes. Also inside was a small pocketknife, a watch, and a wallet with a small amount of currency in it and an ID. I looked at the name: Heinz Schmidt. The picture was of me. *Is this supposed to be me now?* I wondered. I continued to remove stuff from the bag. A passport was next, a small folded map, and a letter clearing me for travel outside of Germany. I couldn't read the signature, but hopefully, I wouldn't need to use it anyway. A suit jacket was at the bottom and another light jacket under that. The jacket felt heavy, so I searched the pockets and pulled out a Luger. I hit the release to remove the magazine. Fully loaded! It dawned on me this was the same Luger I'd had when I was captured. It had distinguishable marks on its frame from the holster which had always been a bit tight for it. I put it back in the pocket, hoping I would not find a use for it.

I changed out of my prison clothes quickly, put them in the bag as instructed and went to the river bank. Scrounging up around ten pounds of rocks, I placed them in the bag and used the twine to tie the bag up again. I made sure I had everything, one last time, and stuffed the new socks in the new shoes and tied them together. I grabbed the burlap sack and side-armed it into the river. *Ker-plunk!* It floated for a couple seconds and sank out of sight.

I picked up the good shoes and slung them over my shoulder, trying to keep them clean until I got out of the woods, figuring muddy dress shoes would raise suspicion. I made my way along the river bank. I felt nervous and looked at my new watch. *It has to be at least thirty minutes by now. I need to get moving faster,* I told myself. I heard traffic up ahead, so I proceeded with caution. An occasional car passed over the small bridge. Then, I spotted an answer to my prayers! A canoe lay upside down under the bridge. I hoped it didn't have any holes in it.

I waited until no one was coming and dashed under the bridge. *It looks good,* I thought. I flipped it over to reveal a paddle tied to the cross members. Taking out the pocket knife, I cut the rope and slid the craft in the water. Not seeing any glaring problems, I jumped in and paddled downstream as fast as I could. I wasn't sure if I heard the faint sound of dogs barking or if it was my paranoid state of mind, but I didn't think it was prudent to hang around. When I got far enough away that I felt safer, I let the canoe drift and pulled out the map. Guessing at my rate of travel, I made some rough calculations. In another hour or so, I'd be about five miles away. There, I'd wait till dark, and go again. The first opportunity I had, I would need to look for some food and water.

About an hour later, I found a spot with good concealment on the bank, pulled the canoe up and camouflaged it, and found some clean ground to stretch out on. The mosquitoes drove me crazy, but at least I was free. On top of that, I was getting closer to my Stella with every mile behind me. I knew I had a long night ahead, so I needed to sleep. I had about three hours before dusk, so this was prime time for a little nap, but my head was all over the place. If I kept following this river, it would flow into a bigger one. Eventually, I'd have to get off the river system and find a different way. At least I'd be far away by then. Hell, I didn't even know if Stella had made it to Spain yet. I wanted so badly to know that she was safe, but all I could do was hope for the best.

Suddenly, a noise interrupted my daydreams. *What was that?* I thought, straining to hear amid the birds chirping and the rustle of leaves in the light breeze. There it was again! Dogs! *Damn, I gotta go! No time to rest. I hope they don't think I'm on the river, or I'll be caught soon.* I rationalized with myself that it was probably just a general search pattern as they widened their net. I uncovered the canoe and shoved it in the river, hopping in as it floated, catching the gentle current. I paddled with long, hard, thrusts, picking up speed. It was critical to put distance between the hounds' noses and me.

It was soon dark, and I felt I was a comfortable distance away, so I slowed it down a bit. The river wasn't big, and I was going at a decent pace, around five miles per hour I guessed. Up ahead, I saw the outline of a house or cabin. No lights were on, so I wasn't sure if it was inhabited or not. I put the paddle deep into the water to stop the canoe, jumped out and pulled it up on the bank. Carefully, I approached from a corner. I glanced at my watch. 2330. Hopefully, if someone was there, they'd be asleep. Slowly, I checked the door. Unlocked. I opened it, being mindful of creaky hinges.

I found myself in the kitchen. Going through the cupboards, I found a few cans of something. I couldn't read the labels in the dark, but it seemed edible, so I slipped them in my pocket. Taking a couple of empty quart canning jars, I headed to the well and gave the handle a pump, thankful as water splattered everywhere. I held the jars underneath, filling them. I took a drink. The water was ice cold and tasted wonderful. I refilled the jar and placed the lid on top when I heard an engine. Boat! I ran out to the river and looked downstream. A searchlight bounced off the trees in the distance. I couldn't see the boat yet, but it was coming.

I grabbed the canoe and heaved it up on shore. There was a shallow depression about fifteen feet up, so I pulled it in there. Grabbing branches from the trees along the bank, I worked at a feverish pace to cover the canoe. The boat was now very close. I ran up and hid behind the house, praying the owner wouldn't wake up.

The boat slowed down and was barely moving when the searchlight played over the area, dancing between the house and trees, striking the house and twice hitting the canoe. Finally, the boat moved off and increased in speed. As the sound faded, I said to myself, "I'm not sure how much more of this my heart can take." Once I was satisfied the coast was clear, I went down to the river and dragged the canoe back into the water. Throwing my goodies in, I shoved off. I decided to wait to eat my mystery surprise until after I stopped for the morning.

Grandma coughed loudly, bringing me back to the dining room filled with relatives. "After he got off the river, he hitched a ride with a truck driver delivering a load of lumber to somewhere in Italy. From there, he stowed away on a cargo ship and crossed the Mediterranean. When he knocked on my sister's door, I couldn't believe it! My prayers had been answered! I remember the day like it was yesterday." Her eyes welled up as she thought about their reunion.

"So, that's the story. We kept the name as it appeared on his new ID and passport, figuring it must be a safe name. With a chance at a new life, my Heinz was afraid someone would find out he was a former SS officer. We didn't even want to think about what the repercussions would be.

"After a few months, my sister and her husband helped us pay for our fare to New York. We arrived weeks later, and within six months, moved here. The only one who knew anything about us before we lived here, besides Aunt Nora and Uncle Juan, was Karl." A sad moment filled the atmosphere. My dad's older brother, Karl, had passed away a year earlier, quite suddenly.

I raised my hand, as if I was in school, asking the teacher a question. I was happy to ask a direct question instead of all the guessing and surmising I had done in my research.

Grandma said, "Yes, Mike, what is it?"

"So, why did Grandpa Heinz want to keep his things from the war if he was ashamed of what he had done?"

"Your grandfather was ashamed of some of the things he was expected and ordered to do toward the end of the war, but he was still proud of his service and still proud of his German heritage. Besides, he was just like you, Mike, a history buff. He thought that history should be preserved; both the good and the bad. And he did not want to forget everything he had been through for us to be together and build the life we had here."

I had another question. "How did you get his things over here to America?"

"He had packed his things in the trunks we took with us when he sent us to Spain. He figured no one would thoroughly search a trunk that had a woman's undergarments or children's clothes and diapers."

My dad spoke up and asked what everyone else was thinking. "Mom, why are you telling us now? After all these years?"

Grandma looked at me and said, *"Kommen sie, Michael."*

I got to my feet and walked to her, keeping my eyes to the floor, nervous I was in big trouble.

She slid her arm around me and said, "Because my darling Michael made me realize it was time, and it was the right thing to do."

Shocked, I looked up her and saw a glow in her eyes.

"I'm thankful to have this over and to have no more secrets." She looked at my father. "With your permission, son, I'd like to give Mike your dad's things. I think he'd be a good steward of the history this family has to tell."

I couldn't believe my ears! "Really Grandma?" I asked.

She nodded approvingly at me.

Looking at my parents, I held my breath, waiting for their answer. Dad and Mom looked at each other, nodded, then nodded at me. I ran to them, giving them hugs.

Lots of excited chatter now filled the room as people continued asking questions, mostly things I already knew about Grandpa Heinz. Now, my question was, "Who helped him to escape?"

Grandma didn't have the answer to that and said she had always wondered that herself. I was intrigued and thought it was time for more research. I had come this far into the story, I might as well dig deeper. Maybe my other grandpa could help me, being as he was on the winning side, and from what I could tell, he had been directly involved with Grandpa Heinz at one point, at least. If nothing else, maybe he could give me a few clues to help me to find the answers I was looking for.

Grandma was getting a little tired of all the talk and endless questions, and we could all see it. Sometimes the same questions were being asked but in different ways by different people. Finally, the family began to leave until only my family remained. We started to put our shoes on when Grandma said, "Arnold, there are three boxes in my bedroom. Will you get those, please? Those are for Mike."

"Sure thing, Ma," he said. Moments later, he returned with a large box that was obviously heavy. "Ma? You sure there isn't an anti-tank weapon in here?"

She smiled and said, "Yes, I'm sure," and we all chuckled.

While Dad loaded the other two boxes in the car, I gave Grandma a long hug, and said, "Thank you, Grandma. Thank you for everything."

"You're welcome, *mein schatz*, Michael. Take good care of it, *bitte*."

I assured her I would and ran to the car. I couldn't wait to get home now.

The ride home seemed to last forever. It was just like Christmas morning when you tried to be patient and wait to open your presents. Dad unloaded the boxes, setting them on the kitchen table. He opened the heaviest one first. It contained a helmet, canteen, gas mask, and leather satchel that had seen better days. Dad's face was like mine, a kid in a candy store.

"I can't believe I've never seen this stuff," he said. "I had no idea, Mike. My dad never wanted to talk about the war. I guess now I know why."

He opened the second box. It held two uniforms, neatly folded. A dress uniform with the pretty silver braided patches, and the cuff title, Das Reich, sewn on the left sleeve. Then a combat uniform, in a camouflage pattern. I knew that they were the only military force at that time to have camo uniforms. They were well ahead of their time. On the top, lay an officer's crush cap and a pair of deep black polished boots that were still shiny.

The third box was much smaller. It had a couple of notebooks, some pictures I hadn't seen before, the *Soldbuch*, the medals, and other awards in it. I spied the ring and grabbed it, slipping it on my finger.

"What's that?" Dad asked.

I told him it was Grandpa's Totenkopf ring. He looked at me quizzically, so I schooled him on the history of the ring.

Dad took a very keen interest in everything now. "Wow," he said, "you've really been working hard on this, haven't you?"

I smiled, feeling proud of what I had learned through my research. One thing concerned me. "Dad, where's the Luger?"

"I have the pistol, Mike. Your grandma gave that to me when you were already in the car. She didn't know anything about it or how it worked so she didn't want to mess with it and thought an adult should handle it. Sometime, we'll go shoot it, but not today." It was as if he had anticipated my next question.

"Okay, Dad," I said. "When will that be?"

He smiled and said, "Be patient, Mike. Don't worry. It's not going anywhere."

"Can I hang the uniforms in my closet?"

"Your mother will have to give permission for that one, son."

Mom didn't like the idea of Nazi stuff anywhere, let alone my closet. She sat down on a kitchen chair and took me by the hands, pulling me closer to her so she could look me in the eyes before she spoke. "I'm going to let you, Mike, because I know how important this is to you. I understand this is family history, but it's important you

281

don't forget the bigger picture and always remember how terrible that ideology was."

"I know, Mom," I said, getting exasperated with this discussion. After all, I probably knew more about this subject than she did!

I hung the uniforms neatly in my closet and sat on the edge of my bed thinking how cool they looked hanging there. I pictured my Grandpa Heinz seeing the same thing thirty-five years ago, only without a ten-year-old's clothes hanging next to them. I really wanted to build a display for all these things. I thought of my other grandpa. He had always been good at working with wood. Maybe he would help me. I could hang the medals he'd given me with the German ones and let the display tell the story. But before I could ask him for help, I would have to tell him about the hidden family history. I worried that he would be angry about me having things that represented everything he fought against. I feared he would talk my mom into disposing of it all. And, of course, I didn't want to cause any rift in our relationship.

I hollered downstairs, "Mom? Could you come up here, please?"

She came over and sat next to me on the bed and eyed the closet. "Wow!" she said. "I think that's the cleanest I've ever seen that closet," she laughed.

I gave a slight smile, and said, "How do you think Grandpa will take this?"

"What do you mean, Mike? Are you worried he'll be upset about you having these things?"

I nodded.

"I don't think you need to be concerned about that, honey. Grandpa loves you a whole lot, and he will understand that what happened was a long time ago and you were not involved. He will understand that this is history, just like the medals he gave you that were his."

I nodded. I knew she was right, but it felt good to hear it out loud.

"But, Mike... I'd like to be the one to tell him about all of this, so don't say anything yet, please."

"Okay, Mom," I said. "Thanks. I feel better."

At dinner, the new family information was all we could talk about. Dad was still in shock. He and Mom discussed changing our name back to the original but didn't settle on it. There was a lot to think about and that would be a really big deal. I, for one, was all for it.

That night, just before I turned off my light, I took one last look at my open closet door and the hanging uniforms.

Pretty cool, I thought.

The next Sunday, Mom woke me up saying, "Time to get up for church. We're a bit behind, so don't take too long."

Groggy as usual, I grumbled and stretched. I put on my dress clothes, and on my way out of my room, my eyes fell on Grandpa's honor ring. I slipped it on my middle finger, but of course, it was too big. Nonetheless, I looked at myself in the mirror, put my hand on my chest, and admired how the ring stood out against my white dress shirt. I decided I wanted the ring with me, so I put it on a chain and slipped it around my neck before heading downstairs. Mom and Dad didn't even notice my extra embellishment, as they were rushing to get out the door.

Still feeling sleepy, I closed my eyes as we drove. I thought of Grandpa Heinz and wished I had been able to get to know him better. *I'll bet he had some amazing stories to tell of his harrowing escape from the German Army!* I thought.

The church bells weren't ringing as we pulled up to the church, so the service hadn't started yet, but we were still late enough that we found our usual seats taken. I chuckled to myself, "Don't people know those seats belong to us?" Taking seats a few rows closer to the front, we had just enough time to get a program from the usher before the bells began to toll and the organ music swelled. Everyone rose to their feet to sing the first hymn.

As per my typical routine, I spent most of the service daydreaming, although the hour went by quickly. As we shuffled to the back of the church, Mom took me by the shoulders and pointed me in the direction of the basement stairs and said, "We'll be here to pick you up after Sunday school." I knew it was pointless to try to get out of it again, so I didn't even try.

The class was smaller than normal, and a few minutes later, the senior pastor arrived. He said, "Good morning, kids. Your regular teacher isn't here today, so I'll be filling in for her."

A faint groan could be heard in the room from a few of the older students. The pastor was a bit dry in his sermons, and his classes were equally as dull. He handed out several sheets of paper with drawings depicting a story in the Bible for us to follow along while he read. He read a few sentences and looked at me in the front row and dropped his book on the floor. *Smack!* "What is that, Mr. Schmidt?" he asked, pointing to my necklace.

"It's an honor ring, Sir," I said, simply.

"I know what it is, Mr. Schmidt." His face turned red. "Stand up, please."

Nervously, I rose, standing on shaky legs, not knowing what was about to happen. I could tell he wasn't happy, but I wasn't sure why.

"The people who wore those did the devil's bidding, Michael," he growled. "They were criminals, one and all!" He pointed toward the other students. "Turn and face the class."

Hot tears welled up in my eyes as I turned around slowly, not only embarrassed and hurt, but confused.

"Remove it now!" he said.

I reached up and slipped it over my head. The pastor stepped to my side and slapped my hand down, the ring dropping from my hand and clanging to the floor.

Bouncing several times, it rolled under a nearby radiator. I stood there, doing my ultimate best to suppress my feelings. I placed my hands in my pockets, wishing my grandpa was here to straighten him out.

"You will not wear that evil talisman here ever again! Am I understood?"

"Yes, Sir," I said, half-heartedly, thinking that not only did I know more about the ring than him, I was certain I knew more about WWII than he did. Who was he to lecture me on stuff?

"Now, go sit down, Mike."

I went to retrieve my ring.

The pastor said, "I told you to sit down, not to go pick up that junk!"

I slowed my steps momentarily but continued over to the radiator, knelt, picked up the ring and crammed it in my pocket. I looked him right in the eyes and deliberately walked toward the classroom door. He began to move toward me. I ran the last few steps to the door, twisted the knob, and got the door open about six inches and then *bam!* The door slammed shut before I could get out, the pastor now leaning against it. "Go sit in the corner, Michael," he said, pointing to the naughty desk. "We'll talk after class."

I walked to the designated desk among a sea of wide-eyed students, shocked at what they had just witnessed. I sat there, staring at the wall with the old green paint chipping off. Like the Rorschach test, I imagined designs in the paint where the cracks had formed.

When class ended, and everyone left, the pastor came over and said, "I think we'll have a talk about your insubordination when your parents get here."

I didn't like hearing that. I knew my dad, especially, wouldn't be happy, and not only would I be grounded, but I was concerned he'd take my newly acquired things away from me. Maybe even for good. So, I grasped for a straw.

"Yes, that's fine," I said. "But you should know that ring belonged to my grandpa, Heinz Schmidt. The same man who belonged to this church for decades and my grandma still belongs here. My grandpa went through a lot to get this ring and then he deserted because he couldn't stand the war anymore. You can talk to my grandma. She'll tell you the whole story." I had been talking fast, worried he might interrupt me. Now, I took a deep breath.

The pastor looked surprised. "So, your parents know you have this thing?"

"Yes," I said.

He looked dejected, knowing he had lost this one. "Okay, just don't wear that thing here again and I'll forgive you. You can leave."

Not saying another word, I got up and walked out the door. I didn't know where those words had come from or where I found the courage to say them, but I was relieved that it had worked. Once in the hallway, I took off running, wanting to get away from him as fast as possible. I let the pent-up tears come then.

I slowed down before reaching the front doors and wiped my eyes with both hands. Mom and Dad were waiting for me in the car. I tried to hide that I had been crying as I got in.

Mom said, "What took you so long?"

"Nothing," I said, with a shaky voice.

She quickly turned in her seat. "You've been crying! What happened"? she asked.

"I slipped on the basement steps and hurt my knee."

"Oh, poor baby!" she said. "Pull up your pant leg and let me see."

"No, Mom, I'm okay, really."

"Are you sure?" she asked.

Before I could reassure her any more, Dad said, "He's a boy. He'll be fine," as he pulled the car away from the curb.

CHAPTER FIFTEEN

It had been over a week since Grandma's big reveal to the family. It was Thursday, and Grandpa was coming over to fly the Mustang. I was up early and thinking of ways I could tell Grandpa the truth about my Grandpa Heinz without causing a heart attack. Mom told me she hadn't had a chance to talk to Grandpa herself about the news, so if it came up while we were together, I was allowed to discuss it with him and that she trusted me to handle it. Dad said he had too much work to do around the house, so he wouldn't be joining us. I suspect that was his excuse to leave us alone, knowing this subject might come up, and he was probably thinking Grandpa wouldn't want to look at the son of a German SS officer.

I went through the motions of my usual summer morning routine, breakfast and TV, although I couldn't recall a single thing I watched. I was too busy devising a plan in my head. I went back and forth with myself whether I should just tell him what I knew, or if I should I ask pointed questions and see if he told me stuff that coincided with what I already knew. I had thought of several questions, so I decided I'd ask those first. Depending on his answers, I could tell him what I knew.

At 10:00 am, I heard his car pull into the driveway and ran upstairs to get dressed. Mom met him at the door and I heard him ask if I was ready. She said I'd be down in a minute, then said, "So this is the big day, huh?"

Grandpa said, "Yes, but I'm worried my pilot skills may be a bit rusty," and they both chuckled.

I bounced down the stairs and into Grandpa's arms.

"There's my boy!" he said. "Whoa, slow down there, champ!"

"I'm just really excited!" I said, jumping a little bit.

"Okay, get the plane and transmitter, and we'll get going."

"Almost forgot that," I said, laughing as I ran upstairs to grab them. I blew past them when I came back through the kitchen. "C'mon, Grandpa, let's go!" I held the door open for him with my leg while delicately holding the plane in my hands.

"I think he's in a hurry," Mom laughed. "We'll talk later, Dad."

"Yes, we better get going! We have bombers to escort, you know," he said, amused.

We headed to a large field only four blocks from home. I hopped out and stood by the trunk, trying to be patient as Grandpa got out our beautiful handiwork. The sun was shining bright, not a cloud to be seen, and just a slight breeze. This was a good day for flying.

Grandpa handed me the plane while he took the remote and a bottle of fuel for the engine. The field where we parked was at the bottom of the hill, and it was going to take us several minutes to get to a spot away from any obstacles, so I decided now was a good time to start with questions.

"Where were you at the end of the war?" I asked.

Grandpa said, "I was en-route to Japan when hostilities ended."

"No, I mean when Germany surrendered," I clarified.

"I was just outside Hanover," he said.

I was in shock, my knees almost giving out. "What?"

"In Hanover, Mike, that's a little town—"

I interrupted him. "I know where it is, Grandpa, I just..." I stopped short. *Not yet,* I told myself.

"You just what?" he asked.

"I just didn't hear you."

We stopped on an oval running track; the hard-packed small gravel would be a good spot for the Mustang to take off.

"So, do you hate Germans?" I asked, expecting to hear Mrs. Graham's voice in my head.

"I don't hate them, Mike. Those soldiers had a job to do, just like I did. It wasn't personal. Both sides fought for their own countries. They fought just as hard for Germany as we did for America. And sometimes, we could look each other in the eye and see just a fellow human being. Like the time that a German soldier actually helped me care for a wounded guy in my platoon."

My interest piqued. He was now putting gas in the airplane, and I was afraid he wouldn't keep going with the story. "Oh, what happened?" I asked.

"It was toward the end of the war, April, I think. I was following a squad from my platoon as we were clearing Hanover of Nazis. The three guys in front of me rounded a corner of a building and a gunfight ensued. The first two guys were shot and killed immediately, the third man was wounded by a German grenade. By the time I got there and looked around the corner, they had left. So, I ripped off my pack and started putting pressure bandages on his wounds from the shrapnel, trying to save his life."

I was so excited, I hardly let Grandpa take a breath before saying, "Then what?"

"I made a big mistake. I was so focused on stopping the bleeding from my patient's wound, I wasn't thinking, and I had my back to the enemy. A German soldier snuck up behind me and pressed his gun to my head. Because I was a medic, I fully expected to die right there and then. He gestured for me to get up, only I decided if I was going to die, it would be trying to save this man's life."

My heart raced as Grandpa told his story.

"But he didn't shoot me! Instead, he let me finish packing my guy's wound, and when I stood up and turned to face him, I realized the man was an SS officer! They were known to be brutal and heartless. I was terrified!"

I started to piece things together in my head. I couldn't believe I was now hearing this story from the other side. "What was his rank? Do you remember?"

Grandpa was engrossed in telling the story and didn't seem to think my question was odd. "I do, vividly," he said. "He was a captain. His uniform was filthy and tattered. I could tell he had been struggling just to survive by the disheveled way he looked. Suddenly, he placed his gun back in his holster and then he did something remarkable. He actually helped me carry the wounded man back to my unit. Of course, he was promptly disarmed and taken prisoner. But I was so moved by this man's actions that it left a lasting impression on me. It restored my faith in humanity, you might say."

I still wanted to press for more information. "So, what ended up happening to him?" I asked.

Grandpa stopped what he was doing and motioned for me to sit down.

I sat cross-legged in front of him as he spoke.

"What I'm going to tell you, Mike, is something I've never spoken of." He paused and looked me in the eyes, showing me just how serious this was. "Do you remember me talking about Corporal Dawson?"

"Yes," I said. "The one who wanted to run the restaurants, right?"

"Yes, that's right. He was the one who was wounded by the grenade and the German helped me carry him back to camp. He had connections in the intelligence community. Plus, his father was a politician in Washington, so I asked him for a favor. And with some

293

behind-the-scenes, underground work, the captain's release was arranged."

"They just let him go?" I asked.

"Not exactly," he said. "They made a fake ID and passport for him. Someone put together a package of civilian clothes and other necessities and left it hidden in a remote spot for him to pick up. I had his Luger from when he was captured, so that was my contribution to the package. It was the unit policy that anyone who brought in a prisoner could take what they wanted as a trophy, so I took his gun. I had thought it would be a good souvenir, the gun that could have taken my life, and didn't. But it felt better to give it back to its rightful owner, as kind of a 'thank you' for not using the gun on me."

I could hardly breathe. I knew this was my grandpa Heinz! It matched exactly with the story that Grandma had told the family. This was amazing! I knew in my bones that there had been some connection between my grandfathers, but to know that my American grandpa had played a part in my German grandpa escaping, and ultimately coming to the United States was fascinating! And for their children to meet and end up married? Unheard of. That was quite a tale!

I knew enough, but Grandpa kept going, and everything he said confirmed I was right.

"I'm not really sure what happened to him. I know he was taken out of camp. The guard said he got a flat tire, and when he got out to fix it, the captain made a run for it. He was eventually tracked to the river, but they lost his trail. They never did find him, as far as I know."

"Weren't you afraid of getting caught and being arrested for helping plan his escape? Wouldn't that be considered treason?" I asked.

"I suppose I could've gotten into huge trouble. But I only asked Dawson if he could help. He knew he owed me for saving his life and the German too. After all, he could have killed Dawson just as easily as me that day and didn't. I hadn't considered the ramifications of being caught at the time. I only wanted better treatment for him. I didn't ask for his escape. And technically, I didn't help him escape, although I did conceal information, I suppose. Anyway, I figured what harm could it do? He was only a captain, and Germany had already surrendered. It wasn't until afterward I learned of the concentration camps. I hope he wasn't a part of that, otherwise, I guess I'll have to answer to God for it. But, again, this man could've killed us, and instead, he helped us, knowing he would be captured. I couldn't see him as an SS, let alone a mass murderer. It's like I was saying, Mike, we were just fellow human beings that day." With that, Grandpa rose to his feet and bent over the Mustang. "Now, let's fly this thing, what do you say?"

I said, "Okay," knowing I had heard enough. I wondered how to tell Grandpa what I knew and how everything was connected.

He turned on the transmitter and gave the propeller a flip. The engine sputtered and died. He again gave it a fling, and the little engine came to life. We walked back about fifteen feet and Grandpa said, "Here we go," giving it full throttle. The plane bounced down the track a few feet before getting airborne and gaining altitude. The plane looked impressive. He performed some basic maneuvers while he adjusted the trim settings. He made it look easy and smooth. I thought Grandpa was a professional pilot. In my mind, though, he could do no wrong. We discussed flight characteristics for about ten minutes while he flew in large circles. Bringing it into land was a little tougher, and the plane bounced a few times before ending up in a nose plant on the gravel, the propeller coming to an instant stop. We walked over and straightened it up, setting it back on its wheels. Grandpa took the fuel container out and refilled the reservoir.

I started in again with questions. "Grandpa, do you know what his name was on his new ID?"

"No, I don't. I was never told any real information. I suppose they thought I might jeopardize everything if I was questioned."

He started the engine up again, pausing any more talk. We stepped back, and soon, the little plane was airborne once more. He performed some stunning maneuvers. I couldn't take my eyes off the plane. A few rolls and loops, followed by a vertical climb and stall, then recovering. He asked me if I wanted to try it and learn. I told him no as I wasn't ready yet. I was content just watching for now.

Grandpa was in serious concentration, beginning another fancy flying trick, when I blurted out, "Have you ever heard the name Dirden?"

He dropped the transmitter like someone had kicked him in the gut, the battery cover popping off and the batteries falling out on the ground.

I pointed to the transmitter, hollering, "Grandpa! The plane!"

He just stared at me, eyes wide. With no one controlling it now, the Mustang went into a dive. I watched in horror as it made a beeline for the ground. *Smash!* Parts flew in all directions. There was a deafening silence.

Grandpa hardly seemed to notice that the plane went down. He didn't even turn his head to see where it had crashed. "Where did you hear that name?" he asked. He sounded out of breath, even though we hadn't done anything strenuous.

I started walking to where the plane lay in pieces. I was so sad, I began to cry. *Why couldn't I just keep my mouth shut?* I thought. I dropped to my knees, gathering the pieces, sobbing while I piled it all up. I knew it was beyond repair.

Grandpa came and stood behind me. Placing both hands on my shoulders, he said, "Mike, I'll buy you a new one, and we'll put it together again. Don't worry about the plane, please. Just tell me how you know that name."

I was crying too hard to speak.

After a few seconds, he said, "Look, let's go get something to eat. You can gather your thoughts and calm down. Then, we'll talk."

Still crying, I nodded. We gathered up the pieces we thought we could salvage. On the walk to the car, I finally quit crying and asked, "Where are we going to eat?"

"I think we'll go load up on pancakes. How's that sound?"

I said, "Good," and tried to smile.

"The hobby store is right across the street from the pancake house. Maybe we'll run in there after we eat."

That made me feel a little better.

We put the shattered airplane and transmitter in the trunk and got in. As we pulled out of the parking lot, I asked Grandpa why he got so upset about that name.

"Because that was the German captain's name that I was just telling you about! The one who helped me when Dawson was wounded. The one I helped to escape."

"So, you never actually knew him?" I asked.

"I never met the man before or after that fateful day in April." He stopped at a red light before turning onto the frontage road where the restaurant was. He ignored the "right on red" rule, kept the car still, and turned to look at me. "Can you tell me how you know that name?"

I swallowed hard, my mouth dry. "He was my other grandpa."

"Arnold's father?" he blurted out. He turned his eyes back to the road and made his right-hand turn.

We sat in silence the remainder of the drive to the restaurant. Grandpa hardly blinked, obviously trying to process this, and it wasn't until we were getting out of the car that Grandpa spoke again.

"How did you find this out, Mike?"

"I found a bunch of pictures, letters, and a journal in my grandma's attic," I told him.

Grandpa held the door open for me, ushering me into the diner.

"Grandma found out that I knew and decided to tell the whole family the truth. She got everyone together about a week ago."

A waitress took us to our table, gave us menus and water, and left to give us time to decide what to order.

Grandpa nodded at me and simply said, "Go on, Mike."

"I just pieced everything together, I guess, and realized that you knew each other," I said, making it sound simpler than it really had been.

"Wow!" he said, shaking his head.

"But, there's more," I said. "I think he was in the pillbox, fighting opposite you on D-Day." Grandpa grabbed his chest in shock, but I kept talking. "One of his letters talked about trying to direct a machine gunner to hit this medic but the American seemed like he had an angel protecting him, or something to that effect. He even describes your friend being hit. He wrote back to my grandma about you."

"That's a lot to digest right now," he said. "I never thought I'd hear that name again, but to think that my own daughter married his son! It's unbelievable!"

"Didn't you two meet or talk after my mom and dad got married?" I asked.

Grandpa said, "I never met the man. I always thought it was funny that he never wanted to meet me. Now it makes sense, I guess. On your parents' wedding day, he had to work, supposedly. Then, when you were born, we always seemed to miss each other at the hospital."

"But why wouldn't he want to see you?" I asked. "That doesn't make sense."

"It could have been any number of reasons, Mike. Could be, he was embarrassed. Maybe he still felt guilty for the things he'd done. Or maybe he was scared. Maybe he thought if I found out he was here, I'd turn him in. After all, he might not have even known that I had something to do with his release." Grandpa spoke as if he was talking to himself more than to me. "I wish I had known all this before he passed away, though. I would've worked harder to try talking to him. I think, deep down, he was a good man but got caught up in a conflict he wanted nothing to do with and was lied to. I think he realized that even before our paths crossed."

The waitress returned, and we ordered our food.

After she left, Grandpa looked at me and said, "Mike, you know I'm not mad at you, don't you?"

"Yes, I know," I said.

"And you know I love you, right?"

"Of course, Grandpa."

"What a small world!" Grandpa said, shaking his head, his mind still trying to grasp what I had revealed. "Do your mom and dad know?" he asked.

"They know a little about his service and Grandma explained how he escaped, but nothing else. Grandma has no idea that you were a part of that. I wasn't even sure until I heard the stuff you told me today."

Our plates arrived, full of pancakes, and we spent a few silent minutes just savoring our food.

"I think it's time we talk about this with the family. Get everything out on the table. No more secrets," Grandpa said.

My mouth was stuffed with soggy blueberry pancakes, but I nodded in agreement.

As he promised, we went to the hobby store afterward and ordered a new Mustang. While driving home, Grandpa said he was sorry for crashing the plane. I told him it was okay and that building another one would just give us more time together.

Mom was standing in the doorway when we drove in. "How did it go?" she asked anxiously. The looks on our faces told the story. She said, "Uh oh... that doesn't look good," watching Grandpa take out the box of what was now nothing more than parts and pieces.

He said, "We had a bit of a mishap."

"I see that," she said. "Are you okay, Mike?"

"I'm fine, Mom," I assured her. "Grandpa ordered a new plane. We'll build it and make it even better. You should have seen him though! It was so cool! Grandpa was doing all kinds of crazy things with it."

"Then what happened?" Mom asked.

I looked up at Grandpa.

"I'll tell you," he said to Mom. "Let's go in the house." He sat down at the table, asked for a glass of water and asked, "Where's Arnold?"

Mom said, "He's out in the garden. Why? What's wrong?"

Grandpa said, "I'll tell you in a minute," and told me to go get my dad.

I ran halfway to the garden and yelled, "Dad, Grandpa needs you in the kitchen for a minute." I ran back in the house and took a seat next to Grandpa.

Dad walked in moments later and noticed the worried look on Mom's face. "What's going on?" he asked.

Grandpa cleared his throat. "It's about time I fill you in on some things."

Mom and Dad looked at each other and Mom said, "You're not sick, are you?"

Grandpa replied, "No, I'm not sick."

Dad said, with sarcasm, "I suppose you're going to tell us you were a secret agent during WWII?"

"No, I'm not," he said, "but it is regarding the war and some things you are not aware of."

Dad looked at Mom again. "What is going on? I'm starting to wonder what is real anymore!"

I was so excited my legs were shaking.

"Mike is quite the investigator, it seems," said Grandpa.

Mom and Dad both looked at me. I tried to look innocent when Dad asked me, "Now what have you gotten into? I hope this isn't more Nazi stuff."

Grandpa asked, "Shall I begin?" and we all turned our attention to him as he took a sip of water.

CHAPTER SIXTEEN

Grandpa told an abbreviated version of the D-Day landing and then went into much more detail about the escape. Dad and Mom were shocked and speechless. They looked at each other, trying to comprehend what they had just heard. There was nervous laughter from everyone in the kitchen.

Mom was the first to speak, putting her hand on my dad's arm. "Just think, Arnold. Our families have a much deeper connection than just you and I being married!"

Dad shook his head. "What are the odds?"

"About a hundred million to one!" Grandpa said. "I'm trying to wrap my head around it still."

Dad turned to me. "So, Mike," he said, "you uncovered all of this?"

Proud of myself, I held my head a little higher and said, "Yes, I did."

Mom said, "So all this time you spent in your room was digging up facts?"

I nodded, grinning from ear to ear, and Grandpa put his hand around my shoulder and pulled me to him. "He's an amazing young man," he said. "Maybe he's got a career in investigation ahead of him!" He looked at my dad. "On a more serious note, Arnold, do you mind if I talk to your mother about this?"

"Of course not! After all, it's about time we get some closure on this and get us all on the same page of our history."

"Talking in person would be better than over the phone, I think. Would you come with me to talk to her?"

"Absolutely," Dad said.

Mom nodded her agreement.

"Can I come too?" I asked.

Grandpa said, "I wouldn't have it any other way, Mike."

Grandpa stayed for dinner that night and we all relaxed in the living room afterward talking about "what if" situations. What if my two grandfathers had met and gotten to know each other here in the States? What if Grandpa Harper had not helped set Grandpa Heinz's escape in motion? There were some somber moments thinking of scenarios that might not have had such a positive outcome.

Grandpa sat in the big rocker recliner with a sleeping Aaron on his chest.

Mom picked the baby up and said, "It's this little guy's bedtime." She looked at me, sitting curled up on the couch, and said, "You too, Michael. It's been a big day."

I didn't argue. I hugged Grandpa goodbye and followed her to the stairs.

She turned around to face us all and said, "You know what I think I am most thankful for? That Aaron will be able to grow up knowing our whole history. Nothing hidden. He'll be able to see how tightly woven our family is." She reached for me with the arm that wasn't holding the baby and hugged me to her.

Dad nodded and said, "You've done a great service to this family, Mike."

Grandpa said, "Your folks are right, and I'm proud of you."

I smiled, thinking this was a great day, despite losing the Mustang. I went to sleep that night with the smile still on my face.

The next day, my waking thought was, "I've gotta talk to Andy!" There was so much to tell him now. I ate breakfast, watching the clock. Phone calls were not allowed before 9:00 am. I paced my mouthfuls of cereal so that I was finished right at 9:00 o'clock. I put my bowl in the sink and grabbed the phone.

Mrs. Petrovski answered and called for Andy once she heard it was me. I told him I had a million things to tell him and asked if we could meet at the pond.

He said, "Sure, but give me about fifteen minutes. I have to finish cleaning my room."

"Great," I said. "I'll meet you down there."

I went to the living room where Mom was folding laundry on the couch next to Aaron in his little jumping seat.

"I'm going to meet up with Andy, Okay?"

"That's fine, Mike, but be home for lunch because you really need to cut the grass this afternoon."

"Sure, Mom," I answered and bolted out the door, so excited that I forgot my favorite baseball cap.

I got to the pond before Andy and started poking around, looking for frogs or snakes.

When he arrived, he asked, "So what's going on, dude?"

For the next hour, I told him all the new information I had learned about my American grandpa on the beaches of Normandy, my German grandpa being an SS Captain in the Das Reich division, my grandfathers facing each other on the beach, one taking the other prisoner many months later, and finally, helping that same one escape. I also told him about the incident with my angry pastor and how I had felt.

Andy was shocked that so much had happened since we'd last talked. "That's unbelievable, man! So, what happens next?"

"All I know is that Grandpa wants to meet with my grandma to tell her he knew my Grandpa Heinz in Germany and that he was the one who put in motion the plans for him to escape. He said I can come with for that, so it should be pretty cool to see my grandma's reaction."

Talking about my grandma reminded me I hadn't talked to Andy since his grandma had passed, so I asked him about it, and he shared what the funeral was like and how much he missed her.

I said I had to get home for lunch and chores, so we gave each other a jab in the arm and said "you hit like a girl" in unison. We laughed and left with smiles on our faces.

I was a few houses from home when I saw Grandpa's car in the driveway. It wasn't his normal day to visit, so I was curious and excited to see why he had come. I walked in the house, expecting to see my new airplane, thinking maybe it had come in early and Grandpa had brought it right over.

Instead, Mom said, "Get ready to go, please. Your grandpa is taking us out to lunch and we're picking up Grandma."

"Really?" I asked. I hadn't expected this to happen so quickly. Immediately, I felt the butterflies in my stomach from the anticipation and excitement.

As we buckled up in Grandpa's car with Mom, baby Aaron, and me, I realized Dad was missing. I felt sorry he had to work and miss out on the fun.

Driving at Grandpa's speed, the trip to Grandma's took us a bit longer than usual. She greeted us at the door, wiping her hands on a dishtowel.

"I'm just finishing up. Come in, please."

We followed her into the kitchen where she and Grandpa exchanged pleasantries while she removed her apron, hung it up on a hook by the stove, and laid the dishtowel out to dry. She announced that she was ready to go, and we filed back out of the kitchen.

"I just need to grab my purse," she said, reaching for it hanging from the doorknob.

Grandma sat in the front seat now, and Mom sat in the back with Aaron and me. The grown-ups discussed where to go and decided on a steakhouse, which was Grandma's favorite. I jumped out of the car first and ran to open Grandma's door for her, then ran ahead to hold the door to the restaurant open for everyone. "What a gentleman!" they all said, but I was really just trying to hurry everything along.

There was small talk at our table, in and around the waitress coming, and mostly between Grandpa and Grandma, but occasionally Mom would contribute. I sat quietly, waiting for the "good" conversation. Grandpa commented that he liked the restaurant.

"This was a favorite of Heinz's," Grandma said. "We would take the boys here a couple times a month. I swear it was the only time they ever got full." She chuckled.

By the time our food arrived, Grandpa was asking about Grandpa Heinz and what he liked to do. Grandma described his love of pheasant hunting, of fishing with the boys, and how boxing and baseball were his favorite sports. Suddenly, she stopped eating, quietly put down her silverware on her plate, and leaned in toward Grandpa. "I know you must be aware of the family secret that Michael uncovered about Heinz, and I know you must have other questions about him." She raised her chin a bit as if to portray that she was determined not to be afraid or ashamed of the past any longer.

Just then, the waitress came to check on our table and waylaid a response from Grandpa.

When she left, Grandpa looked at me, and looked to Grandma. "Do you have any idea why Heinz never wanted to meet me?"

Grandma seemed a little surprised by the question and just shrugged. "He never did say. I don't think it was anything personal. He was just a really shy person, and he took a long time to let anyone in."

"Well," Grandpa said, "I've got an idea of my own."

"Oh?" she responded, puzzled.

"Stella, I was partially responsible for his escape."

Grandma's mouth opened, but nothing came out. She took a few shaky breaths and finally got out, "What... How?"

Grandpa reached over to put his hand over hers and began to tell his side of the story just as he had told Mom and Dad. "I think he knew who I was but didn't realize I had helped him. Instead, I think he was afraid I'd recognize him and turn him in." He nodded in my direction and said, "Michael's the one who figured out that our stories meshed."

Grandma turned to me, tears welling in her eyes. "My Michael. You've been quite the detective. Even more than I realized." She turned back to Grandpa. "And how can my family ever thank you?"

He smiled and said, "I think in light of everything, your family are my family and my family is your family, don't you think? That is thanks enough for me."

She smiled. "I'd like to invite you to church with us on Sunday and to the house for coffee cake with the family after church."

"I would be honored, Stella."

CHAPTER SEVENTEEN

I was awake early on Sunday morning. It would be an exciting day. Grandpa was on his way over, and we would all go to church together. Afterward, he would come with us to Grandma's house to visit with the rest of the family and to reintroduce him, as it were, since none of them had seen him since Mom and Dad's wedding, some thirteen years ago. And, of course, to share this new information and answer any questions.

I sat outside with Dad while he had a cup of coffee and a cigarette, waiting for Grandpa to come. Dad and I both wore suits, and as Grandpa pulled up and got out of his car, I saw he was wearing a suit as well, which was rare for him. Now, this really felt like a special occasion.

We were unusually early for church. Mom led us up to the front, and we slid into the pew behind Uncle Don, but Grandma wasn't there. Dad leaned forward to ask Uncle Don where she was. Just then, she appeared from behind the altar where the pastor's office was and walked to the pew in front of us. Before sitting down, Grandma turned around and shook Grandpa's hand, saying, "It's so nice you could be here today." He repeated her sentiments with a warm smile. She motioned for me to come closer, grabbed me by the back of my neck, pulled me to her and kissed me on the forehead. "Everything is alright now, Michael," she said. I had no time to respond as the organ music crescendoed, and everyone rose to their feet. I was not sure what she was referring to until the senior pastor began his sermon.

My skin prickled at the sound of his voice, initially, as I remembered our last encounter and his anger at the sight of the ring belonging to Grandpa Heinz. But he spoke in a different tone today. He began by talking about illusions and seeing things in a different light. That not everything was as it appears. Sometimes, a little more digging is required for a more accurate picture, he said. Occasionally, he looked right at me and I knew he was referring to the incident with me. He talked about how some people saw Jesus that way but did not understand the whole picture. He admitted that he, too, had recently made a mistake and overreacted to something when he didn't have all the facts about it, and once he was informed of the whole situation, he realized he was wrong. He said, "I only hope that the person I have wronged can forgive me." Again, he looked right at me. I smiled, realizing this is what Grandma was talking about. The pastor had done as I had suggested and talked to Grandma about Grandpa Heinz. It felt good that maybe I had helped to open someone else's eyes and given them a better understanding.

The remaining service went well, and we were ushered outside quickly afterward. Grandpa, Mom, and I mingled with other parishioners while Dad went to get the car, and I introduced Grandpa to everyone I knew, as if it was show and tell at school.

We dawdled so long at the church, I thought for sure we would be the last ones to get to Grandma's house, but as we drove up, there were still family members pulling up to park behind us. I guessed this would be the largest crowd Grandma had, ever.

We walked in the house, and Grandpa found a seat near the coffee cake. Grandma said, "Help yourself," while she placed the paper plates on the table along with several knives for the butter. The coffee cake was cut already, so Grandpa took two pieces and buttered them both. I grabbed a seat next to him and followed suit. After everyone had eaten and had their coffee, Grandma asked everyone to gather in the dining room again. Grandpa and I were already at the far end of the table, and people filled in around us, some standing when there were no chairs left.

When Grandma said, "Can I have everyone's attention, please?" the room became quiet instantly. "So, most of you have now had a chance to meet and talk with Dave by now. For those of you who haven't, this is Sherry's dad." She extended her left arm in his direction. "I've asked you all here today because there is more light to be shed on the recent revelations involving this family. So, with that, I'll turn it over to him."

He stood up and said, "Hello, everyone." Several murmured "hello" or "good morning." He spent the next thirty minutes or so telling everyone his background and about his time in the service, what he did, and what happened when he was in Germany. He went into detail about the incident in which he met Grandpa Heinz, his capture, his subsequent questioning, and his miraculous escape. The family listened intently as if they were watching a gripping movie.

"And now, I have even more information. Something no one knows about." He looked down at me. "Not even you, Mike."

"What?" I said. "I thought I knew everything!"

Everyone chuckled at that.

Looking at everyone around the table, Grandpa continued. "After having lunch with Stella, the other day," he paused, "I called my buddy, Bill, in Texas. He was one of the people who had helped in this operation. I asked him, since it had now been over thirty years, if he could tell me the name that was put on the ID and passport of the prisoner. He confirmed that it was, in fact, Schmidt."

There were several audible gasps around the room. Chatter began as the news sunk in and my dad's younger siblings, ones who had been born in America, realized that they wouldn't be here at all if it weren't for this man who had helped their father escape. Many people began to stand and shake Grandpa's hand, saying, "Thank you."

The overwhelming atmosphere took hold of Grandpa and he started to cry. My mom, dad, and grandma rushed to his side, asking if he was okay.

He said, "These are tears of joy. I'm happy I could help him, to have helped this family. Because I did, I have the wonderful grandson I have today." To Grandma, he said, "I really do wish I could have met Heinz under better conditions." He turned again to address the rest of the family. "As soon as I realized he could have killed me, and didn't, I knew he was a decent man." He sat down again in his chair, as though exhausted, but continued to speak. "I felt bad for the German people. Once they figured out Hitler was a bad apple, removing him wasn't so easy."

Grandma nodded. "We voted for him! The communists were the only other real choice, and they were even worse. That's what we thought at that time, anyway. We all thought that his book, 'Mein Kampf,' was just him ranting, as usual. We honestly didn't believe he'd bring us into another war. When he annexed Austria peacefully and took back other territory without a shot ever being fired, we all thought he was a genius! Oh, how things changed after that," she said. She sat down in a chair next to Grandpa and when she began to speak again, it was as if she was lost in a memory.

"Heinz was excited about serving. He said it was the right thing to do. He left the police force and they took him into the 2nd SS. He was so proud of that, initially. There was honor that went along with commanding his first platoon. However, he quickly became disillusioned with the war and the commanders running it. He wanted out so badly but didn't know how without bringing us all dishonor and hardship. So, he put up with it, trying to change what he could from his position as captain of a company. In the very end, though, he saw no honorable way out, so he deserted. The rest is history, I guess."

Everyone remained quiet for several minutes.

Finally, Grandpa said, "Thank you for sharing that."

I was glad for the glimpse into the mind of Grandpa Heinz.

There were many more hugs and handshakes as the family slowly started to leave. When it was just my parents, Grandpa and I left, Grandpa took Grandma's hands in his and said, "Stella, I wonder if I could ask a favor?"

"Anything for you, Dave," she said with sincerity.

"Could we go to the cemetery where Heinz is buried? Together?"

Fresh tears welled in Grandma's eyes. "Of course, we can!"

We arrived at the cemetery, which was quite large, stately, and well groomed. There was evidence of an upcoming funeral. There was a rectangular hole dug not far from the entrance and workers were setting up a tent-like apparatus over it. The sun was shining brightly, and shadows danced on the ground over the headstones. There were tall, full oak trees scattered throughout the cemetery and a light breeze caused the leaves to show their pale underside.

Grandpa nudged me. "Look, Mike. The oak leaves are turning over. It's going to rain."

"Sure, Grandpa." I still had not figured out if there was any truth to that or if it was just a line Grandpa liked to feed me.

"Park here, Arnold," Grandma said. "We'll walk from here." She led the way, knowing exactly where to go among the sea of grave markers. When she stopped, we all gathered beside her, standing quietly in front of Grandpa Heinz's headstone.

Grandpa took a few steps forward, closer to the grave, and turned back toward the rest of us. He bowed his head and said a little prayer:

"Dear Lord,

We thank you for allowing people into our lives who teach us something.

Guide us in our lives that we may become better human beings,

that we would lend a helping hand to those in need, a neighbor or a stranger,

that we may strive to live closer in Your image.

Help us to turn the other cheek and forgive those who have wronged us.

And please, God, watch over Heinz.

Watch over Stella.

Watch over Sherry and Arnold, Mike and Aaron,

as they go about their lives.

In Jesus' name, we pray,

Amen."

Then Grandpa did an about-face, came to attention, and snapped a crisp salute. He held it for several seconds, and with tears shining on his face, he said, "Rest peacefully, my friend."

ACKNOWLEDGEMENTS

This project means more to me than I realized. I need to thank several people in no order of importance.

I need to thank my grandparents, although they are no longer among us, for instilling pride of a job well done and doing what's right.

To all the veterans of military in the free world, thank you for your service. You keep us free and safe from harm, and allow books like this to be written. Thank you to all that have sacrificed.

To my surrogate father: when I needed a father figure most, thank you, Don, for believing in me.

To two of my co-workers, Craig and Frank, you guys have been by my side when I needed an ally the most. Your belief propelled me forward.

To my father-in-law and mother-in-law, Jack and Virginia, the parents I always dreamed of having, you've accepted me into the family and made me feel special and welcome. Your love for me is evident and I'm better for it. Thank you.

To my publisher, Notebook publishing, and to Ms. Hayley Paige, your hard work and dedication to putting out a superb product had me convinced from Day One that it would be you who would deliver my work to the world, like a baby taking its first breath. I feel like the proud papa of this book. Thank you from the bottom of my heart.

To my editor, Marni, at Notebook Publishing, I don't think I could've imagined a better person to work with. Thank you.

And to Mark on the Notebook team, for designing a beautiful cover. Your creation has instilled a confidence in me that I can't begin to describe. Thank you, sir.

And last, but not least, to my lovely and talented wife, it was you that pushed this. It was you that believed in me and planted the seed. Your hard work has allowed this dream to come true. Your love and support drove me. None of this would've ever seen the light of day without you. Thank you for being a part of its success.